PLEASE TEASE ME

Please Tease Me

Rebecca Ambrose

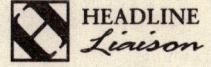

HEADLINE
Liaison

First published in 1997
by HEADLINE BOOK PUBLISHING

A HEADLINE LIAISON paperback

10 9 8 7 6 5 4 3 2 1

ISBN 0 7472 5472 9

Typeset at
The Spartan Press Ltd,
Lymington, Hants

Printed and bound in Great Britain by
Cox & Wyman Ltd, Reading, Berks

HEADLINE BOOK PUBLISHING
A division of Hodder Headline PLC
338 Euston Road
London NW1 3BH

Please
Tease Me

Chapter One

Dressed in a clingy purple sheath of a dress, split from her slim ankle to the top of her thigh, Jayne Sanders purred at camera two, her words picked up by the microphone in her cleavage. It was the midnight hour on ETV, and it was all Jayne could do to keep from yawning as she attempted to whet the viewers' appetites for the tepid fare on offer.

'... starring that delectable hunk, Zach Moran, and stunning newcomer April Showers. So sit back on that comfy sofa, or settle back against that pillow, and prepare to be seduced. Because who can resist ... *Virgins on the Loose?*'

Once the film titles were rolling Jayne leaned back in her chair with a sigh that was half relief and half boredom. What the hell am I doing, spouting this drivel night after night, she asked herself. Well, it was a living. Since Mick's job had brought him to London she'd found it hard to find a job that covered the extra expense of living in the capital. The TV company she now worked for was at South Quays, just a stone's throw away from the smart, but minute, flat which she and Mick inhabited for a crazy rent.

Stella, her producer, lifted an imaginary cup to her mouth with a questioning look and Jayne nodded, rising to join her. They walked through to the coffee machine and were soon sitting in the restroom with their drinks in their hands and their feet up on the neighbouring chairs. The two women had developed an easy intimacy in the six weeks that Jayne had been working at ETV.

'This job is doing my head in,' Jayne confessed. 'I mean, how many ways are there of saying "Hope you enjoy this next offering of tits and bums" without actually saying, "Have a good wank, folks!" Nobody ever watches these films for the plot, surely?'

Stella giggled. 'I hope not – there isn't one!'

Jayne took a sip of coffee, holding it over the arm of the chair to avoid spilling any on her satin dress. 'I suspect they watch them with the sound turned off.'

'Judging from our postbag, most of the men only switch on to see you.'

'They don't get much gratification then, do they?'

'I should think they probably fantasise about you for an hour and a half until you come on to tell them what delicious goodies we have in store for them tomorrow. It's that breathy, little-girl voice you put on. Does wonders for their libido.'

'I wish it had the same effect on my husband!'

'Ah!' Stella pushed her dark fringe away from her eyes and gave Jayne a searching look. 'It's not easy working nights, is it?'

'No. Takes a bit of getting used to. We normally only see each other for an hour or so in the morning and a couple in the evening. But Mick has tomorrow off so he'll probably leap on me the minute I get in and insist on his conjugal rights. Whoopee!'

Jayne's tone was ironic, her smile wry. She knew that Stella didn't have a regular partner. Maybe it was easier that way. She lifted the polystyrene cup to her lips and dropped a spot of coffee down her cleavage. It stung, then dribbled. She wiped it off with her forefinger, feeling the solid swell of her breast as she did so. It gave her a momentary thrill.

'I had a new German film in yesterday,' Stella said. 'But it needed so much editing that the storyline is totally ridiculous. We had to cut it from two hours to one and three quarters. At one point you see her start to give him a blow job and the next minute they're sitting at a table eating sausages and sauerkraut!'

'What did you have to cut out?'

'Close-ups of genitalia, mostly his. And the bit where he sprays her tits then licks it off. Yet we're allowed to keep all the S & M stuff in. Honestly, I don't get this country, I really don't. When you see what the Dutch channels put out we're still in the *Blue Peter* era.'

'Hm, that's an idea. Suppose I dressed up in sticky-backed plastic. D'you think that'll turn them on?'

'Bound to. Personally, I preferred *Rainbow*. I've had a thing about zips every since!'

Jayne's gaze drifted up to the screen in the corner of the ceiling where a woman in a nurse's uniform was giving a man a bed bath. She had enormous breasts and as she bent forward they slipped from beneath her apron and her blouse buttons gaped. A doctor crept up on her from behind and clasped them, making her squeal.

'Oh, Doctor! Fancy coming up behind me like that!' she protested to the amusement of the patient, who promptly leapt out of bed showing the overstated erection in his pyjamas.

'God, it's worse than a *Carry On* film,' Jayne said. 'It's enough to put you off sex forever, watching this stuff night after night.'

Stella gave a wicked grin. 'It's okay if you can find your stimulation elsewhere.'

'Tell me more!'

'I don't think so. You're a married woman.'

'I can still look at other men, can't I? Not that there's much to look at around here.'

'Quite. But the world is bigger than South Quays, fortunately.'

'I wouldn't know where to start looking, quite honestly. If I were interested in having an affair, I mean. Which I'm not, actually. By the time I'm finished here I feel as if I'll never fancy it again for the rest of my life.'

'That's a shame. Why don't you and Mick go away together, next time you have a couple of days off? It would do you the world of good.'

Jayne gave it a moment's thought. On the surface it sounded a good idea. Second honeymoon, chance to rediscover themselves, kind of thing. But Stella didn't know Mick. If they went away together he'd probably spend the whole time watching football on the telly. Even if they got a shag in it would have to be at half-time, and Mick would finish the moment the ref blew his whistle.

'Mm.' Jayne looked at the clock and sighed. Another hour and a quarter to go. If only they hadn't rescheduled this film she would have been able to put her last link onto video and she'd have been home by now.

Stella seemed to read her mind. 'Look,' she began tentatively. 'I know you haven't been home before midnight for weeks. Why don't I do the "goodnight kiss" for you?'

'Wouldn't that be the kiss of death?' Jayne giggled. 'Thanks a bunch!'

'No, I only meant they might think I'd popped my clogs behind the scenes. I appreciate your offer, Stella. And it would be nice to surprise Mick for a change. Do you think it would work?'

'Don't see why not. I'll tart myself up and tell them you'll be back as usual tomorrow. In fact,' her elfin face brightened, 'I can spin a yarn about how you and the cameraman are otherwise engaged and I didn't want to disturb you. That should amuse them – the ones who are still awake, that is.'

'What, me and fat Ted? I'll sue you for slander!'

'Don't be like that. Are you up for it or not?'

Jayne gave a broad grin. Suddenly the idea of surprising Mick was very alluring. 'Okay. Thanks a lot.'

Stella grinned back, getting to her feet. 'I'll call in the favour sometime, you can be sure of that. Now off you go, and start thinking dirty thoughts. Real dirty, mind. Not censored like the stuff we pump out!'

Ten minutes later Jayne was driving through the quiet back streets in a mood of pleasant anticipation. She felt slightly wicked, as if she were bunking off school. Or, more to the point, as if she were meeting Mick clandestinely as at the start of their romance. He'd been dating another girl when they met, and hadn't been able to break if off for two months. Jayne's full lips curled into a smile as she remembered those secret sessions in her Mini parked in a lonely spot on the moors (fellatio, cramped seat), in the lift of a multi-storey car park (cunnilingus, hard floor) or once in the blissful luxury of a friend's flat (full works, soft bed!).

Now that they'd been together two years that early excitement was gone. Could it ever be revived? Somehow she doubted it. Mick had obsessed her every minute of her waking life, and the precious time they had together had been snatched like stolen goods. Jayne had vague memories of attacking each other with hungry mouths, tearing buttons open with eager fingers, that wonderful moment when he first plunged into her with full force and without preliminaries, then the glorious ride towards mutual release.

Afterwards, when they no longer had to run and hide, the sense of freeodm was overwhelming. They made love with slow sensuality, relishing each other like a gourmet meal. They told each other their fantasies, dressed up, explored positions, smoked dope, tried out sex toys. They were always surprising each other, always ready for something new.

Then they moved to London because Mick got a new job, and everything subtly changed. They had neither the time nor the energy to carry on as before, and their lovemaking dwindled from several hours each night to a brief encounter once or twice a week. It will be better when we're settled, they told each other. Then Jayne had got the job at ETV and

Mick had videoed some of the films for them to watch in bed. He had been aroused by them, but it had felt like taking work home with her and she'd found it offputting.

When Jayne pulled up outside the block of flats they now called home, there was still a light in their window. She smiled to herself as she locked the car, feeling a warm throb in the folds of flesh between her thighs. Anticipation quickened her step as she walked to the door, her heels clacking on the concrete, and as soon as she entered the flat she called out ironically, 'Honey, I'm home!'

The babble of the television came from the sitting room and Jayne recognised the tacky soundtrack of *Virgins on the Loose*. When she opened the door Mick was zipping up his fly, his cheeks flushed. She laughed throatily as she rushed in and gave him a kiss on the cheek. 'Naughty boy! I'm surprised at you, watching that trash.'

'What else am I supposed to do?' he asked, his eyes dark, unfocused. Jayne patted his brown, tousled curls. He always looked so boyish when he'd been masturbating. Shades of the school dorm. 'Anyway, why aren't you on the box? I was looking forward to seeing you at the end of this.'

Jayne flopped down onto the sofa beside him and gave him a hug. 'I suppose you were saving the last one for me? Sweet of you. But Stella had pity on my unsocial hours and let me off early. She's doing the honours this time.'

'I wish you could persuade her to get some better films.'

'It's not Stella's fault. Some of the stuff we get is pretty horny, but by the time it's been hacked around to comply with our prissy censorship laws it ends up being utter rubbish.'

As if on cue, the TV suddenly spouted some ludicrously dubbed dialogue: 'Give it to me good and hard, big boy!' . . . 'You slut! You're dying for it, aren't you? I'll teach you to come all prim and proper with me!' etc.

Mick's eyes suddenly lit up. 'Hey, remember that home video we made once, on holiday?'

'God, yes! How could I forget? Where is it?'

Mick leapt off the sofa and soon found it. Slotting it into the player, he came back to pull Jayne onto his knee while the video whirred into action. She found the scenes of them playing on the beach poignant. They'd been so hot for each other then. She watched Mick bring her down in a rugby tackle and drag her, pretending to protest, into the grassy sand dunes. The camera had been on a tripod so there were gaps in the action where they'd had to reposition it.

The bit where they made love in the dunes still looked good. Their bodies had been slimmer then, more finely tuned, and they each had an allover tan. Jayne's dark blonde hair had been lightened by the summer sun, giving it a model-girl sheen. She watched fascinated as Mick ran his hands over her nakedness, his prick rearing visibly as he did so. He made her kneel on all fours and took her from behind, with her breasts swinging bell-like and her nipples pointing downwards. She saw the long, hard shaft burrow into her with its pink nose and then his balls were swinging too as he slapped them against the back of her thighs in his frantic lust.

Mick made an animal noise, put his hand into the low neck of her gown and grabbed her right breast. Jayne wanted to feel wanted, but she just felt tired. His fingers groping for her nipple irritated her, made her flesh crawl. Still, it wasn't fair not to respond. She reached down and undid his fly, feeling the semi-erect penis within. Mick groaned.

'Any chance of a blow job?' he murmured, nipping her earlobe in the way that used to turn her on. Now she found it annoying, but she slid from her seat all the same and knelt before him, pulling a cushion down with her for her knees. Perhaps if she satisfied him now he would let her sleep when they went to bed.

Jayne was disappointed that she didn't feel more like sex, but you couldn't manufacture feelings that weren't there. Carefully she lifted his erection out of his pants and encircled the shaft with her thumb and forefinger. There was an instant hardening and the glans reared up, demanding as a babe in sight of the nipple.

'Oh Jayne, this is far better than DIY!' Mick groaned, as her fingers delicately frotted the loose, sensitive skin of his shaft.

'I should hope so!'

He wanted her topless, and pulled down the satin puff sleeves until she could wriggle out of them exposing her broad shoulders and generous bosom in the strapless bra. Jayne liked being 'a big girl up top' as her mother euphemistically called it. Not only were her breasts large and shapely but, thanks to daily workouts with a bust-improving device, they were also firm. And she had nipples with sizeable areolas, capable of being sucked or tweaked or pulled into a state of provocatively stiff elongation. A satisfying mouthful, as Mick put it.

His mouth was yearning towards them now as, freed from the black lace cups, they began to pucker. Mick seized her breasts with both hands and sucked at her right nipple greedily while she continued to play with his hugely distended penis. There was a tingling in her tits and a corresponding sensation in her clitoris, which felt hard and bulbous against the tight confines of her panties. But she herself felt one step removed from the proceedings.

'Lick me, please!' Mick moaned, replacing his mouth with his hand. He pinched her throbbing nipple, sharpening up her responses, but still Jayne felt oddly detached. Her mouth enclosed the glistening glans and her tongue bathed it in saliva. Then she opened wide and took in as much of the thick stalk as she could, licking her way down it. It tasted savoury. She fondled his balls gently as she sucked him, handling them like delicate eggs. His hand moved to her other nipple and she felt the first sharpness of desire hit her, producing a faint ripple of longing deep inside.

Before it could develop into anything, however, Mick began to thrust into her mouth with the heedless urgency that she recognised as the final climb to orgasm. She didn't try to make him hold back but, just as the first bitter juices hit her palate she withdrew, disliking the taste. Instead she pushed her breasts together and let him nestle between, which always gave him a thrill. While the juice pulsed out of him he spread it all over her bosom with his palms and she groaned sensually as her nipples became viscous. Somehow that made them more responsive and the more he rubbed the more horny she became.

They lay in a heap on the sofa with the video still playing until Jayne began to feel unpleasantly sticky. She got up and went into the bedroom where she stripped, then stepped into the shower while Mick was still recovering. The effect of the water was to dampen down her ardour, so that by the time she was dry and scented, wrapped in her towelling robe, she had lost her transient sexual feelings and now felt utterly weary.

'I'm going to bed,' she announced.

Mick had put his shirt back on but was otherwise in a state of undress. His penis hung semi-flaccid between his lean, hairy thighs. He gave her a rueful look. 'Won't you come and give me a cuddle first?'

Reluctantly Jayne returned to the sofa and took him in her arms. He lay there, childlike, with his head in her lap until she picked up the zapper and switched off the video.

'Put the TV on again,' he urged her, with a yawn. 'I want to see this boss of yours. I've heard you mention her name so often I might as well see what she looks like.'

'Only a few minutes to go,' she murmured as the screen filled with the Vestal Virgin orgy scene that she knew was the grand finale of that particular film. Although she was tired she didn't mind waiting up to see Stella. She was curious too. How would the other woman look and sound in front of the camera? What would she say? A part of her felt ridiculously insecure at having her rôle temporarily usurped.

9

While they watched, Mick began to stroke her breasts through the opening in her gown. Jayne found it distracting. She wanted to ask him to stop, but that would seem churlish. Instead she tried to focus her attention on the television. A writhing mass of female bodies in all shapes and sizes filled the screen. In true Hollywood fashion the action took place on a Romanised set with a large square pool surrounded by colonnades filled with couches. It was supposed to be a lesbian orgy, but none of it looked very convincing with women half heartedly stroking each others' breasts or threading flowers through their pubic hair. A dominatrix was being attended to by three chained slave girls, just to add a bit of variety, and in another corner a black girl enjoyed a lashing on her bare buttocks with histrionic facial expressions.

In an unlikely feat of synchronicity all the women climaxed simultaneously. When their ecstasies had subsided they indulged in some horseplay, pushing each other into the pool until everyone was frolicking in wet abandon. Then the camera moved up to the open and ultra blue sky, from which a flock of doves descended in a bizarre attempt at some kind of symbolism.

'Aren't doves one of the attributes of Venus?' Jayne asked sleepily, dredging up the information from a trip to Cyprus.

'Mm, probably.'

She could tell by his vague tone that Mick was getting hot for her again. But the film was over and the credits starting to roll. She removed his hand from her breast and sat up expectantly as he mumbled a token protest. 'She'll be on now.'

The credits faded and the familiar face of Stella March filled the screen. Familiar, and yet unfamiliar. She looked fatter in the face – and older, Jayne thought bitchily. But she couldn't deny that her boss looked attractive. In the hour or so since she'd left her at the studio Stella had made the most of her dark good looks. Her eyes were done up like

Cleopatra's, with plenty of kohl black eyeliner and sooty mascara. She'd put a dab of terracotta on her high cheekbones and her lips were a rich burnt orange. A search through wardrobe had produced a lime green tunic-style dress trimmed with gold braid that seemed appropriate to the film they'd just shown. In fact, she could well have been an extra on the set.

'Wow, she's a bit of all right!' Mick grinned, sitting up on the edge of the seat with his hands on his knees. His penis was now semi-erect and dangling at an angle of forty-five degrees. Jayne felt vaguely jealous. What right did he have to go fancying another woman just minutes after she'd given him a blow job?

Then Stella addressed the viewers in sultry tones that made Jayne giggle. 'Well, that was quite something, wasn't it? Something for everyone in fact, if you could keep your eyes focused long enough. Now for those of you who are still in the land of the living, let me explain that the lovely Jayne is indisposed right now so your humble servant (producer actually) has stepped into the breach. Hope you like the outfit.' Stella gave a wink and stood up to do a twirl. 'I think it last did service in *Sex Kittens from Mars*. Only kidding.'

Mick was staring at her bug-eyed with his tongue practically hanging out. Jayne biffed him with her elbow. 'Hey, stop ogling my boss!'

He put his arm around her, but she noticed that his erection had grown. Stella went on to tell the viewers about the following night's films. 'She's rambling a bit,' Jayne commented. 'They're all half asleep by now.'

'Well I'm not!' Mick put his hand back inside her robe and got his wrist slapped. 'Hey! What d'you do that for?'

'If you think I'm going to respond to you just because you've got the hots for Stella, you can go screw yourself!'

Jayne surprised herself with the vehemence of her response. Okay, so she wasn't in the mood. Was she jealous? She certainly sounded like it. Yet she wasn't normally the jealous type, so what was going on? Mick continued to stare at the screen, looking sulky.

'I'm tired,' she announced, brushing his hand away firmly from her thigh and rising to her feet. 'You can stay up if you want, but I'm going to bed. I mean it, this time.'

He said nothing and she went through to the bedroom feeling depressed as well as exhausted. What had begun as a rather pleasant evening had turned into something disagreeable and she knew it was all her fault. Was the job at ETV getting to her? Perhaps the daily diet of badly made porn films was putting her off sex altogether. She wouldn't be surprised.

Jayne lay down in the double bed and waited for Mick to join her but he was taking his time. She tried not to think about where their relationship was heading. At the moment it seemed to be going nowhere but with their leisure hours hardly overlapping there wasn't much that could be done about it. She could look for another job, but her qualifications weren't good and she'd only had experience of office work. After the glamorous world of satellite TV the idea of going back to routine anonymity was unappealing.

Maybe she could find an opening with another company, but in the competitive world of the media she knew she was very small fry indeed. It was hard to get up the ladder unless you knew people and, stuck at an obscure TV company doing a low-profile job, she couldn't produce an impressive CV, let alone shine at interview. In many ways she was well off at ETV since the money was reasonable, the work undemanding and the location convenient.

Count your blessings, girl, she told herself with a sigh. Yet once those blessings would have included an active and satisfying sex life. Could she honestly say she was happy with the way things now were between her and Mick? That avenue was too painful to pursue so she gave up on Mick, turned over on her side, extinguished the bedside lamp and waited for sleep.

Jayne's dreams that night were a confused mixture of titillation and frustration. She was on that holiday beach again with Mick, but he wanted to watch the television all the time! Trying to distract him from the nude women on the screen she did a dance of the seven veils, but he ignored her. Then a hunky guy came out of the sea, like Venus rising from the foam and lifted her off her feet. But before he could have his wicked way with her Mick appeared, riding behind a TV camera, and proceeded to film them.

Jayne found the musclebound beach boy very attractive and as he proceeded to oil her nude body she felt herself yielding to his expert caresses. Her thighs fell open and she could feel the delicate tissues within swelling and moistening, ready for whatever he might wish to do to her. She could see his great prick rearing up as he knelt beside her on the sand and her pussy ached for it. But just as she thought he was going to plunge into her Mick rushed up with a kiddy's pail of sea water and threw it over the pair of them, as if they were copulating dogs.

The shock of it woke her up. Mick had got into bed beside her while she slept, and now she cuddled up to his broad back for reassurance. Did she still love him? The question had come to haunt her lately, particularly when she awoke in the middle of the night. Maybe she was suffering from disturbed sleep patterns. It was easy to find reasons for everything, not so easy to find solutions.

To her surprise, Jayne still felt horny after that dream and her fingers wandered down to between her thighs. The thought of pleasuring herself while Mick slept made her feel guilty, but it was an exciting feeling too. Her breasts were hot, and the extended nipples rubbed against the duvet as she laboured down below. She inserted one fingertip between her slick labia as the other hand found her erect clitoris and began to give it the gentle friction needed to increase her state of tumescence.

Soon all other considerations faded and a strong desire for

satisfaction took over, sweeping her along with it wholeheartedly. It was ages since she'd done this, she realised. Maybe it wasn't good to let her sexuality lie dormant, even if she was too tired to do it with Mick. A joyous peace swept through her along with the familiar sensations of arousal, and she began to rub herself more rapidly, her finger inserted deep into her wet vagina.

Suddenly Mick moaned and turned in his sleep. Jayne slowed down, afraid he might awaken, and treated herself to some gentle, sensual stimulation that kept her hovering on the edge of satisfaction but wouldn't disturb the bedclothes. Withdrawing her left hand from her pussy she used it to caress the full globes of her breasts while she continued to stroke her clitoris with her right. She tweaked one nipple and then the other, setting up a tingling circuit that turned the whole of her torso into a quivering mass of erotic tension.

Mick began snoring as he lay on his back, so Jayne knew he was fast asleep. By now the tentative nature of her self-stimulation was becoming unbearable. Her breasts were straining against the slightly rough cotton, nipples like bullets, and a hot voluptuousness filled her veins like mulled wine. In desperation she thrust several fingers into her needy quim while thrusting her mons against her wrist. The secret button in her cleft responded by throbbing violently, sending her libido spiralling up to the next plateau.

Now Jayne wanted to climax with all her being, and her efforts redoubled. She increased the friction on her clitoris and let her fingers move in and out between her labia, simulating the thrust of intercourse. Her pelvis worked to the same end and soon the first sweet waves of gratification hit her, flooding her lower body with spasmodic pleasure, making her inner walls contract again and again over her invading hand.

'How did I ever get along without this?' Jayne thought in wonder, as the glorious feelings began to subside. It was incredible to her now that she had let fatigue overcome her sexual desire to that extent. Had she forgotten what it was like?

Perhaps the problem was that her last few screws with Mick had been less than satisfactory, she reflected soberly as she turned on her side, hugging herself. Was she losing her desire for him? Would a new lover revive her enthusiasm for sex if he came along? These were dangerous questions, and ones that she didn't really want answered. Not yet anyway. She could do without the complication of splitting up from Mick right now.

Chapter Two

Mick woke to the shrill sound of the alarm. Jayne moaned softly beside him then turned over, with the duvet pulled about her ears. He slammed down the clock button and, still half asleep, stumbled out of bed and into the bathroom. This morning he felt like crap. His fuzzy face stared back into his bleary eyes from the mirror on the wall cabinet. It wasn't just tiredness. Something worse. He felt sick inside, his balls hung heavy with frustration and there was angry irritation too. Woe betide anyone who crossed him in the office!

After nicking his neck with the razor in several places Mick was in no better mood. He grabbed a black coffee and a couple of biscuits before dashing out of the door and down the stairs to where his car was waiting. The engine was cold and it took him several cursing attempts to start it. Only when he was crawling along in a traffic jam did he have time to reflect on exactly why the day had started so badly.

'A bloody blow job!' he announced to the woman driver who was creeping up alongside him in the next lane. He relished the alliteration and decided to repeat it. 'She's fobbed me off with fucking fellatio again, the farty-tart!'

Mick couldn't remember when his woman had last given it to him good and proper, the way he liked it. The more he thought about it, the more his indignation grew. He'd been taken in by her excuses. Granted, they didn't have that much time together but last night she'd come home early –

early for her, at least – and she'd still given him short rations.

But Mick could remember how hot they used to be for each other. The days had dragged until the time they could be together, and when they met they couldn't wait to sate their pent-up lust. More than once he'd taken her in the car park lift, flat on the concrete floor, but she hadn't complained even though she'd ached all over next day. She'd got pins and needles from screwing in his car, too. Sex had even taken priority over food and drink in those heady days of mutual discovery, of mutual need. Were they getting tired of each other? It was hard to come to any other conclusion. One thing was certain: he couldn't carry on like this for much longer. His hunger for her had become permanent, but when he begged he only got crumbs.

Mick's thoughts drifted towards that other woman, Stella, and the way she'd looked on the TV last night. He was used to how Jayne appeared on the small screen of course, and got a vicarious thrill out of knowing that thousands of other men were ogling her too as a kind of hors d'oeuvre before the porn. Mick revelled in the idea that they could fantasise all they liked, but she was his exclusive property. At least, he still presumed she was. The thought that she might have gone off him because she was having an affair with someone else struck a chill into his heart. But where would she find the time?

At least she didn't know about his little infidelities. Mick gave a wicked smile as he reviewed his casual conquests over the past few months. Jayne's working late into the night was convenient, and if she suspected anything she'd never said. Not that it made any difference to him wanting her. If anything he desired her more than ever. Those brief one night stands with girls who also wanted a quick thrill didn't come near his passion for Jayne. Perhaps it was just because she'd become so inaccessible to him lately that the flame of his love for her had become dangerously intense, threatening to consume him long before it could harm her.

The open-plan office was buzzing when he arrived, girls gossiping about the night before or what they were planning for the weekend. He'd had half of them, Mick reminded himself, but without any sense of pride or pleasure. Debbie whispered something to Alison with her eyes swivelling in his direction, and both girls giggled. If they were talking about his sexual prowess, let them. He couldn't care less. Only Jayne's opinion of him mattered.

As the day proceeded Mick found himself getting more and more wound up. His colleague, Ben Chapman, had seen Stella on television last night instead of Jayne and began making innuendoes.

'So where was your lovely missus then, Mick? Tucked up in bed at home with you, I hope. Otherwise I expect you're wondering the same thing, aren't you?'

'She came straight home,' Mick snapped. 'Her boss gave her the time off, for a change.'

'Not too knackered for a bit of the other then, I hope?'

'Mind your own sodding business, Chapman. I don't pry into your love life. If you've got one at all, that is.'

'Ooh, we are tetchy today aren't we? If I had a looker like that she wouldn't go begging for it, I can tell you that.'

'What d'you mean, "Go begging for it"?' Mick was unable to keep the suspicion out of his voice and he disliked the way Ben was leering at him.

'Nothing. Just a figure of speech. You're mightily on the defensive though, Mick old chap. Everything okay, *chez toi*?'

'I told you, my private life is just that, none of your business!'

Mick knew very well that Chapman fancied Jayne something rotten, which was why he'd never let them meet. The thought of his colleague leching over her whenever she appeared on TV was disturbing, but he supposed it was the price anyone had to pay for being in the public eye. No one thought about the effect on their partners though, did they?

The lonely evenings were hard to bear. As Mick drove home with his M & S dinner in a bag on the back seat he felt depression creep up on him once more. He couldn't remember the last time he and Jayne had sat down to a decent home cooked meal. Generally on her days off they ate in restaurants, because she didn't want to cook. Maybe next time he would cook for them. Something simple but delicious, like he used to do in the old days, and she would be so grateful afterwards, so very grateful . . .

The image of Jayne sucking his dick came to mind, and he uttered a snort of derision. Not that it wasn't better than nothing, but there were other things their bodies could do together, things their flesh had once delighted in. They even had a video to prove it. Maybe he would run it through later, just to remind him. Or go down the pub to drown his sorrows. On the whole that seemed the less painful option.

By nine o'clock Mick was in the bar of the White Horse. It wasn't a busy night, but there was a rowdy crowd playing darts so the place had a lively atmosphere. He sat in the corner nursing his beer and keeping an eye on the door in case anyone he knew walked in. Even that would be a mixed blessing. Other men envied him his glamorous girlfriend, made constant references to her, and it was getting increasingly difficult to keep up his smug façade. If only they knew what really went on *chez lui*, as that smug bastard Chapman would put it! Uneasily he glanced at the doorway again.

Then someone did walk in, not someone Mick already knew but someone he would like to know. Most definitely. She entered with a girlfriend and gave the pub a sweeping glance, her green eyes lighting up momentarily when they spied him. I'm in with a chance there, he thought, and as his pulse raced his balls began to tingle.

In the old days, Mick never used to have much confidence with women. If he picked someone up it was usually because they came on strong. He and Jayne had only got together through an introduction by a mutual friend at a party. If he'd met her in any other circumstances he would have thought she was out of his league and not even attempted to chat her up. Once he would have thought the same about this woman, but being with Jayne had changed all that. After her, other women seemed ripe for the picking so long as they didn't look the type to get involved. And this one might just fit the bill.

Mick observed her carefully before making any move. He watched her velvet-clad bum slide onto the bar stool next to her friend, saw how the plump buttocks spilled over the upholstery just a little. She crossed her legs at the thighs, displaying shapely calves. Her blonde hair fell casually about her shoulders at the back and, in the mirror behind the bar, he could see that it was swept back from her face. The dark brows suggested she was not a natural blonde, but maybe he'd find more proof of that before the evening was out.

Her friend was smaller and darker, pretty in a stereotyped way but nowhere near as sexy. When the pair of them took their drinks over to a table in the opposite corner Mick was able to compare their faces and figures more accurately. Blondie had wide green eyes with a sparkle of life in them, sweeping lashes and a generous mouth which she'd rendered even more kissable with pink glossy lipstick. Darkie had thin lips and brown eyes that looked vacuous.

Beneath the thin wool sweater Blondie's breasts looked firm and substantial. Mick could see the outline of her bra straps and a suggestion of cups, but the outlines of her nipples were clearly visible and gave him an instant hard-on. By contrast the top the other girl was wearing hung loosely over her boobs, obscuring their shape. She didn't look that well endowed, either. Was there some kind of unspoken pact between girlfriends, teaming up a very sexy girl with an ordinary looking one? Presumably the sexpot got protection from unwanted attention and the other one got the leavings.

The big question was, were they out hunting tonight? Neither of them was wearing a wedding ring. He judged them to be in their early twenties. After a while they noticed Mick looking at them and began whispering and giggling. That could be good or bad, he decided, but the longer he left it before making his move the worse it would look. So he rose casually and strolled over to the bar, passing close to their table. He gave them a nod and a smile. Both girls smiled back. He put his glass down on the counter with a 'Same again please, Charles' to the barman, then turned towards the women. 'Can I get you ladies another drink?' They giggled and nudged each other. Then Blondie said, her eyes challenging and her tone slightly truculent, 'Mine's a Two Dogs.'

Charles spluttered. 'Two Dogs? Not being very flattering to yourselves are you, girls?'

Blondie gave him a withering look and Mick said, 'They're out to ban that alcoholic lemonade, aren't they? Say it makes young girls so tipsy they don't know what they're doing.'

'Oh we know what we're doing all right,' the brunette chipped in, smirking. 'And mine's a rum and Coke, thanks'.

I'm in here, Mick thought with a thrill of anticipation as he ferried the drinks to their table. 'Mind if I join you?' he asked, setting his own beer down. 'I'm Mick, by the way,' he added, before they had a chance to reply.

'I'm Cora and this is my friend Nerissa,' said the dark girl.

'Nice names. I've not seen you two in here before. Do you live round here?'

'We've just moved into a flat together,' Nerissa said. Her voice was soft and seductive. How do I get her away from her chaperone, Mick wondered. It looked like a longer term project which was a disappointment. He needed his oats tonight.

'Students, are you?'

'Student nurses.'

Better yet. He'd had some very nice close encounters with nurses. 'Not on the night shift tonight, then?'

'Not tonight,' Nerissa smiled, her eyes flashing some coded message at him. 'What do you do, Mick?'

'I'm in financial services.' It sounded better than accountancy. 'Bit complicated really. But let's not talk about work. Found your way around this part of town yet? There's a couple of decent restaurants just down the road, and a good disco – *Best Cellar*. Been there yet?'

'We don't have the money to go out much,' Cora said.

'Of course not. Students are all in debt, and nurses are underpaid. Student nurses must be the worst off of the lot, eh?'

'We manage,' Cora said. 'But when nice men like you buy us drinks it helps a lot.'

'Least I can do. After all, I never know when I might be needing your services, do I?'

Cora gave him a knowing smile, and Nerissa giggled. Better and better. Mick glanced down at the blonde girl's chest. She had her arms crossed and her breasts were pushed out provocatively. When she saw him looking she made a mock pout of disapproval and lowered her long lashes at him. Hope she's not just a prick tease, he thought.

When the girls had finished their drinks Mick offered to buy them another, but Cora whispered something to her friend then said, 'Actually we have to get back to our flat now, but you could come with us if you like.'

'Both of you?' It had slipped out before he knew it.

The girls caught his drift and giggled. 'If you like,' Cora grinned.

Mick was afraid they might change their mind if he didn't act quickly. 'Do you want a lift? My car's outside.' He countered their hesitation with, 'I've only had two pints.'

'Okay,' Cora said quickly. She was clearly the more vocal of the two.

Driving felt good with two beddable girls in the back of his car. While Cora gave him directions Mick fantasised about what he might do with the pair of them. He'd never had two women at once before and the prospect filled him with a novel exictement, but he cautioned himself not to expect too much or he'd end up being disappointed. They were just as likely to offer him a coffee and a bit of a chat then kick him out.

They lived in a rundown area of town, full of crumbling terraced houses. Mick followed them up a smelly staircase into their flat, which was decorated in ethnic Oxfam style with lots of Indian embroidered cushions and fabrics, plants in raffia pot holders and dangly macramé bits. The low couch, covered in an elephant-patterned throw, looked comfortable.

Mick instinctively removed his shoes and made himself comfortable on one end of it. To his secret delight Nerissa came to sit at the other end, tucking her bare feet under her and leaning one arm on the back of the couch. Her loose velvet pants clung to her slim thighs and revealed the protruding delta between them. She was surveying him with thoughtful emerald eyes, evoking prickles at the back of his neck. A faint aroma of patchouli wafted towards him.

'Coffee?' Cora asked. 'We only have decaff, I'm afraid. Or there's herbals.'

'Decaff will do fine. No milk or sugar, thanks.'

Beneath the social intercourse there was a definite erotic tension. Mick was still wary. He didn't want to make a prat of himself, but he didn't know how much longer he could keep up this farce. As he took the mug from Cora their fingertips touched and his hand trembled. She smiled at him, faintly condescending, then put some music on – a britpop compilation. The laddish songs blared out, filling Mick with new vigour as he sipped his black coffee.

23

Suddenly Cora said to her friend, 'Does he look the type?'

'Oh yes, definitely,' Nerissa replied.

The girls were exchanging enigmatic looks. 'Are you talking about me?' Mick asked.

They giggled, nodded. He felt the warm embers of desire kindle in the pit of his stomach, but he dampened them down. He had a feeling they might just be making fun of him. Suddenly he felt most uncomfortable in that flat and had an urge to make his escape.

'We were just wondering if we could practise on you,' Cora explained.

'Practise?'

'Mm. We have to practise certain procedures. First aid and stuff. We're training to be nurses, remember.'

'Oh, yes.'

There was still a tightness in his stomach, in his balls. Mick stared from one girl to the other, trying to read their minds. Dirty minds, probably. Yet with two against one the balance of power was uneven and made him feel deliciously uneasy.

'What kind of procedures?'

'Oh, examinations of various kinds. Kiss of life. Bit of massage. Like playing doctors and nurses. Didn't you do that when you were a kid?'

'Can't remember. What would I have to do?'

'Just take your clothes off and lie down.'

'All of them?'

'Don't be shy. You could pretend you're in hospital.'

Nerissa giggled. 'It wouldn't hurt, honest!'

The idea appealed to Mick, but he was still not sure. Along with the excitement there was a real fear. He remembered being tied up by two older girls when he was a small boy and left for ages in the woods. His memory of the event was hazy, but something had happened to him then, something strange. And now those girlie ghosts from the past were troubling him again.

'Can I leave my underpants on?' he asked at last, by way of compromise.

'If you like.'

Cora's noncommittal tone reassured him. He began undoing his shirt but Nerissa stopped him. 'No,' she smiled, her eyes engaging with his to send a wild thread of desire through his body. 'Let us undress you. Pretend you're unconscious if you like, an accident victim, just brought in from the ambulance.'

The soft, hypnotic tone of her voice was impossible to resist. He lay back down on the low couch and the two women knelt at the side, joined in a professional conspiracy.

'I'll do the bottom half,' Cora said quietly, 'And you take the top half.'

Mick gave himself up to them then, his body passive, his mind in a dream. Gentle hands slid his buttons undone, stronger ones pulled off his socks. He was a child again, freed from responsibility, and his soul relaxed. His shirt came off, then his trousers, until he was in his underpants. Inside the cotton pouch his genitals spread themselves, free from constriction. Cool hands were placed on his forehead and began to massage with small, circular strokes. He gave a deep, silent sigh. This wasn't quite what he'd envisaged when he saw the pair of them enter the pub, but it was very nice. Very nice indeed.

Cora's hands were caressing his feet, wakening some dormant pathways in his body and setting his nervous system on tingling alert. Soon they were travelling upwards, towards his thighs, while Nerissa's gentle hands were moving down over the moulded contours of his chest. Would the two pairs of hands meet in the middle? His cock twitched expectantly.

Mick gave himself up to the rhythms of their stroking as they explored his supine body, prodding gently as if they wished to locate his internal organs, check for injuries. Then warm fingers came back to touch his shoulders. He felt his neck being lifted and his head tilted back.

'Will you give him the kiss of life, or shall I?' he heard Cora murmur.

'I will.'

His nostrils were pinched and then he felt Nerissa's luscious mouth on his. Her lips were moist and plump against his own. His stomach quivered as she slipped her delicious little tongue into his mouth and kissed him deeply. Her breasts, still in the thin jumper, were pressed against his chest and he couldn't resist the urge to feel them. As soon as he touched the points of her nipples, however, she sprang back as if stung.

'He touched me lewdly!' she declared, pretending to be shocked. 'Nurse Cora, this patient assaulted me.'

'Did he, indeed? The naughty man! I think we shall have to restrain him don't you, Nurse Nerissa?'

'Hey now, wait a minute . . .' Mick began, but the pair of them already had his hands. While Cora held them in her surprisingly strong grip, Nerissa wrapped his wrists in the chain belt she'd been wearing around her maroon velvet trousers.

'Wandering hands must be curtailed!' Cora said, sternly. 'Now, Nurse Nerissa, time to give him a blanket bath. Fetch the hot water and a flannel, please.'

'Is this really necessary?' Mick asked. He hadn't counted on them actually tying his hands. Now he felt a strange mixture of childlike helplessness and manly aggressiveness. What he really wanted was a good screw, but he'd allowed himself to be inveigled into playing this stupid game while two tantalising females handled random parts of his anatomy, doing more or less as they liked with him.

But then a delightfully hot, moist flannel was applied to his feet and he relaxed with a sigh. Cora worked her way up his legs with brisk efficiency but when she had done his thighs she bypassed his crotch and began to wash first his stomach, then his chest and then his arms. But it was only a temporary reprieve. Nerissa pulled his bound wrists up over his head and held them there, while Cora pulled down his pants, exposing his half risen cock.

Mick gurgled in horror as she enveloped his genitals in hot, wet flannel. 'Hey! I thought you promised not to take them off!'

'You have to be washed, and this is the dirtiest, smelliest part of all. You want to be nice and clean all over, don't you?'

Mick's feeble protest subsided, mainly because the sensations that were coursing through the lower part of his body were so utterly fantastic. His prick was responding readily, much to his embarrassment, rearing and thickening. What were they planning to do to him? If they left him frustrated, with aching balls, he didn't know what he'd do. Already he felt sick with desire. His erection was mammoth, straining up his stomach.

'Get yourself ready, Nurse,' Cora said, suddenly. 'I think the patient has been fully prepared for his therapy. Do you have the dressing?'

Nerissa released his hands and he heard her moving about, doing things. Cora was oiling his dick, her hands passing lightly up and down his shaft, over the throbbing glans. Then he felt her move away from him and Nerissa took her place. He opened his eyes and started in wonder at her kneeling form.

She was stark naked, her blonde hair falling across the tops of her beautiful breasts and a half mocking smile on her face. Mick's gaze was drawn to her closed thighs that led his eyes to the triangle of light brown fuzz at the base of her pale stomach. Then he saw, to his great delight, that in her hands she had a condom. Nerissa leaned towards him, her nipples stiffening into pink swollen buds, and he felt his guts melt.

As she slowly unrolled the latex prophylactic, Cora said, 'That's right, Nurse. Apply the dressing carefully now.'

Nerissa placed the teat over his glans and began to roll the rubber down his extended member, holding it firmly at the base with her other fingers. The confidence with which these women handled him was both alarming and reassuring, as if he really were their patient. Helplessly Mick watched the girl's bountiful breasts swing over his body, tempting but untouchable. He longed to grasp their plentiful flesh, to put those delicious nipples to his lips. They reminded him of the sugar mice he used to get in his Christmas stocking.

Once the condom was securely in place Nerissa straddled him, still on her knees, and Mick's penis leapt for joy. He watched her face as she took it towards her hidden pussy and let his glans nuzzle into the fur-lined cleft. Her eyes were closed in blissful anticipation as she worked his tool up and down her labia, making herself wet. She wasn't going to let him in yet, if at all, but played with him like a vibrator, holding him firmly while she rubbed the enclosed glans over her protuberant clitoris.

Cora sat at his feet still, looking on. There was a smile of satisfaction on her face, too, but she soon tired of being a passive spectator and moved up his body until she was kneeling between his spread knees. Looking down at him over her friend's shoulder, Cora brought her hands round under Nerissa's arms so she could reach her breasts. She began to squeeze and fondle them in mocking emphasis. Her expression suggested that she was enjoying Mick's obvious envy just as much as the love-play. He felt the disturbing mixture of potent lust and impotent anger curdle in his stomach.

'See to him properly, Nurse,' Cora urged, softly, still wearing that horrible smile.

'Mm,' Nerissa murmured, lost in a sensual world of her own. Her tits had grown huge and firm under the other girl's ministrations, and when those nimble fingers came to pinch her nipples she gave a sighing moan of increased pleasure.

Mick held his breath as she raised herself up and positioned his cock between her thighs. Then she slowly sank down onto him, pushing him in through the soft folds of her labia and into her secret heart. He groaned loudly and thrust upwards, feeling her walls clutch at him like a gloved hand, nosing his way down the length of her pussy while the heat of his lust suffused his body and overwhelmed his mind. His hips moved instinctively to provide the friction he needed to take him nearer the brink of orgasm.

But Nerissa was still playing with him, teasing him. She withdrew almost completely and held him there with the ring of muscle around her vaginal entrance, stopping him from going further in. She caressed his balls, scraping her fingernails lightly against the taut skin, tickling them. And all the time she was moaning softly in response to Cora's continued stimulation of her nipples. Suddenly she threw back her head and came in a series of violent convulsions, jerking her pelvis and squeezing the tip of his glans almost painfully.

After that, instead of letting him thrust inside her, she got right off him and lay down exhausted by his side. Mick felt a wave of angry disappointment. His frustration was intense.

'Bitch!' he thought. 'Prick-teasing cow!'

But then he heard Cora say, 'I think this patient needs finishing off, Nurse, but don't worry. I'll do it. You can take a tea-break now.'

The touch of her firm fingers on the base of his cock was very reassuring. She began to masturbate him vigorously and with an air of efficiency, giving him what he so desperately needed. He relaxed into it, letting the powerful tide of arousal sweep him up with ever-increasing speed until the pent-up energy burst out of him in one long, glorious flood of gratification.

'That's much better, isn't it?' he heard a faint, solicitous voice say. 'You'll be feeling far more comfortable now.'

Mick sank into oblivion for a few minutes, and when he came to, his condom and the chain that bound his hands had been removed and Cora was sitting on a chair drinking coffee. His wrists felt sore. He threw her a wry grin, but she stared disdainfully back at him and got up. She left the room and returned a few seconds later with another mug of black coffee.

'Here, you'd better take your medicine like a man,' she said, handing him the drink. 'This'll sober you up for the drive home.'

Any comment on what she had just done for him seemed inappropriate. Nerissa was nowhere to be seen. Mick felt awkward, used. He swallowed the bitter coffee in a few gulps then began to get dressed. Embarrassment made him rush the process, fumbling with buttons, getting caught up in his trousers. He felt relieved when Cora finally said, without ceremony, 'Come on, I'll let you out now.' He followed her down the stairs to the front door and returned her brief, wry grin as he said goodbye, then hurried off to his car.

Once he was in his familiar driving seat Mick felt better. It had been a weird evening and he still didn't know quite what to make of it. He was disappointed that he hadn't been able to give Nerissa a thorough rogering, without that other girl being around, but that nurse-patient routine had been something new, kinky. Smiling to himself he headed off towards home.

Chapter Three

The half hour before she went on air was made pleasant for Jayne by the calming presence of Heather, the make-up girl. Tonight, Heather was even more full of gossip than usual.

'Apparently the phone lines were buzzing all last night,' she said, as she fluffed a smidgen of blusher over Jayne's cheekbones with a cotton bud. 'Your fans were ringing in wanting to know why you'd suddenly gone off air. Switchboard was practically jammed, by all accounts.'

'So absence really does make the heart grow fonder!' Jayne smiled. 'But don't tell me no one said they preferred Stella. I couldn't believe that.'

'There were a few, I think. But the vast majority of the calls were about you.'

Secretly gratified, Jayne said, 'Well, I watched Stella at home and I thought she did a very good job of it.'

'That's not the point though, is it? I mean, you're more attractive than she is. Men always prefer blondes, anyway. And at that time of night . . .'

She didn't have to spell it out. Jayne knew she was an essential part of the ETV package: a bit of class before the tacky smut. Viewers regularly sent in requests to 'see her with her kit off' or some such phrase. There had been a plan to produce a ETV calendar, with a glamour photo of herself along with the porn stars, but it had come to nothing. Stella had explained that Jayne's appeal lay in her inaccessibility, her mystique. If she ever disrobed for the camera she would become just another pin-up, and her pulling power would be lost.

'Okay, gorgeous!' Heather smiled, standing back from her chair. 'You're ready to face the world!'

Just as Jayne was about to leave the dressing room Stella appeared. 'You were great last night,' she told the producer. 'Mick thought so too.'

'I appreciate that,' Stella smiled, her brown eyes glinting merrily. 'You're a hard act to follow though, Jayne. I gather that the viewers weren't too pleased with the swap.'

There was no hint of envy in her voice. If anything, she sounded pleased. Perhaps because it reflected well on her judgement in choosing Jayne from the dozens of other candidates.

The two women walked along the corridor to Studio Four with Heather just behind, chatting as they went. Jayne was wearing a floor-length sheath dress in red satin and had to make three tiny steps for each of Stella's strides while she tugged at her tight-fitting bodice, pulling it up over her cleavage. She was conscious that, on entering the studio, she would be leaving the sisterly companionship of the dressing room and entering a male-dominated zone. Apart from Stella, Heather and Chris, the producer's assistant, all the other personnel were men.

Up in the gallery Tony, the director, gave Jayne a thumbs-up. She walked towards the black leather armchair in the middle of the studio floor and was waylaid by Bill, the sound man. 'Ready when you are, Jayne,' he grinned.

She knew he was referring to fixing onto her body the personal microphone and transmitter that she had to wear. It was a familiar routine, but she disliked his rather slimy manner of pawing her about and grinning while he did so. The tiny mike had to be positioned in her cleavage, while the box that transmitted the sound had to be taped to the small of her back. There was also an earpiece that allowed her to hear directions from Tony.

His fingers were soon groping between her breasts, making his usual heavy weather of the business. 'It's easier to hide this down your front than Stella's,' he informed her, with a lewd grin. 'You've got more up top than she has. I had a devil of a job last night.'

Jayne stood stock still, trying not to betray any emotion. His soft fingers did get her slightly aroused as they moved over the mounds of her breasts, but she would have died rather than admit it. She also had to feign indifference when his hand stroked her rump in the process of fixing the transmitter. He let her put the earpiece in herself.

Jayne was relieved when it was over. Sometimes the tiny mike failed – 'overcome by emotion,' as Bill jokingly put it – and had to be replaced, which would involve another groping session, but tonight she was safe. Everything worked for the sound test. She waited nervously for the countdown to transmission but as soon as the autocue was running, with her own words rolling past her eyes, all nervousness left her and she was as relaxed and easygoing with the viewers as if she were talking to them in her own lounge at home. That she knew, because she had been told it so many times, was her great talent as a presenter.

'Good evening, and welcome to *Cinema Sinmore*,' she smiled at camera two, behind which the dim shape of Stuart, the cameraman, could be seen. 'But before I tell you about tonight's big film – which I'm sure you're going to love, incidentally – I think I should apologise for my absence last night. As Stella told you, I came over all queasy while the film was being transmitted. And in case you're wondering, I'm not in the club! Not in *that* club, anyway! Seriously though, folks, to all of you who phoned in I say thanks for your solicitous enquiries but I'm perfectly all right now.'

Jayne uncrossed and recrossed her legs, as a subtle signal that she was about to change subject. She leant forward and saw her cleavage in the monitor, the tops of her breasts highlighted by the studio lights. Knowing that she looked good, Jayne gave a smile of self-satisfaction before she continued with the introduction.

'Well tonight's offering comes from horny Holland and features that Dutch lesbian sexpot Anna Vandyke, together with dashing Austrian screen hero, Karl Schtonker-Reisen. Without giving too much away, I can tell you that Anna and her two butch vixens have a fine old time trying to subdue the indomitable Karl, but when sexy superstar Delycia appears all hell breaks loose. Anna and Karl both have the hots for the gorgeous Delycia, and do their best to outdo each other in seducing her. Definitely one not to be missed by all you Anna and Delycia fans!'

Once the opening sequence started to roll Jayne heard Tony's voice in her ear. 'That was great, Jayne! Should keep 'em happy, anyway. Want to join me and Stella in a drink?'

She looked up towards the gallery and gave them a thumbs-up sign. Stella grinned down at her and Jayne unclipped the mike from her bosom and stood up, waiting for Bill to release her from the rest of the sound equipment. Again he stroked her buttock momentarily as he stripped off the transmitter and she felt a warmth spread through her lower regions despite herself. She knew that Bill lusted after her, along with the rest of the crew, but she had always been careful not to encourage him.

Tonight, though, she found herself idly thinking about the possibilities of an affair – not so much with Bill, whom she didn't fancy, but with Tony, whom she did. After the previous night's disappointing session with Mick she was beginning to think she would have to look elsewhere for sexual satisfaction.

Not that it was Mick's fault, she told herself hastily. But the lustre had gone out of their relationship and she didn't know what she could do to bring it back. If she didn't start wanting him again soon there was little point in their continuing to live together. They had precious else in common, after all.

Tony, Jayne and Stella met in the hospitality room, where Tony had the key to the small bar. While *Raunchy Rivals* played to the viewers, they sipped their drinks and took a temporary break from the pressures of live broadcasting. Tony grinned at Jayne over his glass as he said, 'Your absence caused quite a stir last night. I hope it was worth it.'

'What do you mean?'

He winked at the producer. 'Stella thought you could do with an early night. But thousands of viewers were deprived of their favourite bedtime lech, so I hope the boyfriend appreciated it.'

Jayne shrugged, embarrassed. 'I don't think he realised.'

Tony's blue eyes scanned her avidly, and her insides started slowly liquidising. 'Don't tell me he takes a gorgeous girl like you for granted. Doesn't he know how many men you turn on each night? Women, too, probably.'

'Don't fish, Tony,' Stella interjected. 'Jayne's relationship with Mick is her own business.'

'It's okay, Stella. I don't mind admitting everything isn't hunky-dory at home. What can you expect if you hardly ever see each other?'

'I'm just glad I'm a night person,' Stella smiled. 'I only need a little sleep. You have to have the right constitution and temperament for this job.'

Jayne remained silent, wondering if she was cut out for it herself. She enjoyed the work, but was sacrificing her private life too high a price to pay? She wondered, not for the first time, about Stella. She had the impression that the woman didn't have a steady partner, that she lived alone. But Jayne also suspected that she didn't go without her share, either.

After a brief discussion of the film programme for the rest of the week, Tony returned to the gallery, leaving the women alone. Stella stretched back in her chair with a sigh, uncrossing her shapely legs, and pushing out her small but equally shapely breasts beneath her silk blouse. She gave Jayne a woman-to-woman smile and said baldly, 'You fancy Tony, don't you?'

Jayne felt her cheeks warming as the blood rushed to them. 'He's quite attractive, yes.'

'Tempted to stray, then? He's hot for you too, you know.'

Jayne shrugged. 'I don't know. Things are tough enough with Mick right now. I don't want to make things worse. And if we do split up, I wouldn't want to get into another long term affair. Not while I'm doing this job.'

'My feeling exactly. Sex without commitment is my bag. Fortunately, I only mix with people who have the same agenda.'

Jayne's curiosity was aroused. 'Where do you meet them? I mean, how can you tell?'

Stella's brown eyes turned evasive. 'I don't believe in leaving it to chance. You can waste a lot of time chatting men up, dating them, and then finding that they're looking for love, not sex. Fortunately I don't have to worry about that any more.'

'You don't? Why's that?'

'Well, I belong to this club. It's very exclusive, and we all agree to abide by the rules so there's no question of mis-understandings.'

Jayne was intrigued. 'What kind of club?'

'I can only tell you if you're interested in joining.'

'How do I know, unless you tell me about it?'

Stella reflected, then she smiled. 'Let me put it this way. You know the stuff we churn out here, soft porn?'

Jane pulled a face. 'Crap, yes.'

'Well the club I belong to provides the real thing.'

'Hard core porn?'

'You could say that. The difference is, we make the videos ourselves.'

Jayne frowned. 'Isn't that illegal?'

'If we tried to sell them in this country it would be. But we make them primarily for our own entertainment, so we stay within the law. Anyway, if you wanted me to propose you as a member, I could. Think about it.'

Stella rose from her chair, smoothing down her black silky trousers. Jayne was surprised at the strength of the fluttering in her stomach. Knowing that her producer engaged in hard porn action put her in a different light. The smouldering sexuality that Stella emitted had to be reassessed. What she had thought subtle and understated now seemed to hide some powerful secret, and she was intrigued.

'It might be just what I need,' she mused. 'I could still love Mick, but find satisfaction elsewhere. And if he didn't know, where would be the harm in it?'

'It's a time-honoured formula,' Stella grinned, rinsing out her glass in the sink behind the bar counter. 'But you'd have to be careful. I don't live with anyone so I don't need an alibi, but you would.'

'When do you go to this club?'

'After work on a Friday, Saturday or Sunday. We could pre-record your links, of course.'

Jayne suddenly realised, that despite her casual tone, Stella wanted her to join the club. Very much indeed. Again her insides reacted to the realisation, throwing her into turmoil. Did Stella secretly desire her?

'I'll have to think about it,' she said, backing off.

'Of course you must. There's no hurry. But I have to propose you to the committee and they meet next week. If you haven't decided by then you'll have to wait another month.'

Now Jayne was sure that Stella wanted her to join. She was bursting with a curiosity that was almost physical in its intensity. She could feel the hard button between her thighs throbbing insistently and knew that she was growing helplessly wet too. For the first time she even saw Stella as a sex object and was surprised by the force of the lesbian attraction.

Confused, she scrambled to her feet and, setting her empty glass down on the counter, mumbled an excuse and hurried to the ladies next door. She sat on the loo seat in a state of trembling excitement. I'm acting like an over-sexed adolescent, she told herself. Fancying first Tony, now Stella. She tried to pee, but her engorged labia wouldn't let it out easily. Feeling horribly decadent she rubbed herself frantically until the release came in a few, short spasms of electric pleasure and the flow of urine followed. Sighing with relief, Jayne heard the door of the ladies open and knew that it was Stella who had entered.

'I forgot to mention that you can use an assumed name,' she whispered, through the door of her cubicle. 'I use my own, but lots of people prefer pseudonyms.'

Jayne made an incoherent noise then wiped herself with the toilet paper and sat back exhausted, her dress tight about her thighs. It was a good job the creases would be hidden from the viewers she thought, irrelevantly. Hearing the tinkle of Stella's water music she got up and flushed her loo, then went out to wash her hands.

By the end of the evening Jayne was full of suppressed excitement. There was an added sparkle to her closing link that even the others noticed. She ad libbed her way through, posing flirtatiously with her lips moistened and her eyes gleaming seductively. Afterwards, when Bill came up to remove the mike, she could see his arousal beneath his cord trousers and hear the deep-throated lust in his voice.

'God, you were one hot bitch tonight!' he murmured huskily, as his hand caressed her behind. 'Made up for your absence yesterday, all right!'

Tony uttered similar sentiments, and Jayne revelled in the sense of power it gave her. Up to now she had always remained slightly aloof from all the hype, distrusting her newfound status as a surrogate porn queen. But now she was no longer ashamed of her rôle. Tony's earlier remark, that he hoped Mick appreciated her, had struck home. If he didn't find her sexy tonight then he was a lost cause in the bed department, she decided, and she would be perfectly justified in seeking her fulfilment elsewhere.

But when she got home she was devastated to find the flat in darkness and her lover absent. 'The bastard!' she said aloud, striking a histrionic pose. 'I give the performance of my life and he doesn't even see it.'

He still wasn't home when, at two thirty, Jayne crawled into bed. She lay awake, miserable and anxious. True he was sometimes out this late, when he and his mates played poker, but tonight of all nights! Somehow she felt he should have known she wanted him. If there was no telepathic link between them, if he couldn't sense when she needed him and be there for her, how close could they really be?

Jayne knew her reasoning was irrational, but she couldn't help herself. Her mind drifted away from Mick and back towards the secret club that Stella belonged to. She wondered what kind of people joined such a club – over-sexed ones, presumably. She thought of Stella, performing sex acts with other members before the camera, and wondered how it felt to be a real porn star. Strange, she'd never wondered how it felt to be Anna Vandyke, or Delycia. Perhaps that was because the films were third rate, the acting unconvincing. It would be different if people acted as if they really meant it, were really turned on by each other. What wonderful films you could make then!

Mick crawled in about half an hour later, when Jayne was on the verge of sleep. Her earlier desire had dissipated and when he disturbed her she merely grunted a little and turned over to doze. He didn't attempt to seduce her, or even talk, but she heard him give a deep sigh. Part of her wanted to take him in her arms, to try and rekindle their physical passion for each other, but her heart wasn't in it. Instead she gave herself up to a confused sequence of erotic and fantastic dreams. The only thing she remembered about these dreams was the name she was known by: *Miranda*.

She woke halfway through the morning to find Mick had already gone to work. It was a familiar situation, but now it only underlined the gulf between them. After a black coffee and croissant she picked up the phone and dialled Stella's home number, but there was no answer. Disappointed, she nevertheless left a message to say she was interested in being put forward as a club member and suggested using the name from her dream. She hoped Stellla would get the message at home. It was not something she wanted to talk about at the studio with types like Bill around.

Although she wouldn't mind Tony knowing. At the thought of the blue-eyed director, Jayne's heart gave a sudden lurch. What if he were involved in this club of Stella's too? It was dangerous having affairs with colleagues, which was why she had kept him at bay so far. But if the rules of this club forbade its members to become involved with each other outside its walls, as Stella had hinted, that put a very different complexion on things.

During the next few days Jayne was on tenterhooks wondering whether her name had been put forward to the committee. Stella had warned her not to mention it again: she would let her know the outcome. Even so, the very thought of joining such a club put a new spring in Jayne's step and a sparkle in her eyes that was noticed by the viewers. They rang and wrote in asking if she had a new lover, begging her to wear certain clothes or making various indecent suggestions, and seemed to have completely forgotten that she went off air the previous week.

'You're flavour of the month again, Jayne,' Stella remarked dryly.

Had she guessed that her appeal was based on the prospect of imminent sexual liberation? Jayne felt a new and subtle tension in her life, both at the studio and at home. Mick was behaving oddly, suspiciously, and she wondered if he had noticed her new aura and concluded that she had taken a lover, but the strange thing was she no longer cared. He'd had his chance and been found wanting. They were friendly towards each other when they met, and she bore him no ill will, but he no longer made her pulse race or her heart throb. Someone else would have to fill that void in her life now – or rather, several others.

Then, just as Jayne was growing impatient, a call came from Stella one afternoon.

'There is a vacancy, and the committee would like to see you,' she said straight away. 'Can you make it on Friday, after work? We could go together.'

'Yes, that's fine. Is there anything I should do? Wear?'

'Wear your sexiest underwear. And be prepared to take it off.'

Jayne's hand was trembling as she replaced the receiver. Stella had sounded so matter-of-fact, but the prospect of appearing before this anonymous 'committee' filled her with a combination of heady excitement, extreme curiosity and sheer terror. She doubted whether she would get much more information out of her producer so she decided not to try. When they met at work that evening nothing was said on either side. But by the time Friday night came around, in Jayne's over-active mind the interview had taken on the awesome dimensions of an initiation ceremony.

She was nervous and fluffed her lines a couple of times, thinking of the trial to come. Stella seemed to sense this and refrained from commenting as they got ready to leave the building. In the dressing room she glanced with approval at Jayne's black lace underwear trimmed with red satin bows but again said nothing. Jayne put a loose turquoise velour top on over her bra and pulled on some stretchy black velvet leggings which she wore with high-heeled black patent sandals. She had agonised for some time over what to wear and settled for what she thought of as 'classy tarty'.

'Do I look okay?' she asked Stella hesitantly.

'Great! You needn't worry, Jayne. The committee will love you, I'm sure.'

'Will they know who I am?' she asked, uncertainly. 'I mean, what if they watch the programme?'

'If any of them does recognise you they won't mention it. We have a kind of unwritten rule that forbids any reference to what we do outside the club. And you'll be known as Miranda, remember. Better get used to that.'

They went by taxi to the address in Hampstead that Stella gave the driver. Jayne felt relieved that they were going to a snobbish area, and not to some sleazy part of town like Soho. As the cab whisked them through the North London streets she felt her apprehension subside to the level of a slight fluttering in the stomach. Below, she was aware of heat coursing through her sex organs, plumping out her vulva, moistening her quim and making her hidden jewel quiver and throb with excited anticipation. Her nipples tingled too, encased in the lacy, uplifting bra.

Although Jayne had become used to appearing before the camera, what she was now facing was a new kind of ordeal. She had no idea what kind of questions they might ask her, what they might make her do. Stella had said something about removing her underwear: would they want to inspect her naked body? The thought sent a wild thrill of shame through her. And what kind of people would they be, male or female, or both?

The taxi drew up outside a house with a high wall around it. They rang a bell by a side gate and Stella had to give a password: *Belladonna*. The gate swung open as if on invisible hinges, adding to the air of mystery. Although it was dark their way along a stone path was lit by low-level lanterns and Jayne could tell, from the shadowy plants and delicious floral and herbal scents, that she was in a beautifully laid-out garden.

At the end of the path reared a large stone house, with one window illuminated. There's money here all right,

Jayne thought, seeing the size of the place and the elegant style. It was completely secluded and, as she entered the tiled porch supported on oak beams, she felt almost as if she were entering hallowed ground.

'This is just one of the places where we hold our meetings,' Stella explained, in a low voice. 'Sometimes it's a hotel, sometimes a private residence like this.'

The heavy oak door yielded when Stella turned the handle and they entered a spacious hallway furnished with antiques. It was all very civilised and not at all what Jayne had expected. They crossed into a small waiting room where there was some interesting reading matter spread out on a side table. Jayne flicked through the pile. There were glossy fetish mags, full of exclusive – and expensive – fashion items in leather and latex; a brochure for a plastic surgeon's clinic in Mayfair; a catalogue of porn videos; a leaflet advertising 'Free as Air' holidays for nudists; a catalogue of 'Whips and Crops for the Discerning Horsewoman'.

At last footsteps were heard in the hall and a pleasant-looking young woman appeared. She was a secretarial type, her light-brown hair clipped back neatly and wearing only minimal make-up. Although the high-necked blue jersey dress concealed her body, it clung to her buxom figure in such a way that its very modesty seemed oddly suggestive. She gave Jayne a smile, ignoring Stella completely.

'Miss Miranda? I think we're ready for you now, if you'd like to come this way.'

It was all so weirdly normal, as if she were being interviewed for a job. Stella smiled and said, 'Good luck!' as Jayne left the room and followed the secretary's trim rump down the faded Persian runner in the centre of the hall towards a door at the end. She had no idea what would be expected of her once she was on the other side of that door, and she regarded it with foreboding. But as they reached it the woman turned round with another friendly smile.

'Don't be nervous. We've all been through this – and lived to tell the tale!'

The door opened to reveal half a dozen people sitting behind a long table. It was a large, high-ceilinged room with elegant furniture and a Chinese carpet. Against the wall, opposite the desk, was a chaise longue draped with a William Morris print throw. Jayne surveyed the faces of the committee, three men and three women. They were all smiling pleasantly at her. The man in the middle, with a dark mane of swept-back hair and square, gold-rimmed glasses, greeted her. 'Welcome, Miranda. Please sit down.'

There was a small gilt chair with a tapestry-covered seat directly in front of the table. Jayne sat down on the edge of it, her nerves starting to betray her. She was conscious of the keen looks everyone was giving her, surveying her from top to toe. Her glances at them were fleet and surreptitious, but she gained an impression of very pretty women and striking men.

'You were nominated by one of our most respected members, so we are disposed to look kindly upon your application,' the man said, in a pompous tone.

This is unreal, Jayne thought, reminding herself of the nature of these people's activities. Anyone would think it was some exclusive gentlemen's club that she had requested to join.

He seemed to read her mind. 'The Eye Spy Club is a most unusual institution, and therefore we have to be very circumspect about admission,' he continued. 'We need to know beyond doubt that any applicant would be prepared to take part wholeheartedly in our activities and also obey the injunction against speaking of them outside. The qualities we are looking for, then, are enthusiasm, discretion and absolute loyalty to fellow members.'

'Those are just some of the required qualities, Quentin,' the woman to his right broke in. 'She also has to be a lewd little bitch with a filthy imagination!'

The others guffawed at the sudden change of tone, and Jayne found herself grinning too. 'Quite,' Quentin said, stiffly. 'But we shall be testing her lubricity in due course. Firstly I wish to stress the moral obligations of membership.'

'Oh Quen, don't be so stuffy!' another of the women, a stunning redhead, declared. 'Can I ask her a few questions?' The man shrugged, conceding the chair. She gave Jayne a dazzling smile. 'My dear, we're interested in your reasons for wanting to join us. I take it that you have some idea of what we're about?'

Jayne nodded. Choosing her words carefully she began, 'As I understand it, you're into sex without guilt, without too much emotional involvement. And you make videos? Well, I like the sound of both those things. My sex life is practically nonexistent, although I still live with my partner, and I have to watch sex films as part of my job. It gets very frustrating at times.'

'I can imagine.'

Quentin took up the thread. 'So you're not looking to replace your lover?'

'Not at all. I'm still fond of him, and I'm hoping that joining your club might revitalise our sex life, but he won't know anything about it.'

'Will you be able to make plausible excuses for the nights you're here?'

'He's used to me working late. It won't be a problem.'

'I hope you're not expecting too much, Miranda,' Quentin said, rather sternly. 'This isn't just another branch of *Relate* you know.'

The others giggled at the absurdity of the idea and Jayne smiled coolly back. She caught the eye of a blond man with gorgeous green eyes, who suddenly winked at her. A flash of lust caught her by surprise and she felt herself blush.

'I want to join as much for my own fulfilment as anything.'

'Ah!'

Her reply seemed to meet with general approval. The red haired woman took up the questioning again. 'How much do you know about your own sexuality, Miranda? I mean, have you ever had a lesbian experience? Do you prefer to be active or passive? Have you taken pleasure in pain?'

Jayne began to feel very naive. She thought about the things that she and Mick had done in the old days, things they'd considered quite adventurous at the time, but she now realised that they would sound pretty tame to these sexual sophisticates. 'I've done all the usual things. I like giving head, I like being licked down below myself . . .'

'We don't use such euphemisms here,' the woman broke in with a smile. 'You can be totally frank with us, Miranda. Repeat after me, "I like having my cunt probed and my clit licked".'

Jayne suppressed a giggle then repeated the phrase solemnly. The words sounded strange coming from her own mouth, although she had heard them uttered many times in the course of her job. Saying them now had a liberating effect on her, and she felt a surge of exhilaration.

'So you like sucking cock, too?' the blond man said, fixing her with his lustrous green eyes.

'Yes, I love sucking cock,' she repeated, pointedly holding his gaze.

'Do you like it up the arse?' another man asked. 'And with two men at a time? Or with a man and a woman, one thrusting into you with his dick from behind while you suck and lick the woman's pussy?'

'I . . . I don't know. I've never tried,' she answered, squirming on her chair.

'But does the idea of it turn you on?' Quentin asked. They were all surveying her closely now, watching her clenched hands and the rosy blush that was spreading over her cheeks. Could they also see her nipples hardening beneath the soft blue top, and sense the way her clitoris was pulsating? The crotch of her pants had turned into a tightly stretched string that rubbed against that fleshy button every time she squeezed her thighs together.

Jayne nodded, speechless at last. She felt a wanton urge to lie down and let them do as they liked with her. Was that what this 'interview' was leading to? The erotic tension in the air was increasing by the second, taking on the properties of a tangible force. She had the impression that every man and woman on the committee was lusting after her, fantasising about what they might do to her, and yet they maintained their cool, calm exteriors.

'Are you feeling sexy right now?' the blonde woman asked, with a smile. Again she nodded, knowing that if she tried to speak she could only utter a croak.

'Good!' Quentin smiled, looking round at the rest of the panel. 'Shall we proceed to the practical part of the examination?'

Jayne felt her heart race, wondering what they would want her to do, or to do to her. Whatever it was she was already half prepared, her body roused and willing, her mind lulled into compliance. Lust was permeating her flesh, flooding her sex organs with throbbing desire, augmenting her breasts within the confines of her bra, lubricating her vagina and moistening the soft folds of her vulva, making her clitoris and nipples bulge and stiffen and strain for the stimulating touch of a fingertip. The time for talk, however lewd and crude, was over, and she was ready for action.

Chapter Four

Mick didn't know how long he'd been feeling jealous. Days? Weeks? Perhaps even months or years. It was like an underground current in his psyche that had only just fully surfaced. Not that he had the slightest proof that Jayne was being unfaithful. It was just that now he needed proof that she was not.

His own humiliating encounter with the two student nurses had been a kind of release from his ceaseless wondering about her, but now his curiosity was eating into him again, taking him back into the old cycle of corroding jealousy. When Jayne had first started working for ETV he used to wait like this in his car for her to appear, and then follow her home. Now he was at it once more.

The street near the tower which housed the TV company's studios was almost deserted, and Mick was parked in a side street from where he could see the entrance to the building. He waited from eleven to midnight, and then to one o'clock, until his mind was as numb as his body. Around half one there was movement behind the swing doors in the small lobby, figures coming and going, and then a cab drawing up. Mick stared through his side window, on full alert, and was rewarded by the sight of Jayne in her long black velvet jacket and matching trousers coming out of the building on the heels of another woman, Stella, the producer. He recognised her from the TV, that slight figure with the dark cap of hair.

To his surprise they got into the taxi together. It was still

48

possible that Jayne was going straight home, of course, that they were sharing the cab. But unlikely. Mick waited until the vehicle had disappeared round the corner of the building before revving his engine and slinking off in pursuit. Fortunately the cab had to wait at a red light about a hundred yards away and he was able to keep it in sight. As soon as it rounded the next corner he put his foot down and sped along in pursuit.

They were heading up Hampstead way. Was that where Stella lived? Maybe they were going to her place for a nightcap and some shop talk. Unlikely. Were they having a lesbian affair? He laughed aloud at the thought. Jayne had never shown the slightest tendency in that direction but you never knew these days. Bisexuality was the in thing, wasn't it?

This is better than sitting at home, Mick told himself gleefully. But was it better than last night's little escapade? He was still unsure about that. There was a residual feeling of resentment in him that he hadn't managed to get the blonde girl alone. If he had, he was sure they wouldn't have got involved in all that nursey nonsense, but she would have let him make love to her straight. He'd never even got to see her tits, he thought resentfully. They had promised a great deal, sticking out so round and firm beneath her sweater. He felt cheated, and it had all been that other girl's fault, that Cora.

Even so, he'd kind of liked some of the things they did to him. Being tied up, for instance. And not knowing quite what was coming next. It had been very arousing, in a masochistic kind of way. He wouldn't say no if some girl turned him into a passive victim again – not if she had tits like that!

But now Mick was on a new adventure, and it promised to be quite exciting. If Jayne was seeing someone he would bide his time about saying anything, let her make a slip so she would land herself in it. He liked the idea of seeing her trying to squirm out of it, making up silly excuses, telling futile lies, while he knew about it all along. And if he was wrong, and her late nights were quite innocent then he must look elsewhere for the cause of her lack of enthusiasm for him. Maybe he had bad breath.

The taxi drew up at the far end of a residential street, near a green gate in a wall. Mick stopped the car at the kerb behind a parked van, making sure he was away from the street light. He got out and positioned himself behind the van, peeping round the back. The two women got out of the cab and rang a bell by the gate. He could hear its faint tinkle in the still night air. Then they disappeared through the gate and he heard it close behind them.

'Damn!' Mick walked cautiously up the road until he came to the gate, but was too wary to ring the bell himself. The wall was high and made of smooth brick, so there was no hope of scaling it, and it stretched to the end of the road. He followed it and turned the corner, seeing the same brick wall run along until it was broken by a small shopping parade. Over the top of it he could glimpse chimneys and the tops of trees. It must be some house. If Stella lived there she was a very wealthy woman indeed.

He heard a cough coming from a doorway in one of the shops, followed by the flash of a flame. As he turned to go a woman appeared, wearing a short skirt and boxy jacket and drawing on a cigarette. Mick looked away and started to walk back towards the corner but he heard the quick clack of her heels coming after him and a brief shock of desire took him by surprise. She fell into step beside him and murmured, 'Are you looking, love? I can give you anything you fancy, within reason.'

Mick turned and looked at her. Although she was heavily painted, beneath the thick mascara and thicker lipstick she was rather pretty. And young, no more than twenty-two. He was tempted, very tempted.

'A quick one in the dooorway won't cost you much,' she offered, blowing out smoke.

He frowned. 'No, if we're going to do it my car's just around the corner.'

She smiled, showing rather good teeth. Something told him she was a cut above your average street walker. But this was Hampstead, after all. Maybe she was on her way home from her patch in a less salubrious neighbourhood and he was a chance she couldn't resist. He admired her opportunism.

'Okay, but we must agree terms before I get into your car. What do you want, a blow job?'

'Okay. But will you sit in my lap and wriggle as well? Let me touch you?'

'It'll cost you extra.'

They agreed a fee, which was just about all Mick had in his wallet, and then started to walk back along the brick wall. When they came to the green door he paused. 'Know what's behind there?'

'Yeah, it's some kind of sex club,' she said, casually.

Mick felt his pulse race and his heart leapt painfully. 'Sex club?'

'Yeah, members only.' She tittered. 'No pun intended.'

'Is that all you know about it?'

She shrugged. 'I'm not a member, am I? It costs a lot to join. Snobby types with more money than sense, I expect.'

'And you've no idea what they get up to?'

She looked bored, puffing away on her fag. 'Usual stuff I expect, flagellation, bondage. Stuff I do, only they dress up and ponce around and get off on the idea of it instead of getting down to it. Bunch of wankers if you ask me.'

Mick found her attitude oddly refreshing. He felt himself warming to her, fancying her even. His appetite for the diversion ahead increased. They stopped at his car and he counted out the money into her hot little hand then unlocked the door, leaned over and opened the door to the back seat. She scrambled in.

After pushing the two front seats as far forward as they

could go, Mick climbed in after her. She'd already taken off
her jacket and plonked it in the driver's seat and now she
was slipping off her shoes. Mick shut the door carefully, so
as not to make a noise, then took off his own jacket.
Embarrassment suddenly overwhelmed him. 'I'm not used
to this,' he said.

'That's okay, just let me do all the work.' She pulled off
her cotton top to reveal small breasts encased in a see-
through nylon bra. Her fingers went to his fly and she began
to pull down the zipper as he reached out for her nipples,
prominent beneath their flimsy covering.

'You can take it off me if you like.'

Mick fumbled behind her back and soon her breasts were
free, the brown nipples contracting to hard little cones. He
grabbed the two handfuls of warm flesh with a sigh, just as
she pulled his penis free of his pants. Her handling made it
grow twice as big in seconds.

'Wait, let me get down on the floor,' she told him.

Carefully she squeezed her small body in between the
seats until she was kneeling before him, her mouth poised
over his erection. Her breasts were out of his reach, but the
minute her lips closed over his glans Mick was oblivious of
all else. He fell back in sensual delight as her tongue went
into the groove at the tip of his organ and tickled him
slowly.

'Mm, that's good!' he groaned, feeling his cock rear
further into her mouth. She was cupping his balls too now,
levering them out of his pants to dangle in the cool air.
There was something pleasantly relaxed and unhurried
about her, unlike the few other whores he'd known. Maybe
he was benefiting from being the last trick of the night.

Before he could really get into it, she suddenly got up off
her knees and moved onto his lap, hitching up her short
skirt so that his prick could rub against her smooth nylon
panties. Mick took his erection in his hands and tried to fit it
in the groove between her labia but without much success.

She was moving around on his thighs like greased lightning, her breasts bobbing within reach of his lips. He caught one nipple and sucked hard. She moaned and writhed with renewed ardour, and his cock slid along her increasingly wet crotch.

One of her hands was on his shoulder while the other took hold of his penis at the root and began to move it up and down between her thighs. Mick could feel himself on the verge of coming, and his breath came in short gasps. He chewed on the small bead of her nipple, his hands caressing the rest of her breasts. Her bottom made circular motions over his thighs, her pussy making only intermittent contact with his penis through the nylon panties.

'Suck me again!' he begged her, needing more direct stimulation.

She slid off his lap onto the seat and skewed herself round so she could take all of his swollen member into her mouth. Her tits were still within reach of his fingers and he stroked them more feverishly as the desire mounted in him, making his organ thrust into the warm recesses of her mouth. Her tongue played up and down his shaft with the skill of a musician, taking him nearer and nearer to the climax in one long crescendo of sensation.

In his mind Mick was thrusting into the warm hole between her thighs, Jayne's thighs, any woman's thighs. He felt the force gathering in him like a storm until it suddenly broke out, heat cascading through his pelvis, balls shuddering in one long frenzy of release. He was scarcely aware of her mopping up after him with tissues from the box behind the back seat. Nor did he notice her putting her bra back on and then her top. It was only when he heard her opening the car door that he realised she was about to leave him.

'Can't you stay?' he asked her, craving a bit of a cuddle.

'No, I've got to get home. It's late.'

She sounded hard, dismissive. Mick raised his head and saw her bum slide off the seat and out into the night. 'Bye!'

she called, then slammed the car door in his face.

Mick lay there, head down on the seat cover he'd bought last Saturday from Halfords, and almost fell asleep until he remembered where he was and what he was supposed to be doing. Then he sat bolt upright with a start. He looked at his watch, holding it up to the back window to catch the faint glimmer of street lighting: four a.m. There had been no sound of a taxi arriving down the street, unless he'd been so taken up with his whoring that he'd missed it. A worried frown crossed his face as he considered the possibility that Jayne might have emerged from the green door without him noticing. Perhaps he'd better just drive home and forget it.

Quentin sat facing her with his hands clasped in front of him, looking as if he took the business very seriously indeed. Jayne could feel the suspense in the room and licked her lips, nervously. She was going to have to do something, or take part in something, but what?

'What we want you to do now, Miranda,' he began, speaking with slow precision, 'is to take your clothes off for us in the manner of a striptease. Make it sexy, erotic, arouse us. We are all red-blooded men – and women.' He looked round at the others, smiling, and they smiled back. 'Then we want you to go over to that couch, make yourself comfortable, then make yourself come.'

Jayne felt her cheeks burning at the thought of masturbating before an audience of six people. She thought first, 'I can't do it!' But then she realised that it was a fair test of her willingness to take part in the club's activities. If she wasn't up to this, there would be no point in her joining.

Besides, Jayne did feel a thrill of wicked delight at the prospect of indulging her latent exhibitionism. Already she felt horny, especially when she looked into the green eyes of that hunk at the end of the table. If she imagined she was doing it for him alone she was sure she could put on a convincing show.

Quentin and the others were watching her face closely, waiting for her response. At last she gave a nervous smile. 'Okay.'

'Good! To make it a bit easier for you we'll play some music. Then you can imagine you're performing in front of a camera. Just you and the cameraman. You can use the chair you're sitting on as a prop, if you like. Stephen? Start the music, please.'

The dark haired man on Quentin's left pressed a button on the desk and some raunchy music filled the room. Jayne took a deep breath and closed her eyes, trying to imagine herself as a striptease artiste in a club. She'd seen so many such performances on film that it should come as second nature to her if only she could overcome her initial shyness. Mentally she reviewed her clothes and decided to start with her shoes and work her way up.

'When I stand up, that's when I'll start,' she told herself. For a few more seconds she sat there, psyching herself up to it, then rose dramatically to her feet pulling herself up to her full height, and went round to the back of the chair. She rested on it with her legs apart, bottom swaying seductively as she boldly surveyed the faces of the panel. Each of them was regarding her with polite interest, one or two of them scribbling on the pad in front of them. 'Oh God!' she thought. 'I didn't realise they'd be taking notes!'

Although it made the whole business seem more like an examination Jayne wouldn't let it faze her. She put one foot on the seat of the chair and pulled up her loose trouser leg a little, displaying her shapely ankle. Her mouth was stuck in a permanent pout, her eyelids lowered seductively. The adrenaline was rushing through her veins, powered by the twin forces of sex and fear. She eased off one shoe and held it up like a trophy.

Soon that shoe was under the chair and she was taking off the other one. Without her heels she felt less commanding but it couldn't be helped. She wouldn't have been able to remove her leggings without them. Now she had her hands in her elasticated waist band and turned her back to her audience as she eased the velvet trousers down over her bottom. There were murmurs of appreciation as she wiggled her bum at them, knowing her taut buttocks looked good in the minuscule black panties.

With the leggings off Jayne felt freer, showing off her well shaped legs in a few stretchy poses. Again she turned her back and slipped her hands down the back of her knickers, caressing her buttocks as she swayed and thrust, before she turned her attention, and theirs, to her upper half. She rolled up her turquoise top until it lodged over the shelf of her bosom, exposing her navel and her slim waist. Then she began to stroke her stomach, rolling her hips around as she did so.

The music swelled and Jayne put her hands beneath the roll of velour to feel her breasts beneath. She moaned slightly and thrust out her pelvis, watching the reaction of the committee through half-closed lids. The blond man's eyes were smouldering with lust and she felt an answering pang in her crotch, making her gyrate her hips even more. Within the lacy pouch her clitoris swelled and throbbed, giving her performance even more credibility. 'I'm starting to get into this,' she thought, with a thrill of pride.

Crossing her hands over her front, Jayne slowly pulled the top up to her neck and then over her head. Her breasts felt pert and full, almost overflowing their cups, and she was sure they must be able to see the outline of her rigid nipples beneath the lace. She had always been rather proud of her breasts and was looking forward to displaying them, but not yet. She would make them wait for it.

Turning her back on them again, Jayne reached up and unhooked her bra but left it in place. She stroked her own buttocks, enjoying the feel of the smooth round flesh through the thin material of her panties. One hand slipped round the front and found the hard nub of her clitoris. She rubbed it briskly with her forefinger and felt the buzz of sexual energy lift her a little higher. Still with her back to them she put one hand inside her bra and tweaked her nipples in turn.

Facing front again Jayne put both hands beneath her loose bra cups and clasped her breasts tightly. She stared straight into the eyes of the blond man for a few seconds, challenging him to find her sexy. His green eyes blinked lazily and she felt her quim convulse with desire. Getting into this club would be worth it for the chance to screw him alone! The thought inspired her to be more daring. She covered as much of her two breasts as she could with one hand and whipped off the bra with the other, tossing it in his direction. He caught it with a smile and pressed it to his lips.

With both hands now covering her nipples, Jayne writhed and bucked her pelvis suggestively, clad only in her black lace panties. She turned away and let her breasts hang free, out of their sight, while she stood open legged and placed both palms on her buttocks, massaging them round and round. She pulled them down at the back until the deep cleft was exposed, then ran a fingertip up and down it, making herself shiver with longing. Soon she would be able to satisfy herself and, by God, she would be more than ready for it! Her lust was taking over, driving her on, making her more and more wanton and uninhibited.

Jayne took a few steps forward, making for the chaise longue where she would perform her finale. She got onto the red velvet seat and, still with her back to the committee table, eased the pants down her thighs and past her knees until she could hop nimbly out of them. She whirled the scrap of lace around her head several times then threw it as hard as she could onto the floor behind. Completely naked, she caressed her breasts and then stroked the hairy mat over her mons, feeling the hard core of her clitoris just below. She was thoroughly roused now, and more than ready to pleasure herself. The committee continued to watch her impassively, taking notes from time to time, but there was an electric charge in the air that was bound to be affecting everyone in the room.

A smile hovered on Jayne's lips as she slowly turned around on the springy upholstered seat, both hands covering her breasts but with her pubis laid bare. She opened her fingers a little and took the peeping nipples between her thumb and forefinger, rolling and pinching them while she continued to gyrate her hips. She squeezed her buttocks and thighs rhythmically, enjoying the heightened sensation in the area between them. She passed her tongue over her lips, making them slick and glossy in imitation of the way her vulva felt.

Then she looked straight at green eyes again and relished the pure lust she saw in them. Smiling more broadly Jayne sank down onto the sofa and raised her left knee, letting the other thigh dangle, so that beneath the fluffy bush of pale brown hair her pink folds were open to the air. She thrust her head back, feeling the heavy blonde curtain of her hair fall across the sloping deep-buttoned back of the chaise longue. A feeling of voluptuousness swept over her as she let her right hand fall casually to her stomach where she began stroking herself gently. The convulsive shudder that this titillating treatment evoked deep within took her by surprise, making her back arch and her pelvis thrust urgently into the air.

They were all watching her, waiting for the real action to begin, but she took her time. Aware of being the sole focus of six pairs of eyes, Jayne revelled in the attention, used it to feed her own auto-eroticism. She gave each of her nipples a firm tweak with her left hand, accompanied by a squeezing of her buttocks and an upward thrust of her mons, and the tight furled bud at the top of her labia hardened and expanded into throbbing life. Lazily she reached down from her belly to part the soft, swollen lips of her vulva and give access to her open quim.

Jayne's eyes, still dreamily hooded, turned back towards the man who had most taken her fancy. His emerald gaze was scintillating beneath the lock of blond hair that fell carelessly across his brow. Slowly she reached down, still half mesmerised by the jewel-like clarity of those eyes, and with a sly smile slipped a finger into herself. He blinked lazily, like a lizard, and Jayne imagined it was his finger that was stirring up her pot, his lust that was driving it deeper into the warm, liquid heart of her pussy. She moved her finger round and felt the protruding clitoris, thrust hard against her wrist, vibrate hotly. Her breasts were straining upward, nipples stiff and red from her pinching, and she knew that she was not far off her climax.

Some exhibitionist instinct was urging Jayne not to come too soon, was making her prolong the show for them. She took her finger out and put it to her lips, sucking the musky moisture from it, and all the while she was looking at green eyes, making him want her more and more. If it was up to him I'd be allowed to join this establishment right away, she thought, her smile widening. Was he thinking about what he would do to her? Her insides lurched at the thought of those full, curving lips tasting her pussy. Was he hot for her, hard for her? Beneath the level of the table top, was his erection already visible beneath his trousers, jerking and thrusting like a live animal in captivity?

Jayne sat up, her breasts huge and taut, crested with the bright red buttons of her nipples. She opened her thighs wide so they could get a full frontal view of her pink, inviting pussy. There was a faint groan from one of the men, but she wasn't quick enough to tell which one. She hoped it was her favourite hunk. Balancing her feet on the chaise longue she opened up wider, making the dark slit at the centre of her pussy more visible.

Using her pubic muscles she made herself open and close as she rubbed herself gently. The green eyes were smouldering at her now – enviously, she imagined. Her desire for him grew and she felt the upward swoop of her arousal take her towards the brink. Unable to hold out any longer, she gave an involuntary moan as the first of a series of sharp spasms flooded her system with violent pleasure, making her judder and gasp.

Jayne was dimly aware of a brief flurry of applause as her climax reached its bliss-inducing zenith, then she sank in exhaustion onto the couch. Bathed in a light film of sweat, she could do no more than lie there like a rag doll with her eyes closed. There were noises of people leaving the room, but she was incapable of taking any notice. When she finally managed to open her eyes Quentin was sitting alone at the table, writing. He smiled at her warmly.

'Well done, Miranda. That was a quite spectacular display. I'll ring for Helen. She'll bring you a robe and take you to the bathroom.'

The secretarial type appeared as soon as he'd summoned her with a button on the desk. She entered, smiling. Jayne put on the white towelling robe then, unsteadily, got to her feet.

'If you'd like to follow me, I'll take you where you can have a shower,' Helen said.

The bathroom suite on the first floor was luxurious. Jayne opted to soak in the huge square tub and as the room filled with hot steam she poured in a generous measure of exquisitely perfumed oil. Once she was in there soaking, however, fatigue took over and she almost fell asleep. The thought of the journey home was not appealing.

After about twenty minutes Jayne emerged, dressed again in her own clothes, and went back downstairs. The waiting room where she had left Stella was empty. When she came out into the hall again Quentin was standing there. 'I'm afraid Stella is otherwise engaged right now,' he said, smoothly. 'But I'll have Raymond call you a cab.'

'Raymond?'

Quentin pressed a button set into the wall. 'He's our

factotum. Makes everything run smoothly around here.'

'I see.' Jayne smiled faintly. The place was run like a stately home, it seemed, with an army of servants at the master's beck and call.

'I'm afraid club rules prevent me from letting you know the result of your audition straight away,' he continued. 'Talking of rules, please read through this copy of our club contract before you leave. We will require you to sign it if you become a member. But we will be in touch through Stella as soon as we have come to a decision. Thank you for attending tonight. May I wish you a safe journey home?'

He smiled, gave a slight bow, and was gone. Within a few seconds a tall, dark man in evening dress took his place. 'I have called you a cab, Madam,' he said. 'It should be here directly. Perhaps you would care to wait in the ante-room?'

Jayne read through the simple list of club rules while she waited, but she didn't have to wait long. Raymond ushered her back down the garden path and through the gate to where a smart limousine was waiting. This will cost me, Jayne thought sleepily. But when the driver drew up outside her flat, waking her with a start, he told her the fare had already been paid. Smiling wryly, she staggered from the car and went up to her door.

It had been a night to remember, but all was forgotten once she fell into bed. She didn't even notice the time, and her exhausted mind scarcely registered that the bed was empty.

Mick had been stunned to see Jayne emerge from the green gate accompanied by a suave type in evening dress. It had seemed to confirm his worst fears. But then she got into the cab alone and he had to get into gear quickly to follow her.

He drove through the deserted streets trying hard to keep up but, at the same time, remaining unseen. The absence of other traffic made it both harder and easier to achieve both goals. As he drove, Mick wondered what Jayne had been doing inside those walls for a good couple of hours. And what had happened to Stella? A part of him wanted to confront her the minute they got home, but he knew that would only make her clam up. No, he would have to use guile and stealth here.

The prospect of playing detective appealed to him. The idea that Jayne was having an affair with someone didn't. Still, he would have to pursue it. Mick waited until she was indoors then followed cautiously. He slid in through the door and heard her switch off the bedroom light. Taking his clothes off in the hall, he tiptoed in after her, dumped his things on the floor then slid into bed beside her hunched-up form.

Jayne was already fast asleep, her breathing slow and regular, her body scented with some exotic perfume. Mick sighed into the darkness. Had she become some rich man's mistress? The signs were all there: the Hampstead mansion, the hired limo, the smell of luxury about her. The memory of last night's romp floated back to him and he gave a wry smile. To think he'd felt guilty about betraying her with those two tarts! Resisting the urge to take her now with brutal force, while she slept, Mick turned his back to her and was soon asleep.

Chapter Five

Every day for the rest of that week Jayne was on tenterhooks at work, wondering when Stella would take her aside and tell her the verdict of the committee. She didn't dare bring up the subject herself, and since her boss didn't mention it either it was quite hard to act normal, especially as one of the films they were showing that week was called *Club Erotica*.

At home, Mick was still behaving strangely. She often caught him looking at her with a thoughtful expression, as if he were trying to read her mind. Not that she had a hope of reading his. There was a gulf between them and it was widening, but Jayne felt helpless to do anything about it. During the week they saw so little of each other and at the weekends he usually went off with his mates during the day. If he stayed indoors he'd be watching sport on TV most of the time.

In the back of her mind Jayne had the idea that she wouldn't be with ETV for much longer. She was on a short-term contract which expired in a couple of months. Maybe now was the time to rethink her career. After two years there surely she'd be able to find another job, one with less unsocial hours even if she had to take a cut in salary. Or there was always the family that she and Mick agreed they wanted – some day. But until things changed one way or the other her relationship with Mick was on hold.

Then, on Thursday night, Stella greeted her casually with the words, 'You're in, Miranda!'

'What? Oh!' Jayne blushed in confusion as she realised what the cryptic message meant, but there was no time to discuss it since she had to be on air in five minutes. She found herself in front of the camera without a script, since they'd had to change the film at the last moment, and her ability to ad lib deserted her. She spent a couple of minutes floundering uncomfortably while she tried to recall what the new film was about.

'That wasn't like you, Jayne,' Tony frowned at her afterwards. 'You usually take changes of programme in your stride. Time of the month or something?'

She glared at the director, wondering whether to charge him with gender discrimination, but thought better of it. Suddenly he didn't seem quite so attractive as before. Instead, Jayne found the image of a blond, green-eyed Adonis swimming before her eyes.

Stella gave her a wink, perfectly aware of what it was that had thrown her normally unflappable presenter into confusion, but she was busy with the rearranged schedule so Jayne had to wait until the show was over before gleaning any more information. The two women coincided in the dressing room. As Stella closed the door behind them Jayne turned to her with a smile. 'Well? What happens now?'

'It's up to you when you want to go to your first meeting. There's one tomorrow night. I'm going, so if you wanted to come along . . .'

'I'd love to!'

'Then I'd better explain that we don't meet at the same place each time, for security reasons.' She opened her bag and drew out a small plastic card. 'This is your membership card, by the way. You'll need it every time you attend a club function.'

Jayne took the card and examined it. There was a hologram of a couple embracing through a keyhole, her pseudonym – Miranda – and a three-figure number.

Nothing more. It was about as discreet as you could get. She smiled and slipped it into her purse.

'Is there anything else I should know?' Jayne asked, uncertainly.

There was a look in Stella's dark eyes that she'd never seen before, a secret, wanton look that made her shiver in response. 'I'm glad they accepted you,' she said, softly. 'You'll find out everything in due course.'

She was standing very close to her and, for a breathless moment, Jayne thought her boss was going to kiss her. But then she turned away and took a hairbrush out of her bag. She began brushing her hair with languid strokes, staring at herself in the mirror.

'We'll video your closing remarks tomorrow night,' Stella went on, changing back abruptly into her professional tone. 'Then you'll be free to leave with me around nine. I'll tell Tony. He can hold the fort if anything goes wrong. And if he complains I'll tell him we're entitled to a girls' night out once in a while.'

'He . . . he doesn't know, does he? About the club, I mean.'

Stella laughed scornfully. 'Of course not! They wouldn't take a guy like him!'

For a moment Jayne felt aggrieved. She'd found Tony attractive, not long ago. But she had to agree that if the rest of the club members were as good-looking and sophisticated as the committee then he definitely wouldn't fit in.

As Jayne drove home that night she was filled with a feverish excitement at the thought of being accepted into the Eye Spy Club. It was strange not being able to share it with Mick, though. Once they'd shared everything, she thought wistfully, but those days were long gone. They just didn't seem interested in each others' lives any more. She wondered what he would say if he knew of her involvement, how he would feel if he knew she'd masturbated in front of six strangers. Would he be annoyed, or intrigued? It disturbed her to realise she just didn't know what his response would be.

On Saturday he was around all day, unusually. Perhaps prompted by guilt, Jayne cooked him a decent lunch for a change and they spent the afternoon in the private garden attached to their apartment block. They were the only people there and, relaxing in the lazy sunshine, Jayne felt some of their old companionship return as they shared crossword clues and drank beer. Around five she went indoors to get ready for work and, after showering, Mick saw her putting her white lace undies on in the bedroom.

'You never wear those for me these days,' he complained wryly.

'What? Oh!' Jayne blushed guiltily, bending over to hide her pink cheeks as she fastened her stockings to her suspender belt.

She felt Mick's arms around her waist and held her breath. His lips brushed her hair as he whispered, 'Shall I take you right now, from behind?'

'Don't be daft, you'll make me late for work.'

He slapped her bum and turned away. 'It's always work, isn't it?' he growled. 'I thought we agreed, when you took this job on, that if we couldn't put up with the hours you'd stop.'

'You know I can't afford to. We can't pay the mortgage on your salary alone.'

'But what's more important, this flat, your job, or our relationship?'

'Not now, Mick, please! We'll talk about it tomorrow, maybe.'

'Yeah, maybe!'

He stomped from the room, compounding Jayne's feelings of guilt. But there was nothing she could do about it now. Sunday was the one day in the week when they really could be together, if they both wanted it. Maybe tomorrow they would sort something out.

After you've been to the club, she reminded herself soberly. Somehow that seemed significant. She had the feeling that she might regard her life quite differently after tonight.

'I may be home a bit later than usual,' she informed him casually, just before she left. 'We've been invited to a launch party – some new porn star that *Hot Screen* is hyping. I'll try to get back before dawn, though!'

Again he gave her that half amused, searching look before saying, 'Okay, enjoy yourself. But don't do anything I wouldn't do!'

He kissed her briefly on the lips. Jayne felt a pang of regret that she was deceiving him, but it was too late to back out now. Her curiosity had got the better of her, and her libido was longing for some new outlet. Maybe after she'd sown her wild oats she'd be ready to settle down with Mick again.

They'd been so young when they got together, she reflected as she left the flat. Jayne had been just eighteen, fresh from school in her first job, and he'd only been her third serious boyfriend. At twenty he had been at the end of an affair with an older married woman. Jayne soon realised that she had cause to be grateful to his former mistress, who had taught him a great deal about making love!

Smiling to herself, Jayne walked towards the Underground. There was no point driving tonight, not with all the booze she intended to drink to give her Dutch courage! When she got onto the train the men in her compartment kept giving her covert looks. Did any of them recognise her? She hoped not. The few times she'd been accosted in public had been mildly embarrassing. Usually, though, the fake glasses and dark wig she wore by way of disguise did the trick.

Jayne had spent ages deciding what to wear. She couldn't look too tarty for work, so she'd settled on a pink dress with spaghetti straps that crossed over the low back, and wore a navy blazer over the top. Her underwear was ultra sexy, though. A strapless bra in white lace and tiny lacy panties with a matching suspender belt to complete the set.

It was a relief that she only had to do one live session that night. Jayne recorded her brief link and summing up of the evening's showings, introduced the main film and then made for the cloakroom where Stella was already awaiting her. She watched as Jayne ran a brush through her loose blonde hair, retouched her lipstick and put on her jacket.

'Ready?' she said, looking her up and down with obvious approval. 'We have to go to Richmond tonight. Better make a prompt start.'

'Richmond?'

'Yes. I told you we meet at different venues, didn't I? Got your card?' Jayne nodded. 'Good, you couldn't get in without it even if I vouched for you. Let's go then, shall we?'

The taxi was already waiting for them by the time they got downstairs from the studio. The two women sat side by side on the back seat and, as they raced westwards, Jayne was unable to suppress her bubbling curiosity.

'What's going to happen tonight?' she asked, in a low voice.

Stella shrugged. 'I don't know the full programme. But you will be presented to the other members in the course of the evening, and there will be both live and video entertainment. Plenty to eat and drink too, of course.'

'I'm really nervous,' Jayne admitted. 'You won't leave me to sink or swim, will you?'

Stella laughed. 'Of course not! Though I expect you'll soon make a crowd of new friends. New members tend to be fêted by everyone, especially if they're as pretty as you.'

The compliment made Jayne clam up. She wasn't used to hearing such direct language from a woman, let alone from a female boss. Was Stella a lesbian? Bisexual? Even if she were, surely it wouldn't be a good idea to mix business and pleasure? The sense that she was on an unstoppable roller-coaster ride towards heaven-knew-what intensified as the first road signs to Richmond appeared.

The house where they alighted was another splendid mansion, set on high ground with views of both the river and the park. Jayne followed Stella in through the wrought-iron gates and up to the Georgian-style porch. There was a faint sound of music and a buzz of voices coming from deep within the building. When the door opened Jayne recognised 'Raymond' at once.

'Your membership cards, ladies?' he reminded them.

Stella had hers ready, but Jayne had to fumble in her bag. As she held it out to him she dropped it then bent to pick it up at the same time he did. His nose was practically in her cleavage as they bumped heads, and she felt herself covered in blushing confusion as she straightened up.

Raymond didn't lose his Jeeves-like poise. His smile was cool, urbane, as he handed her back the plastic card. 'Everything is in order Miss Stella, Miss Miranda. You may enter.'

The hallway had six doors leading off it, all of them closed. Raymond opened one at the far end and they found themselves in a large room with wardrobes lining two walls. There was a full-length mirror too, and a dressing table with a couple of chairs.

'The costumes are to your left, ladies, and there's room for your own clothes on the right,' he told them, bowing respectfully as he shut the door. Stella slid back the door on the left and smiled as she revealed a dazzling display of clothes in all colours and materials. 'Take your pick, Miranda!'

'You mean we have to change into something else?'

'Of course! Party clothes. Now let me see, where's the latex gear?'

Jayne's mind boggled as costume after costume was presented to her. There were sexy clothes of all

70

descriptions, some with strategically placed cutouts, others that clung to every curve. There were garments in leather, vinyl and latex, outfits that seemed to consist mainly of chains and steel plates, others that were obviously designed to afford the wearer as much pleasure as the viewer since they incorporated various stimulating devices. Jayne marvelled at a catsuit with a dildo in the crotch that was designed to fill the wearer's vagina, and roughened plastic areas to stimulate clitoris and nipples.

'Fancy that one?' Stella smiled.

Hastily Jayne replaced it on its hook. 'Not tonight, thanks. I'm going to be excited enough without extra stimulation!'

'Well, I'm going to wear this!' With a decisive air, Stella took out a black rubber bustier and a see-through plastic skirt. 'I'll need some help with the lacings,' she smiled, already taking off her high-heeled shoes.

Jayne pulled out a long pale blue dress in soft vinyl. It felt wonderfully soft and liquid in her hands. 'This is for me,' she murmured.

She'd never experienced such sexy material before. It was so thin and sleek, like skin. The style was plain, almost prim with puff sleeves and a square neckline with a band below the bust, 'Empire' style. Taking off her shoes Jayne pulled down the zipper of her pink dress and stepped out of it. When she was standing in her underwear, Stella asked for her help so she went over and laced up the rubber bustier as tightly as she could.

'That's good,' Stella smiled approvingly at herself in the full-length mirror. The corset pushed up her small breasts so they bulged over the cups and her nipples were clearly visible, moulded by the latex into sharp points. She pulled on the skirt and then slipped her shoes back on. The image she presented was weird, but certainly effective. Beneath the transparent skirt her black nylon panties could be seen, and beneath them the flat, neat mat of her pubic hair. She wore a black suspender belt and dark stockings, which also showed up effectively.

'Want any help with yours?' she smiled. Her eyes travelled to the full curves of Jayne's breasts, packed tightly within the white bra, then to the sleek dress that she had hung on the front of the wardrobe. 'I think you'll find it looks best without underwear.'

'What, none at all?'

Stella laughed. 'Yes, none whatsoever! Try it and see.'

Tentatively Jayne reached behind her back and unfastened her bra. When she took it off she saw Stella's eyes flash with interest as her full breasts were exposed, but she pretended not to notice. She unfastened her suspenders and removed her stockings, then the rest until she was completely naked.

'You have a lovely body,' Stella said, appreciatively.

Once again it felt weird to have another woman compliment her like that. Yet Stella made it sound perfectly natural, matter-of-fact almost. Jayne reached up and took the long dress off its hanger, then held it over her head. It fell down over her nude body like a shimmering waterfall, touching her skin silkily all over, making her shiver.

'It feels fantastic!' she exclaimed, turning to the mirror excitedly.

'Yes, doesn't it?' Stella came up behind her, smoothing the material down over her bottom. It felt deliciously cool and thin as clingfilm, moulding to her curves, slipping into her crack. The gown wasn't just enrobing her, it was invading her!

Stella's palms moved up to her bust and smoothed over that too, cupping her breasts gently. Jayne felt her nipples harden at the tentative contact and the effect was magnificent in the mirror, the Jane Austen innocence of the style contrasting with the revealing cling of the material. She stood still, hardly daring to breathe, wondering where this was leading. But then the other woman turned away and picked up her shoes.

'Here, put these on. And let me do your hair. I think you need to wear it up . . .'

Stella soon had her sitting in front of the dressing table while she hot-brushed her fair curls into casually styled ringlets, fixing them with diamanté-studded combs and letting a few strands bob about her face.

At last she stood back from her handiwork. 'Gorgeous!' she pronounced with a smile.

'Yes, it's lovely. Thanks, Stella.'

'She went for her lipstick but Stella took it from her hand. 'No, I think you should go for the virginal look. It's appropriate for your first appearance at the club, don't you think?'

'If you say so.'

'Right. Well there are one or two rules and regs you ought to know about before we make our appearance. Sit down a moment.' Obediently, Jayne perched on the stool while Stella sat in a tub-shaped chair opposite.

'The main purpose of our meetings is to watch the videos that other members have made,' she explained. 'Of course we get aroused while watching, and sometimes we feel the need to relieve ourselves in various ways. But we are all, basically, voyeurs. That's not to say there isn't some live action too. And when it's your turn to be on stage, or make a video, I can promise you plenty of sex.'

'How often do members get to do it, then? And who decides?'

'It's done by lottery, with one exception that you'll find out tonight. But if someone hasn't had a turn after three months they can take part in some live action with all the other poor deprived bodies!'

'What an odd way to go about things!'

'Not really. It adds to the fun, you see. If we just turned up and had sex every time it would soon get to be too predictable, too . . . samey. There's always titillation, though. And if your need is great it is possible to make assignations upstairs. The main thing is we're here to explore the subtler, more erotic aspects of sex. It's not just a bonking club.'

'But don't you get tired of looking without touching?'

Stella smiled. 'No, because I know my turn will come, eventually. And the longer I have to wait for it, the more I enjoy it. Most of us are quite content with the way things are. I suppose those of us who aren't into it leave to join some other club.'

'And these videos, who directs them?'

'Quentin and the other committee members. The participants work out a storyline together. Usually there's no dialogue. Anyway . . .' She got up from her chair. 'That's enough talk. The best way to find out what's on offer is just to take part. Shall we go?'

They went back into the hall, their heels clacking on the wooden floor, and Raymond appeared as if by magic. He raised his black eyebrows seductively at them. '*Very* nice, ladies! You're just in time for the start of the proceedings. This way, please.'

They followed him down a corridor until they went through another door and into a large room full of people. Jayne stared around her, trying to take everything in. There were around sixty people there, all dressed in fantastically sexy costumes, talking and drinking or smoking, laughing and flirting while they waited for the fun to begin. At the end of the room was a platform with dark blue curtains behind it, fringed with gold. In front of it there were tables and chairs, a few of them occupied.

A red-haired woman in a black leather bikini studded with silver and thigh-length boots to match, came up with a smile. 'Oh Stella, you chose the latex bustier! I almost wore that myself!'

'I'm glad you didn't,' Stella smiled back. 'It feels wonderful! This is Miranda, by the way. It's her first time here. Miranda, meet Dana.'

'First time, eh?' The tawny eyes met hers with a glint of amusement. 'I remember my first time as if it were yesterday. You're going to enjoy yourself tonight, my pet!'

Suddenly Quentin appeared on the platform, wearing evening dress and a cloak lined with red silk like some stage magician. He clapped his hands. The buzz stopped and everyone looked expectantly towards him. He beamed at the assembled company.

'Welcome fellow libertines, young and old, old and new!'

Jayne imagined he was looking straight at her when he uttered that last word. She blushed, feeling conspicuous in her figure-hugging blue gown. Stella nudged her and winked.

Quentin beckoned the crowd towards him. 'Come and fill up your places, one and all! The show is about to begin. Although I often consider we have no need of a floor show with all you fantastic creatures decked out in your finery!'

Jayne followed Stella and Dana to one of the tables, and they were soon joined by a man called Sten who was heavily into body piercing. His blond hair reminded Jayne of that other man, the one with the green eyes, but although she looked searchingly about the room she couldn't see him. Her heart made a disappointed dive.

Again Quentin clasped his hands to gain their attention. 'Just to whet your appetites for the main features, ladies and gents, we have an unusual juggling act that I'm sure you're going to enjoy. So please give a big, welcoming hand to Danni and Annie!'

The curtains parted as he left the stage, music played and a red headed girl in a stripper's outfit dashed on. She was very well endowed, and as she began to gyrate and tease the audience the atmosphere in the hall became charged with sexual tension. 'I wonder what she juggles?' Sten remarked, with a smirk. He was playing abstractedly with the nipple-rings on his naked chest all the time.

A smattering of applause and a few whistles rang out

when she finally revealed her tasselled breasts. Although large, they were firm and well toned. She began to work the tassels expertly, making them spin like Catherine wheels. The control she had over her bosom was very impressive. Then a second, dark haired girl appeared, also in a spangly bikini, and carrying a drawstring bag. After posturing for a while and playfully tugging on the other girl's tassels, she opened the bag and drew out four coloured balls which she proceeded to juggle.

Suddenly, to everyone's astonishment, she threw a ball towards the other girl who managed to catch it on her breast by manipulating it from below. Applause broke out, but then, with a deft flick, she bounced it back up into the air. A second ball was thrown and she caught it on her other breast. The process was repeated until she had four balls bouncing from breast to breast, up into the air and down again in a rhythmic cycle.

Thunderous applause broke out and Stella murmured, 'God, that's amazing!'

'I suspect you ain't seen nothin' yet!' Sten said, with a wry smile.

The other girl turned round and presented her rear view to the audience. She waggled her bottom then began to remove the lower half of her bikini, revealing a minuscule G-string. Her buttocks were large and firm, evoking more appreciative whistles from the audience. She turned to one side and presented her posterior to her partner, who was now eyeing her intermittently, sizing up her position. An expectant hush fell over the audience. They knew something spectacular was about to happen, but what?

The redheaded juggler suddenly flipped her breast hard propelling one of the balls towards the dark-haired girl. A gasp rang round the hall as the ball bounced off her right buttock and onto the left, then returned to sender. Laughter followed, accompanied by applause as everyone realised the amazing skill of the two women. It wasn't long before they had a good flow going with the balls, from breast to breast, from buttock to buttock, from girl to girl. The audience clapped in time to the rhythm amidst much laughter. Jayne giggled too, feeling more relaxed. If this was the style of entertainment provided she was going to have fun!

The two jugglers ended their act with a bow and skipped off stage to be replaced by the MC. Quentin held up his hand for silence after the rowdy applause. 'Weren't they fantastic, folks?' he beamed. 'Just one more example of the high standard of entertainment we provide here at the Eye Spy Club! Those of us who have been members for some time already know this, but I hope we've managed to impress our new member, the lovely Miranda. Stand up please, Miranda, and let us all have a good look at you!'

Jayne blushed, but there was no way she could avoid it. She got to her feet, smiling shyly, and everyone clapped. She was briefly aware of many pairs of eyes scrutinising her body in the long, clinging gown, then she hurriedly sat down again. 'Whew, I'm glad that's over!' she whispered to Stella, who gave her a peculiar smile.

The hall quietened, with everyone expectant again. A slow grin spread over Quentin's ruggedly handsome face. 'Once again, those of you who are longer term members know what manner of ordeal you had to go through to join our club.'

He smiled directly at Jayne, who glanced around uneasily as she realised that many pairs of eyes were still looking in her direction. Had they all been obliged to masturbate for the committee too? She wasn't exactly comfortable with everyone knowing what she'd done, even so. Then Quentin pulled a cord at the side of the stage and the curtain at the back opened to reveal a large screen.

'I think we're in for another treat tonight,' he said. 'In keeping with our tradition, we shall now show the new member video.'

Jayne sensed the excitement in the air, but there was a sinking feeling inside her as a dark suspicion grew. Surely they couldn't have filmed her 'performing' for the committee, could they? But it was easy to conceal a camera. She fought the hot tide that threatened to flush into her cheeks, clenched her fists tightly in her lap in an effort to keep a tight rein on her emotions. The title of the film flashed onto the screen: 'New Member Initiation No. 79. *Miranda*'.

It was then she let out a stifled gasp. Stella gripped her forearm, whispering, 'Don't worry, Jayne. We've all been through this. It's nowhere near as bad as you imagine.'

Jayne wanted to rush from the room in shame as the image of herself in the centre of the floor, posed for her striptease, filled the screen. She didn't know where to put her eyes. She couldn't bear to watch herself, but neither could she bear to watch the audience. And as for catching anyone else's eye, she'd rather die!

Realising she would draw more attention to herself by leaving than by staying still, she resigned herself to sitting through it. Reason took over, once she got used to the idea. Although she was horribly embarrassed she told herself that this was a sex club, after all, and if she was going to be shy about performing in front of the others she might as well resign on the spot. But it wasn't easy. From time to time she glanced back at the screen to see herself in a state of undress, and horror seized her.

Then, realising that everyone was absorbed in her performance, she sneaked a look at the faces around her. Although she was used to having an audience, this was entirely different. She wasn't just a pretty face, as she was on the box. Now the rest of her was exposed in graphic detail and it was clear, from the approving smiles of both the men and women members, that they liked what they saw.

The hall was filled with silent concentration as Jayne, alias Miranda, had them under her spell. She could see from the unmistakable bulge in Sten's red pants, and from the way that Dana was clenching her naked thighs, that even the people at her table were aroused by her performance. Curiously she glanced at Stella. She had hitched up the transparent skirt under the table and was stroking her pussy. Jayne blushed and turned away, pretending she hadn't noticed, but it was too late. Stella leaned over and whispered. 'You're really turning me on, you know! A wicked performance, totally wicked!'

Jayne felt she could suffer no worse humiliation now. Here was the woman she worked with, the woman she saw almost every day of the week and whom she'd have to face again on Monday morning, getting turned on by a film of her masturbating. As she heard herself moaning towards a climax the whole audience seemed to be murmuring in sympathy. Their faces riveted to the screen, they were turning through all shades from pink to purple as their libido worked overtime to keep up with Miranda, the rampant sex bomb that they now had in their midst.

Suddenly everything flipped inside Jayne as she realised that no one was thinking any the worse of her for her performance. On the contrary, their faces were filled with admiration. When the video came to an end, with a close-up of her lying exhausted on the chaise longue, they leapt to their feet with one accord to give her a standing ovation.

Shyly Jayne also got up, bowing demurely. All around her table they were muttering compliments, congratulations, turning what had begun as a mortifying ordeal into an achievement to be proud of. She looked boldly into their smiling faces and beamed broadly. She had passed her initiation with flying colours. Now her full membership of the Eye Spy Club had begun.

Chapter Six

'What the heck am I doing, stuck here in my car in the middle of the night again?' Mick wondered, as he kept his vigil outside the imposing Richmond mansion. He'd tried to resist the urge to follow Jayne but it had been impossible. His curiosity had been unstoppable. Besides, he had to admit to rather liking playing the sleuth. Was this how stalkers felt when they followed their victims everywhere, obsessed with their every move?

He looked at his watch: ten past midnight. Suppose Jayne had been telling the truth and she was attending a launch party after all. But then, who knew what went on at those parties? When she'd first been offered a job presenting porn films he had been dubious about the company she might keep, but his doubts had subsided over the months. Now they'd returned with a vengeance.

Mick took out the book of soccer stars' lives he'd been reading, switched on his torch and tried to get through the rest of Georgie Best, but it was hard to concentrate when you had to keep an eye out all the time. Although a couple of people had gone through those imposing gates just after Jayne and Stella had arrived, there had been no comings and goings since. He glanced up at the top floor of the house, which was all that was visible over the surrounding wall. No lights on. Yet he could hear faint musical sounds wafting towards him on the night breeze from time to time.

Around half past one a couple emerged, laughing, and

Mick was on full alert. But they wandered off arm in arm and then there was a long pause. Soon after two a taxi arrived and some more couples appeared, six of them getting into the same cab. Then, around half two, a steady stream emerged and disappeared into the night, ferried away either by cabs or one of the expensive-looking cars that were parked nearby. Mick stared wearily at the gates from his corner position, fed up with waiting. It was hard to keep his eyes open, but he was reluctant to leave now after wasting a whole evening.

Then, just as he began nodding off, Stella and Jayne emerged. He sat bolt upright, rubbing his eyes and peering to make sure it was them. They were in a huddle, discussing something. Then they appeared to say goodbye. Jayne got into a waiting cab and Mick heard her clear voice say, 'South Quays, please.'

Mick started the engine, ready to follow her. But then he saw Stella move towards a parked car, probably her own. He edged out into the road, watching Stella fumble in her bag for her keys. As she did so something fell out onto the road but she didn't see it. He slowed, as if he were waiting to pick up someone, his mind racing.

There was little point in following Jayne, he decided. He imagined she was going straight home. But if he picked up what Stella had just dropped he would have an excuse for approaching her. Chances were he would glean far more from her about the evening's activities than he would from Jayne. His mind made up, Mick hung back waiting for her to pull out, then once she was away, he inched slowly forward to see what she had dropped. It was some kind of credit card, by the look of it. His luck was in!

After looking behind to make sure there was no other traffic, Mick opened the passenger door and picked up the plasticised card. He turned it over with a frown. There was some kind of hologram, the number one-five-six and the name Stella, that was all. Funny credit card. He held it towards a street light and squinted at the hologram, managing to make out two figures. Maybe it was a membership card of some kind. At any rate, it didn't look like the sort of thing you could afford to lose. Slamming his car into gear he followed the fast disappearing vehicle up the road.

Mick drove eastwards through the semi-deserted streets in the wake of the small red car, hoping Stella wouldn't realise she was being followed. It was far harder than he'd imagined to keep her vehicle in sight without exposing his own. He almost caught up with her at some traffic lights but they changed in the nick of time, allowing him to keep his distance. She headed off towards Blackheath and eventually drew up outside a large old house. He shut off the engine and slid to a halt about thirty yards away.

Stella got out and locked her car, then walked up to the front door, jingling her keys as she went. Mick knew he had to act quickly. He got out of his car and sprinted up to her. She looked round in alarm, and hurried up to the front door but he waved the card at her and she paused, looking puzzled.

'I found this!' he called, in a hoarse whisper, aware that all around people were sleeping in their beds. 'It's yours, I saw you drop it.'

He slowed down as he came up the path and she took a step forward. 'I dropped it?' she repeated, dazedly. He held it out to her and her mouth dropped open. 'My God! Where did I drop it? Don't tell me . . .'

He nodded. 'Yes, back in Richmond.' He smiled sheepishly. 'I hoped I'd catch up with you before this, but . . . anyway, you've got it now.'

'Yes, and I'm very grateful to you. I hope you haven't come too far out of your way.'

Mick shrugged, still grinning foolishly. She hesitated, sizing him up. Evidently she came to the conclusion that he was both genuine and harmless because she smiled and said. 'Look, can I offer you a coffee or something? I know it's late and you must be tired, but I feel it's the least I can do before you drive home.'

'That's kind of you, great. Better lock my car up first, though.'

'Right. I'll leave the door on the latch. My flat's on the ground floor. Oh, and my name's Stella, by the way.'

'I know,' he grinned.

She looked flustered. 'Of course you do! Well, I'll get the kettle on.'

He couldn't believe how easy it had been. No wonder women got themselves into so much trouble, he thought as he returned to his car, they were too trusting, far too trusting. It was a good job he only wanted information.

Or did he? The sight of her trim, petite figure and her attractive face with those big, dark sexy eyes had got him going. But he wouldn't make a move unless she did. There was no way he was going to incur a rape accusation from Jayne's boss! He would see what he could get out of her about that card. Somehow he thought it might be connected with where she'd been that night and, if it was, that would give him a clue as to what Jayne was up to.

The smell of freshly made coffee greeted him as he entered the hallway. The doorway to the right was open and he entered tentatively to find himself in a large sitting room with a kitchen leading off it. Stella popped her head round the door. 'Almost brewed.'

'That was quick! I'll take mine black please, two sugars. I need waking up a bit.'

Mick sat down on the battered leather sofa and looked about him. There was an oversize television set in one corner with a video beneath it, the only hint of her profession. If there were any dodgy videos around she kept them well hidden. Stella came through with two steaming mugs and set them down on a low table.

'You looked relieved when I gave you that card,' he began. 'Didn't know you'd lost it, eh?'

She smiled, her dark eyes flashing. 'No, and I'd have been devastated when I found out!'

'I thought it was a credit card at first.'

'Oh no, nothing like that! It's just a membership card, actually. But not the sort of thing you want a stranger to pick up. I mean . . .'

She looked flustered again. Mick laughed. 'I know what you mean. At least I was an honest stranger. But to tell you the truth I wouldn't have had a clue what to do with it. Doesn't give much away, does it?'

Her eyes turned to her coffee. 'No. Well anyway, as I said, I'm really grateful to you . . .?'

'Mike,' he said without hesitation. It was the version of his name that his old schoolfriends used. He'd changed to 'Mick' when there had been another 'Mike' in an office where he worked, but the new name had stuck.

'Cheers, Mike!' She held the mug up with a smile, then had second thoughts. 'Want anything stronger with it, a dash of brandy perhaps?'

'That would be nice. Thanks.'

She rose and went to the wall unit, taking a bottle out of a small cupboard. When she opened up another section to retrieve the glasses Mick glimpsed a row of videos along an inner shelf. He smiled to himself. So that was where she kept them! He tried to peer at the titles but they were too far away. Maybe she had some of the uncensored ones in there, the ones Jayne told him were too hot to show on British television!

They sipped the brandy in silence for a few seconds, then Stella asked him where he lived. When he replied 'South Quays' she said, 'A colleague of mine lives there. In one of the new luxury flats.'

Mick nearly choked on his drink. 'Oh, I can't afford one of those!' he said, hastily.

'What do you do for a living, Mike?'

There, at least, he could tell the truth. 'I'm afraid I'm in boring old financial services.'

'Not boring for those of us who have money to invest, I assure you. But now's not the time to talk shop. Are you married?'

He shook his head and quickly threw the question back at Stella. She laughed, waving a hand around the room. 'Hardly! Does this look like a married woman's flat? No, I like my freedom, my independence, too much.' She leaned forward, her glass poised on her crossed knees. Mick saw the top of her shallow cleavage appear in the neck of her black roundnecked T-shirt and his stomach lurched with unexpected lust. 'How about you, Mike?'

Her dark eyes were drawing him into her orbit. It was a blatant invitation, but now it came to it he was wary. Already he had some explaining to do when he got home. He'd wanted to see where Stella lived, pick up some clues, but soon it would be time to beat a hasty retreat.

'Like I said, I'm not married,' he told her, swilling down the last of his brandy. 'But that doesn't mean I don't have a girlfriend.'

'Going steady?' She made it sound like a disease.

'Sort of. Anyway, I must get back. Long drive, and all that.' He got to his feet leaving half his coffee in the mug. 'Er . . . can I use your loo before I go?'

Stella had a separate toilet and bathroom. As he used the loo he could hear her running a bath next door. He finished and flushed, but when he appeared she was still in the bathroom. Stealthily he made his way back along the hall to the sitting room. The cupboard of the wall cabinet was still open. On impulse, he reached in and took a video at random off the shelf, managing to conceal it beneath his jacket just as he heard her footsteps return.

He picked up his mug of coffee. 'Thought I'd take another couple of swigs before I left,' he said as she entered. 'Sober me up for the drive.'

'Are you sure you're okay to drive?' her big, brown eyes were looking at him with innocent appeal. 'You could stay here for what's left of the night if you like.'

Mick thought, 'You don't give up easily, do you, darling?' But he just thanked her and declined her kind offer, then made for the door.

'I hope you get home safely,' she said as she opened the heavy front door. 'I'd hate to think of you having an accident after your good deed to me.'

'I'll be fine,' he assured her, eager to get away now. He turned at the end of the path and saw her standing in the doorway, arms folded across her chest, a wistful look on her face.

'I'm the one that got away!' Mick thought, with some satisfaction, as he turned towards his parked car. As he started the engine he threw the video on the passenger seat. There was a picture of three semi-naked women on the front and he saw the title: *Three Girls Called Les*. He gave an amused grunt, but then the significance struck home. Was Stella a lesbian? Not after the way she'd gone for him tonight, surely? She must swing both ways. So what was going on between her and Jayne? Driving through the already lightening streets, Mick realised that his encounter with Stella had raised more questions than it had answered.

Mick entered the flat quietly, peeped in at the bedroom to satisfy himself that Jayne was sound asleep, then went into the sitting room and switched on the video player. As often happened, he had passed the point of maximum fatigue even though it was almost five in the morning. Good job tomorrow – correction, today – was Sunday.

Before he inserted the video that he'd stolen from Stella he turned it over to read the blurb on the back. Along with the usual salacious prose he was surprised to see a hologram similar to the one on that membership card. Light dawned: she must belong to some dirty video club! She was bound to have a professional interest in such things. He smiled as he slotted the video in and pressed play.

The quality of the video impressed him at once. Mick wasn't exactly a connoisseur of porn but he'd watched enough of the stuff that ETV pushed out to know that this was streets ahead of it. The girls were gorgeous, for a start. And although the dialogue was minimal there was a definite storyline. In *Three Girls Called Les* they all belonged to the same health club. The film started with them lounging in a sauna, wrapped in white towels, then they got to chatting and discovered they all had the same name. When blonde Lesley said she was a qualified masseuse, the other two requested her services. They locked the door, discarded their wraps and the story proceeded from there.

Mick watched the steamy action from beginning to end and by the time it was over he could hardly contain himself. But fatigue had also caught up with him, and he was ready for bed. He hid the video amongst the others in their collection and crawled into the bedroom, where light was already filtering through the gap in the curtains. After pulling off his clothes he slid in beside Jayne, but she was evidently in a light sleeping phase because she moaned and sighed as his body cuddled up to her naked back and buttocks.

Despite the fact that he'd gone a whole night without sleeping, Mick found himself roused by the silken feel of her flesh. He moulded his stomach to the curve of her back and felt his prick harden, sneaking up the crack between her buttocks. His mouth came to rest on the nape of her neck where the skin tasted sweet, and he couldn't resist bringing his hands up to cup her slack breasts. The nipples were soft and delicate at first, but he felt them harden at the brush of his fingertips.

In her sleep, Jayne gave an unequivocal moan of desire and Mick squeezed her breasts harder. He was unsure whether she'd woken up or not: if she had, she was keeping very quiet about it. His right hand slid down the gentle curve of her stomach to the springy curls at its base and she made a little, guttural noise, letting her thighs fall open. Encouraged, he let his hand slip between them to find her vulva giving him a warm, wet welcome.

Mick gave a low moan as his fingers parted her labia and went on in, deep into her velvet-smooth interior. He felt Jayne squirm against him, her clitoris swelling with excitement, and wondered if she were having the female equivalent of a wet dream. It was hard to believe that she could still be asleep but if she wanted to pretend that was up to her. There was something very satisfying about taking her in this semi-passive state, seeing how far she would let him go.

His cock was hot for it now, making it very difficult for Mick to ignore his full-blown erection. He brought both hands round to cradle her bum and then parted her thighs to gain access to her pussy from the rear. She was compliant, moving around to a more accommodating angle, which made him think she was quite definitely awake by now. But he wasn't going to push his luck by saying anything.

Mick's penis slid into her with ease, making him utter a long sigh of contentment as the silken sheath closed around his shaft. For a while he contented himself with making only small thrusts, feeling the walls of her vagina caress his shaft with blissful tenderness. He reached up for her breast again and found the nipple taut and hard. When he fingered it she clutched at him with her pussy and his movements became more urgent, taking him rapidly into sensual overdrive. His lips kissed at her neck and shoulders, teeth grazing gently over the smooth surfaces, and she began to moan almost continuously as her libido synchronised with his.

Soon the pair of them had set up a gentle rocking rhythm that was both arousing and soothing. Jayne's body was like a warm cradle for his penis, lulling him blissfully in his sleepy state. The leisurely pace of their lovemaking was a pleasant surprise after the brief and somewhat frantic couplings that had become their norm. Mick loved the sensation of being afloat in her warm body, of allowing himself to drift with the tide that was rising in a gentle swell towards the ultimate pleasure beach.

His orgasm, when it finally arrived, was in keeping with the slow buildup. Instead of erupting from him in a burst of fire the hot waves of ecstasy pulsed gently through his body, taking him into mindless rapture and beyond. When the last throbbings ended, and he felt his prick slip out of her, sleep overtook him at once.

Mick awoke to find the sunlight streaming in through the gap in the curtains. The rest of the bed was empty, but there was still a warm depression where Jayne's body had been and the scent of her hair on the pillow. Remembering their fucking he rolled over with a sigh and embraced the plump pillow. How much of the time had she been conscious, he wondered wryly. Had she come as well? Where was she now? The rest of the flat felt silent, deserted. He glanced at the clock: it was eleven thirty.

After a while he heard the front door open. Jayne went straight into the kitchen and he heard her put the kettle on, clatter mugs and plates around. It was a good sound. Maybe they could go back in time after all, back to those days of domestic bliss when they spent Sunday mornings in bed together, making love.

Suddenly she put her head round the bedroom door, grinning when she saw he was awake. 'Hi! What time did you get back this morning? Never mind. I've got coffee in the pot and croissants in the oven. Thought you might like breakfast in bed for a change.'

'Wonderwoman!' He sat up, smiling, and held out his hand to her. Slowly she came over and sat on the bed, holding his hand lightly in hers. 'Did you enjoy our lovemaking?' he asked, softly.

The expression in her eyes turned wary. 'I was half asleep.'

'I know, me too. That made it all the better in my opinion. We were more relaxed.'

She sighed. 'That doesn't say much for our relationship, does it? We can only enjoy making love when we're practically comatose!'

Mick knew she was only half joking and his mood of optimism dissipated. All he wanted now was to repeat their earlier performance, but when he saw her look harden and she drew away her hand it seemed unlikely to happen. He just couldn't make her out these days with her blow-hot, blow-cold manner. The old anger welled up in him but he did his best to curb it, saying as casually as he could, 'Didn't you say something about us having a talk today?'

'What about?'

'Us, of course.'

'Oh!' She stood up, looking vacant. 'I'm not sure talking does any good, does it?'

The anger he'd been damming up inside himself now burst through a leak in his defences. 'Do you have to be so defeatist, Jayne? This is life we're talking about, yours and mine. Not one of your stupid porn films!'

'I'll get the coffee,' she said stiffly, and walked out.

Mick lay there cursing his peevish outburst. For a few brief moments around dawn he'd thought their love life was on course again, believed they could make a go of it after all. But now he'd been thrown back into the state of uncertainty he'd been in for the past few months. If Jayne wasn't prepared to pull her weight in this relationship there was no hope. He couldn't do it all alone. They might as well call it a day.

She didn't wait with him while he ate his breakfast, just brought in a tray then exited at once. The coffee tasted like liquid mud in his mouth, the croissants like wood pulp. Mick was tempted to lie there feeling sorry for himself but he got up and went to have a shower, hoping that would make him feel better. When he came out, clean and dressed in jeans and a shirt, Jayne had left the flat. There was a note on the kitchen table saying she'd 'gone round to see a friend' and would be back at six.

'Just in time to get ready for work,' he told himself, gloomily.

Was she deliberately trying to sabotage things? Maybe she wanted him to leave first, so she could stay in the flat. But she could never afford the rent on her own. What if she had a lover waiting in the wings, ready to move in the minute he moved out? Mick tormented himself with such thoughts for a while, but then he decided to go and see Stella. He could suggest an afternoon drive, or something, maybe take up her implied invitation to sex. That would serve Jayne right, he thought viciously. She might take him a bit more seriously if she knew he was screwing her boss!

Anything was better than staying in the flat, he decided as he grabbed his jacket and opened the door. At the last minute he went back for the video. It would give him an excuse to call, and Stella might just admire his cheek for lifting it. She might also ask him what he'd thought of it, which would provide a handy opening. It could also work against him, of course, but he'd have to take that risk. It was no big deal either way.

The area where Stella lived looked different by daylight, with guys tinkering with their motors and kids rushing about on skateboards. Mick walked up to her door in slight apprehension, wondering what kind of reception he'd get. To his relief, the minute she saw him Stella's face broke into a smile. 'Hello again, Mike! What have I lost this time?'

'Er . . . not lost, exactly. I've been a bit of a naughty boy, I'm afraid.'

Her grin widened. 'Oh good, I love naughty boys! Do come in.'

'You might not be so pleased when you hear I stole something of yours. Well, borrowed it really since I've brought it back.'

'You did?'

'Yes, one of your videos.'

'Oh!' Her smile dropped, and for a moment Mick was afraid she was going to be cross with him. There was an ambiguous tension between them. He held it out to her and her smile returned. 'Ah, that one! You mean to say you took it out of the cupboard? Now that *is* naughty.' She sighed. 'If I had the time I'd devise some fiendish punishment for you, but I'm afraid I have to go to work in a few minutes.'

'To work?' Mick frowned, wondering why she had to be there so much earlier than Jayne.

'Yes, there's a bit of a crisis on. But I was just having some tea. Will you join me, just for five minutes?'

She led the way into a large kitchen, lit the gas under a kettle and put a second tea bag into a mug. Then she sat down on a stool, legs crossed so the short skirt she was wearing rode up above her knee. Pity there's no time, Mick thought. The idea of 'punishment' at her hands was oddly exciting.

'So, what did you think of *Three Girls Called Les*?' she asked with a giggle, picking up the video that she'd tossed on the table. 'It's not one I've seen yet.'

'I think it was pretty high quality. Not like that rubbish they put out on ETV.'

She threw him a keen glance. 'Oh, you watch that channel do you?'

'Used to. Don't bother much now. The stuff's pretty pathetic, really.'

'Well we are . . . do have some pretty strict censorship laws in this country, compared to the rest of Europe.'

Mick smiled. He'd nearly caught her out there. She got up and made his tea then sat down, picking up the video again. 'So, was there a lot in this drama then?'

'Yes. It takes place in a sauna, actually.'

'How original!'

'It's okay, really. Bit of a massage session leading on to

91

other things. Oh, and there's a bit where two of the girls tie the third one up and start beating her with birch twigs.'

'Turned you on, that bit, did it, Mike?' she grinned, taking a sip of tea.

'Yes it did, as a matter of fact.'

'And who did you most identify with, the girls dishing it out or the one on the receiving end?'

'The receiver, I suppose. It's always been one of my fantasies to have a girl with big breasts give me a walloping.'

'Has it now?' She looked thoughtful, finished her tea quickly and stood up. 'Excuse me a moment, Mike, but I have to get ready. Don't rush your tea, though.'

Left alone in the kitchen Mick looked around him. On the mantelpiece was her scheudle at ETV. He recognised the printing and layout, the company logo. Jayne had an identical one. Smiling to himself he wondered what she would say if she knew who he really was. It gave him a buzz to be sitting there in her kitchen when she had no idea how much he already knew about her.

Stella returned, in an obvious hurry, just as he was finishing his last mouthful of tea. 'Awfully sorry, but I have to throw you out now,' she grinned. 'But do visit another time. Here's my card, with my phone number on. I work nights, but if you're around during the day or in the early hours of the morning . . .'

She gave him another of her wicked grins as he took the card. 'I might just take you up on that,' he said.

'If you look on the other side of the card there's another number I've written down for you. Someone who's a dab hand with birching!'

He stared at her dumbly. She laughed. 'Her name's Lady Odile, and her rates are quite reasonable. I can thoroughly recommend her. Look, I really must dash now!'

Mick followed her out and she got into the waiting taxi with a farewell flutter of her pale fingers. He stood on the pavement for a few seconds, feeling slightly dazed. His lack of sleep was beginning to take its toll, or was he just fazed by Stella giving him that prostitute's number? It was as if she'd taken one look at him and worked out just what he needed to satisfy his most secret desires.

By the time he got home Mick was quite excited by the idea of visiting Lady Odile, but he was also quite scared. He'd never done anything quite like that before, taken the initiative with a whore. The few girls he had been with had all solicited him. He picked up the phone and set it down again, several times, before at last dialling the number on the card.

It was a relief to get her answerphone. The confident, educated voice speaking the message was also reassuring. 'Thank you for calling Lady Odile,' it began. 'I'm sorry I am unable to come to the phone right now, but allow me to describe my services. I am London's foremost disciplinarian, guaranteed to provide you with any kind of treatment your heart desires. I have a range of costumes and implements to satisfy your every wish. My standard range includes cowgirl, nurse, spacegirl, French maid, horsewoman, and a variety of exciting dominatrix outfits. There is a supplementary charge for topless. My implements suit most tastes and are made from the finest materials. My Standard Service is for half an hour, the Special Service lasts one hour, and the Premier Service allows you a full three hours of punishing pleasure. If there is something you particularly require, I shall do my best to provide it. Just tell me your fantasies when you book your appointment and I shall devise a stimulating and satisfying scenario. If you wish to make an appointment please ring this number again between the hours of eight and ten a.m., or four to six p.m. Thank you once again for calling Lady Odile, London's leading dominatrix.'

When he replaced the receiver Mick could feel his heart racing and his cheeks were flushed. Despite his disappointment at not being able to talk to the Lady herself, he knew instinctively that the 'services' she had outlined were just what he had always wanted. He'd never been able to speak to anyone about his secret longings before, had hardly even acknowledged them to himself, but now that he was on the verge of venturing into unknown, and yet strangely familiar, territory he felt very good about it, very good indeed.

Chapter Seven

As Jayne walked into the offices of ETV on Sunday night she saw Stella in the foyer. 'Hi!' Stella grinned, beckoning her into the ladies where they stood at the vanity unit. She said, eyeing her reflection, 'Well, did you have a good time last night?'

'Oh yes!' Jayne didn't have to pretend to be enthusiastic. The memory of that extraordinary evening was with her still, making her feel warm and sexy inside. 'When's the next meeting?'

'Next weekend, but after we left they held the draw. Remember I told you they draw lots for the members who are to appear in the videos? Believe it or not, your name came up and so did mine!'

'What?' Jayne frowned. 'Isn't that a bit of a coincidence?'

Stella gave a sly grin as she reapplied her lipstick in the mirror. 'Some people say it's a fix, but it's never been proven. Anyway, we have two gorgeous partners to work with, Dean and Ralph. We have to meet to talk about what we're going to do, maybe rehearse a little.' Her grin became even more wicked as she stroked her full lips one more time with the red lipstick. 'How about Wednesday before work, my place?'

Jayne nodded. 'Sounds good to me.'

'I'll get some food and booze in. We can work from around six to around nine. I'll get Tony to do the early shift here.' She snapped her bag shut and looked straight at Jayne. Her eyes became glowing hot coals for an instant and

Jayne felt suddenly self-conscious, knowing that Stella had seen her at her most nakedly uninhibited. Then she gave a friendly smile, easing the tension. 'I think you'll really enjoy it!' she said before she slipped through the door.

But as she drove home that night Jayne felt nervous. So far she hadn't actually been unfaithful to Mick, but now it looked as if she was going to. And after what happened in the early hours of that morning she felt mean. Had it been unfair of her to let him make love to her and then rebuff him? Not that she could have helped herself. The minute she felt Mick's erection between her buttocks and his hand crept round to her breast she was lost, especially after the stimulating time she'd had earlier!

When she'd first returned from the club and dropped into bed she hadn't been able to resist the urge to bring herself to a climax. Then she'd had erotic dreams for the rest of the night, dreams of performing naked before huge crowds, of having several men make love to her at once, taking her in succession. There had been a wild abandon about her dreams that she'd never known before and they had kept her at a high level of arousal even in her sleep.

So when Mick's member had slid into her she'd been more than ready for him, wet and engorged. It had taken only a few gentle thrusts of his to make her come, but she had the impression he didn't notice when it happened. So much for his sensitivity! Still, she mustn't blame him. They'd both been half asleep. It had been churlish of her to refuse to talk to him later, but since she'd joined the Eye Spy Club there was little she could say to him about her sexual feelings without mentioning it, and she was sworn to secrecy.

Maybe the club activities will satisfy my curiosity and libido for a while and then I'll feel ready to settle down with Mick, she thought as she drove into South Quays. But it seemed unlikely. A more probable scenario was that, faced with hunks like Dean and Ralph to play with, Mick would be even less likely to turn her on. She'd been trying, just lately, to remember what it was about him that she'd once found so attractive. But it was like trying to recapture an elusive childhood memory.

Jayne could hardly contain her excitement over the next few days. She was distant with Mick, not wanting to enter into any serious discussion with him, and he seemed alternately cold and conciliatory towards her. Some day we'll have to sort out our relationship once and for all, she reflected sadly. But right now she was going to have some fun!

On Wednesday Jayne drove to Stella's flat in Blackheath feeling ready for some excitement. She'd put on a new cropped top that emphasised the high roundness of her breasts and showed an inch or two of midriff above her jeans and drenched herself with her favourite perfume, a blend of floral and amber with strong musky overtones. In a bag on the back seat was the low-necked dress she would be wearing for work.

Stella opened the door to her smiling. She looked sexy in an understated way, with her slight figure looking even slimmer in a black dress scattered with floral sprigs. The V-neck showed a slight cleavage and the dress was nipped in at her slender waist.

'Dean's here already,' she said, her eyes dancing. 'He's looking forward to seeing you again. He was on the selection committee.'

As soon as she heard that Jayne's heart leapt. Somehow she knew that it was *him* – green eyes. When she entered the room he turned from the window and smiled, his face lighting up.

'Miranda! How lovely to see you again.' He came forward and kissed her cheek, formally. 'I'm looking forward to performing with you,' he added, seriously.

The doorbell rang again and Stella went to answer it, leaving the pair alone. They sat down opposite each other, and Jayne felt awkward. She could sense the powerful male signals that were throwing her system into disarray and her libido into overdrive. Her palms felt sweaty and her pulse was leaping erratically. It got so bad she couldn't look him in the eye.

Dean did his best to put her at her ease. 'I expect you're almost as nervous about this as I am,' he smiled. 'Although I'm on the selection committee this is the first time my name's been drawn. But at least Ralph's done it before, and so has Stella.'

Jayne swallowed hard. 'Really? That's good then.'

She felt uncomfortably like being in the throes of a schoolgirl crush. Dean was so incredibly good-looking that just the thought of seeing him naked, let alone having that tuned-up, athletic body do things to hers, was quite overwhelming. Then Stella entered with a vaguely familiar-looking guy in her wake.

'Hullo folks!' Ralph grinned, his eyes scanning Jayne's face and figure automatically. She knew she'd seen him in the audience at the club, but she was relieved to find that she was no longer embarrassed by the fact that he'd already seen her naked and pleasuring herself, on screen.

'Let's get the noshing over with first,' Stella suggested. 'I've got pizza in the oven, salad and red wine. Is that okay for everyone?'

It was hard to be formal with tomato sauce and mozzarella running down your chin. Jayne soon felt relaxed, especially when the talk turned to last night's TV movie. It had been one of the worst, a limp tale about two girls' holiday flings in Greece, and the men lampooned it mercilessly.

'I hope our effort will be better than that!' Jayne said at last, wiping the tears of laughter from her eyes.

'I've got an idea that I think might work,' Stella said, and everyone was instantly attentive. 'Our session will be happening at Freebody's.'

'Is that the Health Club we hired last summer, with the pool and stuff?' Ralph asked.

Stella nodded. 'You got it! If you remember, in the basement there was a full-size badminton court. Well I remembered that famous poster with the girl playing tennis with no knickers on . . .'

'What, where she's scratching her bare bum? Oh, yes!'

'So I thought we might base our little drama on a tennis game. Call it *Love All* or something.'

'I like tennis,' Jayne grinned. Come to think of it, she couldn't remember the last time she and Mick had a game. But it wouldn't have been anything like what Stella described. The thought of putting all that adrenaline to good use was turning her on already.

'Me too,' Dean smiled, knocking back his glass of wine. 'What exactly did you have in mind though, Stell?'

She outlined her idea and it met with instant approval, each of them chipping in with further details. Then Jayne had to go to the loo. When she came out, Dean was standing in the hall and he beckoned her in through a nearby door with his finger on his lips. Mystified she went with him into what she quickly recognised as Stella's bedroom.

'Look, Miranda, I just had to . . .'

Their eyes met and there was no need for further explanation since Jayne recognised his naked lust as the reflection of her own. They fell upon each other hungrily, lips and hands exploring mouths and bodies at reckless speed, knowing they only had a few moments to take what they could from each other.

The sudden violence of their passion overbalanced them and they toppled onto the bed, where they each undid the zip of the other's jeans. Jayne felt his hard, thick finger probe into her wet pussy at exactly the same moment that she grabbed his erection. Staring into each others' eyes they proceeded to rub each other up the right way.

Jayne was already aroused by an hour or so of merely being in his presence, exchanging flirting glances and imagining what it would feel like to kiss those sensual lips and run her fingers through his silky blond hair. Well now she knew, and it was heaven! His lips were crushing hers with urgent longing while one of his hands played with her nipples beneath her top, and the other hand eased her internal hunger. She could feel his dextrous fingers dabbling in her juices while the fleshy pad of his thumb rotated exquisitely around her clitoris, propelling her towards a climax.

As her arousal gathered force Jayne tried to focus on his rigid erection, which was jerking out of control in her hands. She felt the hot length of his shaft straining between her finger and thumb and knew it longed to be somewhere else, cushioned within her own vaginal walls. The thought of it sent her stomach into a flurry of brief convulsions. She groaned and bent to lick the smooth surface of his glans: at the same moment he probed deep inside her, triggering the first sharp spasms of ecstasy that soon mellowed into a long, voluptuous orgasm.

On the outer rim of her consciousness Jayne was aware that he was coming too, moaning out his relief as warm splodges fell onto her hand. She collapsed with his hand still inside her, making her feel whole, satisfied. A few seconds later she opened her eyes to see him looking at her, his face very near to hers.

'That's better,' he smiled, placing a kiss on her lips then slowly extricating himself from her embrace. He reached over towards the box of tissues by the bed and threw her a handful, then wiped himself. She mopped herself then sat up, slowly returning to normality.

'I'd better go back to the others. You take your time,' he smiled at her, getting off the bed. Then he put his finger to his lips. 'But keep this as our little secret, okay? It's against the rules to get too friendly outside the club.'

'Okay.' She threw him a questioning look, needing to make sense of what had happened now that the madness had passed. Rules or no rules, the overwhelming strength of their attraction for each other was obvious, and would not be denied.

Again he bent over and kissed her, this time on the forehead. 'Now we'll feel more comfortable with each other on Saturday,' he smiled, moving towards the door.

Jayne watched him go, smiling at his tousled hair and the way his eyes now looked like cloudy emeralds. She lay back and stretched like a lazy cat, wallowing in the softness of the duvet and wondering what he looked like without his clothes. A delicious languor crept over her, which she promised herself to indulge for a few minutes only. Her body felt warm, alive.

Even when she told herself that time was up and she should return to the others, Jayne lay there for a few more seconds, feeling the warm glow still in her veins. Although she felt exhilarated by the encounter she knew that its fierce brevity had awakened more desires than it had satisfied. Dean had succeeded in making her want him even more than before, if that were possible. She wanted his prick to take the place of his fingers and plumb her to the depths.

At last Jayne made a determined effort to get up. She went into the bathroom and washed her sticky vulva then splashed cold water on her face, running Stella's brush through her tangled hair. She could repair her make-up at work, she decided. By the time she returned to the front room the three of them were sitting round drinking coffee and Stella appeared to be making notes on a clipboard.

'Oh, there you are!' she said. 'I was about to send out a search party.'

Her smile said she knew exactly what had been going on, and it was only to be expected. Jayne returned it with a wry grin and looked over her shoulder at what she had written. It was set out like a television script, but her mind was too fuzzy to take in the detail. She was glad to leave the detailed planning to Stella, who was evidently putting her experience at ETV to good use.

The meeting broke up soon after, since the two women had to get to the studio and do some real work. Jayne offered her boss a lift, which was gladly accepted as Stella was staying on to do some viewing and would be getting a taxi home anyway. As Jayne followed Stella's directions across London her mind was still on Dean and the devastating impact he'd had upon her libido, so she wasn't surprised when the conversation came around to him.

'I gather that you and Dean got it together in my bedroom earlier on,' Stella smiled, quite unperturbed. 'You don't waste any time, do you?'

'It just sort of . . . happened,' Jayne said, lamely.

'He told me he'd had the hots for you ever since you came in front of the committee,' Stella chuckled. 'Do I take it the feeling's mutual?'

'You could say that!'

'Good, that'll make things a lot easier on Saturday night. But just don't make a habit of seeing men outside club hours, okay? It's okay this time, because we were at my flat, but you could get into trouble if you were indiscreet.'

Stella paused and Jayne sensed a sudden change of mood in her. 'Look, I hope you don't mind me giving you some advice. I know you're a grown up girl, and all that, but I also know you're new to this scene and I don't want you to get hurt.'

'Is it about Dean?' Jayne asked, her voice wavering.

'Yes, but not just him. Most of the guys in the Eye Spy Club are out to make love to as many women as they can with no strings attached, and Dean is no exception. Okay, you're flavour of the month right now but as soon as the next pretty set of tits and arse comes along he'll be straight in there. I just don't want you kidding yourself, okay? The club is not the place to find romance, just sex.'

'It's all right, Stella. If I want more than just a fuck I can get it at home. I suppose,' she added, as an afterthought.

'You never talk much about that guy you're living with. Are you sure he's okay with this?'

'He doesn't know.'

'It's none of my business, I know, but I hope you've thought this one through.'

Jayne sighed. 'I'm confused about me and Mick right now. I was pretty inexperienced when we got together, and I suppose I want to spread my wings a bit before making any long term commitment to him.'

'Hm.' Stella kept her eyes on the road in front and said nothing more, but Jayne sensed her misgivings. They echoed her own, but now that she was scheduled to perform with Dean there was no way she could back out. It was the most exciting prospect she'd had in ages, and even if she decided to go no further with the club she would at least have known what it was like to lust after a man and have him satisfy her again. She realised how much she'd been missing that special buzz since the fire had dampened down between her and Mick.

By Saturday night she was raring to go, and as she got ready for work she tried to prepare Mick for her late return. 'One of the crew is leaving, and there's going to be a bit of a party after the show,' she lied. 'So I'll be back late.'

'Oh, really?' Mick's expression was one of scepticism. 'Well my Great Aunt Lucy's died and I have to go to a wake.'

'Don't be ridiculous, Mick! What are you trying to say?'

'Only that I don't believe you for a minute.'

He scowled at her, and her heart sank. She'd been a fool to imagine that he didn't suspect anything. Remorse stung her for a few seconds, but then she decided to brave it out. 'I seem to remember that you came home after I did last Saturday night, but I didn't make a fuss.'

'I'm not making a fuss, I just said I don't believe you. But it's entirely up to you how you spend your time, Jayne. We're leading more or less separate lives now after all.'

His words saddened her, but there was no time to get into a debate. There was never time, she reflected wryly. She kept putting off the inevitable showdown, but how much longer would Mick stand for it? Maybe it would be better to call it a day.

She travelled to work in a sombre mood but lightened up when Stella greeted her in the cloakroom wearing a mini-skirted tennis dress. 'What do you think?' she asked with a giggle.

'It looks great! Have you got one for me, too?'

'You bet.' She held up a dress with a low V-neck and short pleated skirt. 'I've got us rackets too. But the men are supplying the balls!'

Jayne got through the TV business in a dream that evening. Fortunately she'd anticipated that she would find concentration hard and had prepared a detailed autocue for herself so she didn't have to ad lib too much, but she was relieved when it was over all the same. As she made her way to the exit she wryly reminded herself that once she had been as excited about her work as she now was about the activity to follow. Well, almost!

Stella was waiting for her in the foyer and they took a taxi to the hotel. Quentin was on reception and beamed broadly as they walked in. 'Evening, ladies! Your partners are already downstairs with Charles. He's your cameraman for the evening, Miranda, and Joe will be directing you. Not that you'll need much of that, I'm sure. We're all looking forward to your performance. Good luck!'

Somewhat mystified, Jayne followed Stella into the lift. She hadn't imagined that their little scenario would be taken quite so seriously. Down in the basement they followed the signs to the Indoor Court and saw the three men as soon as they entered. They were standing on the edge of the astro-turfed area in earnest discussion, wearing white shirts and shorts. Both men had lightly tanned bodies, and Jayne's eyes were drawn to Dean's strongly muscled thighs and well developed calves.

'Ah, here they are!' Dean exclaimed, his face lighting up when he saw Stella. 'We were just wondering if we could put some gym mats down here at the edge, Stella.'

'Good idea,' she smiled. 'Would you like to scout round for some, Joe?'

Both Ralph and Dean gave them a hug of welcome, but as Dean took Jayne in his arms he murmured, 'I've missed you!'

'Me too!' she whispered back, her heart already racing.

'Can't wait to see you two in your tennis togs,' Dean said aloud, with a grin. His green eyes scanned Jayne's body and she knew he was imagining how she would look. Smiling, she paid him the same compliment.

Both women went into the changing room and stripped. It seemed strange going into hiding, seeing as they were soon to bare all to the men, but they had to put their clothes somewhere and there was no room around the court. This was the first time Jayne had seen Stella in the nude and she couldn't help glancing at her small, firm breasts and the tiny dark smudge of hair below her navel. She had shaved so there was just a thin line from the top of her pussy. How intimate would she be with that secret cleft by the end of the night?

While Jayne was in the loo, clad only in her underwear, she thought about her one previous lesbian experience. It had been with an older girl at school and not very satisfactory since neither of them had known what they were doing and they'd restricted their foreplay to above the waist. Stella, on the other hand, was sure to be more experienced. A wicked shiver went through her as she imagined tasting female juice for the first time. Would she like it, or hate it?

It might not come to that, she told herself as she came out

of the cubicle. The men might be so rampant that they wouldn't let the women get near each other, despite the two episodes where they were supposed to be making love in a foursome! Although Stella had outlined the general pattern of the script there was still plenty of room for improvisation. And no doubt Joe, the director, would want to intervene from time to time as well.

He was out there instructing Charles when they re-emerged, clad in their tennis whites. A burst of applause greeted them, and they made mock curtseys, then Stella flipped up her skirt to show that she was wearing no knickers and Jayne followed suit. They weren't wearing bras either, and as they lobbed a few playful shots over the net she could feel her unencumbered breasts thud heavily against her chest.

'Right, let's make a start!' Joe called. He was a short, tubby man, half bald, with very blue eyes and wicked grin. 'They're ready and waiting for us upstairs.'

Jayne had forgotten that this video would be shown to the other members as it was being made. The intercom had been turned on and she could hear the excited buzz of subdued voices and the clink of glasses as they waited in the conference room for the entertainment to begin.

'Any chance of a drink?' she asked Stella.

'Sure! I think we could all do with one.'

They walked over to the mini-bar and Jayne chose a quarter bottle of champagne. 'Might as well push the boat out,' she said to Dean, offering to share it with him. 'I've never done anything like this before, and I don't know if I ever will again.'

'Cheers!' He raised his glass to her, his eyes sparkling green fire.

'Hey, how about you two taking off your shirts and playing bare chested?' Stella suggested, as they walked back on the court swinging their rackets.

'We will if you will!' Ralph grinned.

'Later, later!'

'What d'you think, Joe?' Ralph called.

'I think it would be good if they worked up a bit of a sweat,' Stella said. Joe agreed with her, so the men stripped off. Dean displayed a deeply contoured set of pecs, with a smattering of fair hair between that Jayne found quite a turn-on. Her palms itched to run over all that firm-packed flesh. She couldn't wait to see – and feel – what his bum was like.

They were supposed to be playing mixed doubles, so Ralph took up his position on the other side of the net with Stella, while Jayne and Dean remained at the end nearest the camera.

'Okay!' Joe called. 'Action!'

They were to play a bit of a game first, so Stella served to Dean. When she missed the return shot and had to bend down to retrieve it her bare buttocks were clearly visible beneath the white mini-skirt.

'Great!' Joe chuckled, as a gasp of appreciation followed by a burst of applause came from the loudspeaker on the wall. He called out the score and then Stella served again.

This time the play lasted longer, and Jayne got a chance at the ball. She tried to lob it over but it hit the net, losing them a point. Dean acted angry, following their script, and when she missed again he threw his racquet down in disgust. 'Thirty-love!' called Joe.

When they lost the game, again thanks to Jayne's poor play, Dean came up and pretended to harangue her. She answered back and he beckoned the other two to help him force her to bend over the net. Jayne kicked and protested, but her short skirt was pulled right up around her waist and she felt the first stinging impact of the racquet on her naked buttocks.

'Here's one for every point you lost us!' she heard Dean say, thwacking her again.

After Jayne's chastisement the game continued, and she

found herself rubbing her behind with a rueful grin whenever there was a pause in the action. The crowd upstairs was warming up and she found their spontaneous responses encourging as they laughed and applauded. Again she and Dean were beaten hollow, but this time it was Dean who lost the game for them and, gleefully, Jayne insisted that he should take his punishment like a man. He tried to wriggle out of it but Stella and Ralph backed her up, debagging him and holding him over the net while she brandished her tennis racquet.

He stood there in his white Calvin Kleins, the taut curves of his bottom looking very inviting. Jayne imagined biting into the smooth skin of his bum cheeks, and the muscles of her own still-throbbing bottom clenched, making her clitoris throb in sympathy. She slapped the gut strings against his rear end with a satisfying twang, finding the act surprisingly enjoyable. Her whole body seemed to be coming alive with the exercise and her libido was rising as well. She couldn't wait to get down to the real action!

The game proceeded, this time with the other couple losing and administering punishment to each other, but Jayne felt that the joke was in danger of wearing thin. She was glad when the two men started arguing about whether the ball had been in or out, because that was the start of the next phase. It didn't take long for Dean and Ralph to come to blows and then the women joined in, tearing at each other's hair, until all four of them were engaged in a wrestling match on the mats at the side of the court.

Jayne was dimly aware of Charles moving in with his camcorder as the action grew hot. Ralph had already had his shorts ripped off so now both men were in their underwear, although still wearing their white shoes and socks. Stella began to undo the zipper at the back of Jayne's dress and soon the top half was hanging off, exposing her breasts. This proved too much for the men. They fought to gain access to this newly discovered bounty and soon each man was suckling contentedly at a nipple while Stella did her best to pull the rest of the garment down over her hips. Within a few minutes she was completely naked, and lying on her back with her legs open to the camera.

'That's good!' she heard Joe exclaim. 'Move in now, Stella! That's right. Down with that right hand. Shift round a bit, you're hiding her. That's better! That's great!'

Jayne could hear the appreciative noises of the crowd sifting through the wall speaker. Gentle hands spread her thighs even wider and then the most delicious sensations began to fill her pussy as something wet and delicate began to probe between her labia. She didn't need to look at what was happening to know that Stella was licking her down there, probably with her bare arse in the air for the benefit of the audience.

There was something sweetly different about the way the other woman was licking her, coaxing her eager clitoris into standing up for itself and making her lubricate copiously. Stella's tongue was very gentle against her hot, swollen tissues, in balmy contrast to the way Dean had taken her the other night, with his rough and ready cock. Not that she preferred one or the other, she reflected dreamily. Both were very nice indeed.

'Now into her mouth, Ralph!' she heard Joe say, as if in a dream.

Something warm and musky nudged at her lips and once again she didn't have to open her eyes to know what it was. Ralph's prick was a bit thinner than Dean's, but she worked her tongue energetically around it and heard him groan somewhere in the wings. The champagne had made her head fuzzy, her body compliant, and when she felt the entrance to her quim being plugged by Dean's substantial glans she almost fainted with bliss.

Slowly he was working his way inside her, letting the thick stalk of his penis fill her, inch by wonderful inch, until she felt fully stretched. Her walls expanded to accommodate the girth of his organ, sucking at him, squeezing him, until he groaned aloud at the pleasure of it.

For a few seconds Jayne opened her eyelids. Dean's place had been taken at her breast by Stella, who was now nibbling at her nipple with relish while she had her own pussy licked by Ralph. Jayne put out her hand and felt the shallow slope of Stella's breast, moving up until her fingers found the small nipple which she proceeded to flick with her fingertip. She looked up to see Dean towering over her, his green eyes hidden behind closed lids, his magnificent body working overtime to please her.

Jayne watched him thrust into her, saw the thick root of his cock buried in golden hair as it pounded in and out of her, saw his biceps straining to take the weight as he supported himself on his arms. The sight of so much rampant masculinity made her feel almost faint with desire and her eyelids fluttered shut again. Now the world she inhabited was entirely one of sensation. She could still hear the sounds at first – heavy breathing and soft groans from the bodies in close proximity to hers, Joe's occasional muttered encouragement and instructions, the appreciative murmurs of the crowd that filtered from the walls – but they gradually faded as the more primitive senses of taste, touch and smell took hold.

Now she could smell the combined odours of sweat, male and female musk, a perfume more potent than the most powerful of aphrodisiacs. She could also taste the slight bitterness as Ralph's glans put out the first dewy drops of milk-white essence. But the sense of touch was paramount. Her own hands slid over Stella's smooth thighs and belly, then felt the rougher contours of a manly chest. Her fingers felt the contrast between a man's nipple and a woman's: her huge ripe berry, and his hard little seed.

'Miranda . . .' A man's voice whispered in her ear. With a shock she realised he was addressing her. It was Dean. She knew him from his smell, his natural signature. He had fallen forward, sweeping Stella aside in his eagerness to encompass her body, and now he was thrusting hard inside her, over and over, making her gasp and moan as the air was forced out of her lungs and her clitoris responded in throbbing rhythm to the relentless pace of his cock.

Someone was licking her toes – Stella, probably – and she felt a slow heat start to work its way up her legs, making her thighs tingle, mingling with the deeply pleasurable sensations that were taking place within her vulva. She recognised the hot surges that were gathering force and heard herself moaning, as if from far away, at the slow onset of supreme pleasure.

It crept up on her with extraordinary stealth while her whole body was tensed, waiting for the release, every cell and fibre of her being poised on the brink of the cataclysm. So that when the gentle shudders gathered force and swept her into the maelstrom she cried out at the sheer force of her climax. All around she could hear vague echoes of her own cries, from the other lovers and from the invisible crowd that filled the room like ghosts. But soon she was oblivious to everything but the hammering impact of the great rod that was filling her with such ecstasy, such relief.

And it took her a long while to come down, to her awareness of her surroundings. Even then she found herself gazing up at an alien ceiling, wondering where she was and what she was doing there.

'That's a wrap, folks!'

The familiar phrase in such an unfamiliar context brought her abruptly to her senses. She sat up and saw that Stella and Ralph were walking off towards the cloakrooms with towels around their necks while Dean lay, still exhausted, beside her. She caught Joe's eye and he walked over to her. 'Okay, Miranda? That was a great performance you gave there. And you, Dean. Well done the pair of you.'

Performance? Jayne stared at him dumbly as he put out his hand to help her to her feet. She'd completely forgotten about the video, the club, the fact that she had been making love in a foursome for the first time ever. All she'd been aware of was Dean's prick inside her, taking her to places previously unvisited, undreamed of even. She looked down to see him stirring, his green eyes still unfocused, and smiled like an angel.

'Wow, you're such a star!' he breathed in admiration.

'You too,' she replied, shyly.

He was not the only one to congratulate her that night. It was the custom for the actors in the video to appear upstairs, before the assembled company, and receive a standing ovation. Jayne felt absurdly proud of herself as she stood on the tiny stage lapping it up. There was champagne afterwards, and caviar. Dean stood beside her making lewd suggestions about how he'd like the stuff served up to him, and Jayne giggled her way through the rest of the evening on cloud nine.

There was a fashion parade of the latest in fetish wear by a famous German designer, then the company began to disperse. They were gathered in small knots around the hall, chatting about all kinds of inconsequential matters before they left, and Jayne suddenly had the feeling that, without the bizarre clothing, they might be members of any kind of club: model railway enthusiasts, perhaps, or birdwatchers. She still hadn't got used to the idea of sex purely as entertainment, an amusing pastime. Perhaps she never would.

As she rode home in the taxi, however, a feeling of unreality took hold. Just what did she think she was playing at? Her life seemed to have gone off the rails, but how bizarrely! Tonight she felt as if she had been playing out some absurd parody, cheating on her lover with her boss!

Now, speeding towards South Quays, the prospect of

sleeping with Mick was depressing her. It was true, she thought with a sigh: you could be lonelier sleeping in the same bed with someone than sleeping by yourself.

Chapter Eight

Mick almost didn't bother to phone again. The voice of
Lady Odile spelling out the details of her services had
intimidated him, and yet he had to admit to a certain
fascination. He missed the morning appointments slot
through wavering, but then his determination grew during
the day and by the time he reached four o'clock he was like a
cat on hot bricks. He left work at five and hurried to the
nearest public phone booth where he dialled her number
again. This time she answered in person. 'Hullo, this is
Lady Odile. How can I help you?'

'Er . . . I phoned yesterday and got your recorded message.'

'Good. Do I take it that you wish to make an appointment?'

'Yes, please. At least, I'm not sure . . .'

'Which particular services attracted you?'

Her tone was brisk, but also quite pleasant. Recognising
that she was running a business and couldn't talk to him all
day, Mick tried to be brief. 'I'd . . . er . . . like to try the
spacegirl, please. And topless, if that's possible.'

'Not with spacegirl, I'm afraid. She has to wear her
decompression suit at all times. But you could have
cowgirl.'

'Oh yes, of course. Cowgirl will do, then.'

'And what about the recreational activities, sir? A
favourite with my clients is the Bucking Bronco with a taste
of rawhide.'

Mick gulped, nervously fiddling with his cuff. 'That sounds good. I'll try that.'

'Cherry has a slot tomorrow evening, ten o'clock. Would that suit you?'

He said it would, imagining a face and figure to go with that delightful name. The madam went on to quote him a figure four times what the street whore had cost him. But then he supposed that Lady Odile was more upmarket. Telling her his name was Mike, he scrawled down the King's Road address she gave him and replaced the phone. When he came out into the air it was like surfacing from another world, and he gave a huge sigh of relief.

'I've done it!' he thought, gleefully. Striding towards his parked car he gave a little skip.

As he drove home Mick reflected on the fact that this was his second prostitute in a couple of weeks. Was it becoming a habit? Once he would have scorned the very idea, but after enjoying a regular sex life with Jayne he couldn't bear to be without it for long. Besides, he wanted to experiment. Although he and Jayne had been passionate towards each other, had done it in novel places, discovered their favourite positions and so forth, there were dimensions of sex that they had never explored and he had always been afraid to suggest things that seemed really kinky.

When he walked into the flat he found Jayne not long out of the shower and smelling sweet. Mick kissed her and she clung to him for a few seconds, but no sooner were his expectations raised than she dashed them again by saying she was in a hurry. Even so she'd prepared them a pasta and salad supper and seemed in a good mood for a change. He was disposed to be amicable too, forgiving even. If she was carrying on with someone else at least he wasn't just taking it. He was, in his own fashion, fighting back.

'What's the film about tonight, then?' he asked as he attacked his spaghetti.

'Oh, usual rubbish!' came her habitual reply. 'Something from Amsterdam. It's called *A Sex Comedy of Manners*. I ask you!'

'Can't be worse than *Two Hours of Arctic Lust*, surely?'

She giggled. The film about making love in the Nordic Ice Hotel had been one of the alltime turkeys of the porn world. 'We'll see. At least the girls are pretty in the *Hot Shot* films.'

'Ever thought you might like to appear in one yourself?'

Mick was startled by her reaction. She stared at him piercingly for a few seconds then looked away as a flush rose in her cheeks. For one crazy minute he thought she might be doing exactly that. Were she and Stella involved in making those films, not just showing them? But the notion struck him as absurd.

'No, I've never thought about it,' she said with deliberate casualness. 'Although it might be a bit more exciting than what I'm doing at the moment. Honestly, Mick, I don't know how much longer I'll be able to stand it. Do you know, last night I actually had to help with the editing because Tim was off sick. And did anyone say anything about overtime? Not on your life! I'm getting sick of being taken for granted.'

'That was quite a speech! You really mean it, don't you?'

For a moment hope dawned in him. If Jayne got herself a job with normal hours maybe they could start rebuilding their relationship. He looked at her as if seeing her for the first time. In her black silk kimono covered with pink and white flowers, her face devoid of make-up and her hair still damp from the shower, she looked young and appealing. He'd take her to bed there and then, given the slightest encouragement.

'Oh, I'm just a bit fed up with working there, that's all. But the money's good and you know we need it for the mortgage on this place, so . . .' She shrugged.

Mick said, 'We could always move.'

'Do you want to? Out of London, I mean?'

'Not at the moment, no.'

There was a lot he was leaving unsaid. Like how he'd always dreamed of raising kids in the country, for instance. But the way things had been between him and Jayne lately it didn't seem a good idea to mention such things. He thought of his appointment with Lady Odile and smiled to himself as he finished his spaghetti. That was something to look forward to, anyway.

Lady Odile. Already he had an image of her in his mind, based on the way her voice had sounded. She would be very tall and blonde, the willowy sort, but strong because she worked out. If only he could get an appointment with her, instead of one of her girls! But he suspected she came expensive, and she was probably choosy too. Still that didn't stop him dreaming!

He imagined she would be quite efficient and business-like, taking charge of the proceedings completely, but that wouldn't matter because she'd know exactly what to do to please him. She would tease him unbearably until he was in torment, not knowing if she would satisfy him or not. Then, when his release came, it would be all the more sweet. Oh yes, she would know exactly what to do all right!

Mick thought about her and Cherry alternately for most of the next day, which got him into a bit of trouble at a VAT meeting when he let his mind wander off the point. He delayed his return home after ringing to tell Jayne he was working late, for no better reason than not wanting to be distracted from his sweet mood of anticipation. By the time he got home at eight thirty she had gone to work and left him a salad which he consumed rapidly, almost without tasting it. His appetite was for sex now, not food.

Afterwards Mick showered diligently, dusting himself liberally with Chanel talc afterwards, and put on clean clothes. He didn't want to give Cherry any cause for complaint when she was riding him like a cowgirl, now did he?

The thought sent tingles down his spine as he pulled on a cashmere sweater that slid smoothly over his back and shoulders. He stared at his reflection in the mirror: not bad looking for a guy of thirty-two who'd never gone out of his way to look after himself. Then he chided himself for acting as if he were going out on a date. Who ever heard of trying to impress a prostitute?

Around nine thirty Mick found himself cruising down the King's Road. It was quiet at that time of night and he had no difficulty parking outside the mews-style house that was situated in its own private yard. Because he was early Mick strolled round the corner and into a pub, where he downed a Scotch and soda. Dutch courage, he told himself. But he only had one. Something told him that Lady Odile wouldn't take kindly to him turning up reeking of whisky.

Mick presented himself at the door promptly at ten. At first he thought the doe-eyed, dark-haired beauty who opened the door dressed in a maid's uniform was Cherry, but he soon realised his mistake.

'Please follow me,' the girl said. 'Cherry will be with you shortly.'

'Ah, yes!'

'Her name's short for Cherokee. Like Cher, you know?'

The maid led him into an elaborately furnished lounge, all gilt mirrors and red plush. When Mick turned to face her she was holding a silver tray. 'For your contribution, sir,' she reminded him. He put the notes down and then, rather self-consciously, added an extra tenner. 'That's for you,' he smiled.

'Why thank you, sir!'

She bobbed him a curtsey and walked back towards the door on her high heels, her well shaped rear bobbing sexily. Mick sat down on a settee to wait. He was impressed. The place had the feel of a high class bordello and there was nothing tawdry or embarrassing about it. Even the maid had spoken as if she'd been educated at Roedean.

Suddenly the door opened and a tall woman entered at speed, flourishing two pistols.

When Mick found himself staring down the twin barrels he automatically raised his hands in the air. Then he felt utterly foolish, and gave a sheepish grin. His eyes travelled incredulously over the woman's well stacked body. She was wearing a very short fringed bolero affair in light brown suede that only just skimmed her generous breasts, and her midriff was bare except for a thin, beaded belt. The lower half of her was clad in a mini-skirt of the same buckskin material, also fringed, and her long legs were encased in thigh high leather boots. He realised that she owed much of her height to her very tall heels.

The areas of her skin that were visible were tanned a rich honey brown, and her very black hair was in two plaits. Probably fake tan and a wig, Mick surmised, seeing her very blue eyes. She was giving him a haughty stare beneath her thick lashes, her luscious red mouth pressed into a firm line.

'Turn right around, cowpoke!' she said, poking him in the back with one of the guns. 'Now go through that door and kneel on the floor, with your hands above your head.'

He did as he was told, wondering just where all this was leading. As he sank to his knees in front of the large, brass bedstead his arms were pulled roughly behind his back and his wrists secured with a length of hairy rope that chafed his skin. Despite his discomfort a thrill of excited anticipation went through him at the thought of his helplessness before this domineering woman. She came to stand before him, unbuckling her gun belt which she threw onto a chair. 'You deserve to be pistol-whipped, jerk!' she exclaimed, in a fake American accent.

Mick wondered what he was supposed to have done wrong. This was a game where only she knew the rules, and it unnerved him. At the same time it was tremendously arousing. He could feel his erection developing rapidly in his pants. His chest felt tight, making it hard to breathe freely, and yet he felt strangely liberated.

Cherry sat on the bed and stared down at him, her blue eyes cold with contempt. 'You're a no-good bastard, and you need taming,' she muttered. 'How best to do the job, that's the question.' She got up and pulled down a whip from the bedpost. 'Same way as I break in a mule, I guess. Get on your feet, cowpoke!'

It was hard to get up without using his hands. Mick tottered to his feet and stood there while she surveyed him thoughtfully, brandishing the whip. Suddenly she lashed out at him, catching him on the seat of his pants with the stinging leather. He winced and she laughed.

'That hit the spot, didn't it? I'll have you crawlin' to me before sundown, cowpoke!'

She flicked out the whip again and this time it curled around his ankle, the unexpectedness of the assault making him stagger then fall forward onto the bed. She grabbed him by the seat of his pants, hoisting him further up the bed. Mick realised how strong she was. She must work out, he thought, but then he felt the snakebite attack his other ankle and he gasped with the acute pain.

Cherry threw the whip carelessly across the pillow and came to sit beside him, pushing his shoulder until he rolled over onto his back. In a couple of minutes she had reduced him to a useless sack of bones, he reflected ruefully. Her cornflower eyes surveyed him with a glint of amusement, and there was the hint of a smile about her lips.

'Whew! This is darned hot work!' she said, slipping off the buckskin bolero.

She was nude underneath, her brown breasts thrusting proudly from her chest, crested by dark pink nipples that were gradually stiffening as he watched. Mick felt his prick leap in his pants, eager to know what lay beneath the tiny skirt. She had her legs tightly crossed so he didn't know whether she was wearing panties or not.

'Well now, guess it's time to find out jest how much of a man you are!' she drawled. Reaching out for his belt she quickly unbuckled and unzipped him, pushing down his trousers over his hips until his packed-out red pants were revealed. She went to the foot of the bed and took off his shoes, then pulled his trousers down his legs. Mick felt stupid in his socks, but she didn't take those off. Instead she returned to sit beside his pants, running her hand delicately over the bulge within them. 'Hm, not bad for a guy that's been broken in. But it's time I got you all trussed up so you won't try any of your tricks again.'

Mick watched her fetch another length of hairy rope from a chest of drawers. She tied his ankles together tightly and tethered them to the rail at the foot of the bed. Then she tied the rope that bound his wrists to the opposite post on the bedhead until he was strung between them, immobile. A twinge of fear crept up from his feet to his head. His lips tasted salty.

'Okey-dokey!' she said conversationally, sitting back on her heels beside him. 'I don't think you're gonna cause any more trouble, are you, mister? Maybe we can put you to service now.'

She got to her knees and began to roll down the top of his pants, exposing his penis. 'Now that's one mighty fine organ you got there!' she grinned. 'Guess we can find a use for that.'

Giggling, she took off the hat which was slung around her shoulders and placed in over his erect prick. 'Mighty fine hat stand, don't you reckon mister?'

She lifted up his cashmere sweater until his chest was exposed then suddenly straddled him, the short skirt riding up her thighs. In an instant Mick discovered that she was definitely not wearing underwear. She began to slide up and down his torso, her naked quim smearing him with her juices.

'Hey, ain't you gonna give me a rough ride, bronco?' she

challenged him. 'C'mon, cowboy! Shift that hat!'

She slapped at his thighs and he began to shift his hips, bucking until the hat slid off his penis and it began to rub against her naked buttocks. His excitement grew as she slid back and forth on her own slime, anointing his chest and stomach with wet kisses from her open pussy lips. He glanced up at her face and saw she was getting into it, her eyes closed and lips parted as she 'rode' him like a horse.

Mick could feel his own imminent climax gathering strength, but before the release came she suddenly slid off him and began to masturbate, rubbing her big breasts with her own wet fingers and then plunging into herself again. Helplessly he watched her doing what he longed to do himself, his penis aching for satisfaction at the same time. But before she reached her own orgasm she suddenly straddled his chest and lifted up her fringed skirt, showing him her red, distended vulva.

'Okay, Trigger, lick my sugar lump!' she commanded him.

Mick didn't need a second bidding. He put out his tongue and tasted the sweet fruit between her labia, sucking strongly to make her squirm with delight. He sensed that this would be his one and only chance to get at this hot female, to prove that he could bring her off, and he took full advantage of it. The agility of his lips and tongue amazed him as he licked and flicked, sucked and tongue-fucked, without any help from his hands.

Suddenly Cherry arched back with a cry and Mick saw the wracking shudders pass through her body. He had no reason to suppose that her orgasm was not genuine. At any rate, it hastened his own. As soon as she slid down his body again and thrust her naked buttocks against his straining erection he felt the force of his climax gathering within him. She deftly slipped a condom over his glans and soon he felt himself explode in a molten burst of energy that filled his head as well as his crotch with indescribable sensations.

It was good, very good. He came down with a long sigh to find that she was already wiping him up, sliding his pants back on. The realisation that his session was at an end hit him with cold shock and he tried to sit up, then yelped as he ricked his shoulders. He'd forgotten that he was still tethered like an unbroken calf.

'Hang on a minute, fella!' she said, kindly now. She quickly untied his bonds and rubbed the places where the cords had cut into him. 'I'll get you something for that.'

She got some ointment from a drawer and rubbed it tenderly into his skin where the rope marks were. He caught her eye and saw a pleasing friendliness there.

Suddenly he wanted to talk, wanted to bring things back to a more normal plane. 'That was really good,' he began, as if talking to a waiter about a meal.

But she cut him off. 'Now get your things and get outta here!' she snarled. 'I ain't got all day. If you want more of my time you gotta pay for it.'

Mick stared at her, uncertain how much of it was an act. It was impossible to tell. Ruefully he pulled on his trousers and shoes, got up gingerly from the bed and walked towards the door. When he got there he said, 'Thanks a lot, Cherry. Maybe I'll come back for another of your services soon.'

'If you want me again, ask for Cheryl. That's my real name. Now get going. I've another appointment and I got to get changed.'

Mick hurried out into the ante-room and then into the hall in a state of minor confusion – and major satisfaction. That little piece of play-acting had done things for him that no amount of straight sex could do. But it hadn't been the silly talk, or the dressing up that had done it for him. What he'd most enjoyed was being treated as a plaything by that nubile female, of being midly abused in her pretty, capable hands.

On the way home, however, his disappointment grew at not seeing Lady Odile herself. His curiosity about her was intense. Something about that smooth, cool accent on the phone had really got him going. Was there any way he could get to be one of her clients, he wondered. There was one person who could tell him: Stella. But it was too late to try and see her tonight. She'd be working at the studio, and he didn't feel like waiting until two or three in the morning just to talk to her. But he would see her before long, he promised himself that.

The desire to see Lady Odile grew over the next few days, but Mick was wary of approaching her himself. He felt sure she would be choosy about the men to whom she granted her personal services and he wanted to be sure he qualified before risking rejection. So after Jayne had returned from work one night and had fallen asleep, he crept out of the flat and drove to Stella's place. He was relieved to see her light on when he drew up outside.

Once again she seemed pleased to see him. 'I thought you might get back to me,' she smiled, standing back to let him in. It didn't seem to faze her at all that it was two thirty in the morning. She was wearing a mauve kaftan-style robe in some clingy material that suggested she had nothing on underneath. Although his libido level rose automatically at the sight of her thrusting nipple points and the visible contours of her delta, Mick was more eager to talk – about Lady Odile.

Once he was seated in her room, with a whisky in his hand, Stella raised the issue herself. 'Did you phone that number I gave you?'

'Yes. That's what I've come about actually.'

Stella grinned. 'I thought it might be. You got one of her girls, right?'

'She was fine. Very professional, knew what she was doing and all that. But I was wondering about Lady Odile herself. Does she have personal clients?'

A secretive look came into Stella's dark eyes. 'Not exactly. You can't get an appointment with her just by ringing up. She's in a position to pick and choose, you see.'

Mick felt his shoulders sag with disappointment. 'I see. No chance for me, then?'

'That depends . . .'

'On what? Money?'

Stella chortled. 'Lord, no! She earns more than enough from her business.'

'What, then?'

'Oh, if she likes the look of you I suppose.'

'But how can she . . . can I . . .?'

'Hold on!' Stella laughed, tilting back her head to drink the dregs of whisky from her glass. 'It's not that easy. First you have to apply to join the club she belongs to.'

His face fell. 'Club?'

'Yes. That card you returned to me, remember? That was the membership card.'

Hope dawned again. 'So you're a member too?'

She hitched up her skirt and pulled her feet up onto the couch beside her, giving Mick a glimpse of her lean, smooth thighs. All the time she watching him with her dark, amused eyes. Playing cat and mouse, he thought. 'Yes. I can propose you, if you like. But you'd have to go before the committee.'

'What kind of club is it?'

'It's only for the sexually adventurous. But I've a hunch that might include you, am I right?'

Was she making some kind of pass at him? Mick felt very unsure of himself. He wanted Stella, but at the same time he wasn't sure what she was into. And her description of the club was a bit vague.

'I liked what Lady Odile's girl did, and I could fancy more of that. But it's her I really want. Her voice on the phone, it did things for me. I can't explain.'

'You don't have to. I think I understand. You want to be dominated by a queen of the art, and Odile is that all right. But the club has other diversions to offer too, things you probably haven't dreamt of. The main thing is, how willing are you to participate?'

'I don't know. It's all a bit new to me, quite honestly.'

She regarded him thoughtfully. 'But I think you have potential. Tell me, Mike, do you like watching sexy videos?'

'Mm. But they're nearly always a bit tame for me.'

'Ah!'

'Why do you ask?'

She shrugged. 'Just to see how curious you are about other people's sex lives. And what about yours: any girlfriends?'

Mick scarcely hesitated. 'Not so as you'd notice.'

'I mean, I wouldn't want you to get into any trouble by joining our club. It's strictly for people who enjoy experimenting with sex in a "no strings, no complications" environment. There's no room for jealousies or rivalries, either inside or outside our circle. And members are sworn to secrecy about our activities, which is why I can't go into detail.'

'Of course. Well I have to admit I'm intrigued.'

'You find the idea exciting, do you?'

Before he realised what Stella was doing she'd slid off the sofa and come over to him, her hand moving to his crotch. She found his erection and squeezed it gently. 'Mm, you are excited, aren't you?'

Mick felt his breathing accelerate as her slight, but sexy, body hovered over his. But then she moved away and he felt a mixture of disappointment and relief. She smiled down at him for a few seconds in that same enigmatic way, then nodded slowly. 'Okay, I think we'll give it a try. I'll propose you to the committee and see what happens. If you'll let me have your phone number . . .'

Mick panicked. If she phoned him at home and Jayne answered, the fat would really be in the fire. 'I'd better give you my work number,' he said. 'I'm hardly ever at home and I don't have an answerphone.'

'If you're quite sure that's okay.'

'Yes. Just pretend you're a client, make it sound like a business appointment. No problem.'

'Fine. I should hear in a week or so and I'll let you know right away.'

There was a pause, and Mick wondered if sex was on offer right there and then. Yet the signals she was sending out weren't quite sexual. It was more like a game, a game of 'I know something you don't know'. He wondered if she was aware of his relationship with Jayne and, for a moment, his blood chilled. What if he were walking into a set-up?

Then Stella got up and the slight tension was dispelled. 'I'm tired, Mike, I've had a long and busy day. If you don't mind, I'll ask you to go now.'

He leapt to his feet. 'Yes, of course.'

'I have a rule that I never entertain fellow club members outside meetings,' she explained. 'And I must admit that I've regarded you as a potential member from the start. You finding my membership card seemed like a kind of omen.'

'Is that why you recommended Lady Odile, to see if I liked my sex a bit more . . . adventurous?'

Her laugh tinkled through the apartment. 'Spot on!'

He grinned, ruefully. 'Maybe it takes one to know one.'

'Maybe.' She moved towards the door and he followed. There were many questions in his mind but now was not the time to ask them. A powerful aura enclosed them both, the air between them filled with secrets. Mick's head felt light and giddy, but he knew it wasn't just the alcohol. He was half drunk with elation at the thought of joining some secret society devoted to the uninhibited enjoyment of sex in all its forms.

More sober considerations surfaced as he drove home

through the silent streets, foremost of which was the effect membership of such a club might have on his relationship with Jayne. The craven part of him tried to justify it, imagining that he would learn a few more bedroom tricks to reawaken her interest in him. A more realistic voice argued that if he was getting his sexual satisfaction elsewhere he would no longer bother with her, and they would drift apart. The nightmare scenario was that she would eventually find out, probably through Stella, and be so furious that both her professional and her private life would be ruined in one fell swoop.

That must be prevented at all costs, he decided. He still loved Jayne, and wouldn't wish her harm. But his sex drive was in danger of extinction if he didn't take steps to revive it. Given the option between starting an affair with someone new and joining this club, the latter seemed less likely to rock the boat, long term. Mick sighed. If someone asked him what he wanted more than anything he would have to say he wanted Jayne back as she used to be, loving and lusty, with all the time in the world for him. If improving his technique in bed could bring back those wonderful times then it would be well worth it.

He got back around three and snuggled in with Jayne's warm body, hoping she might prove compliant as she had before. But when his hand crept to her breast she snorted furiously at him, and moved over to the far side of the bed in an uncompromising rebuttal. Mick decided not to push it. He wanted to make love to her when she was fully awake and sharing in the experience. It was too long since that had happened, far too long.

Maybe she just found him boringly predictable. Maybe she was just exhausted. Either way, he couldn't do much about it right now. His only real fear was that she might have fallen in love with someone else. If so, did Stella know about it? Was she encouraging him to join her club so the blow might be softened when Jayne eventually told him?

His mind raced on, inventing all kinds of fantasy scenarios until he wore himself out with speculation and drifted into sleep.

Chapter Nine

'Want to come to Frankfurt for the Fuck-Film Fest?'

Jayne blinked at Stella incredulously. 'What?'

'It's in two days' time and we'd go as guests of *Hot Shots*. Should be good for a laugh, at least. We get flown over in Harry's private jet first thing in the morning, spend the day there and return in time for you to present the programme at ten.'

'Sounds good to me.'

'The idea is that we help Harry promote the club compilation video. You know he's included our tennis romp, so we'll be shown off as the stars.'

'Will Dean be going?' Jayne felt her pulse suddenly race. 'And Ralph?'

Stella made a face. 'Afraid not. They only want the women to go, not the men. But it's our first commercial enterprise, so a lot's riding on it.'

'Okay, I'll come. Like you said, it sounds fun.'

They were in the cloakroom at work again, but just as Stella was halfway through the door she shut it again and came back in. 'Oh, by the way. Quentin wanted me to ask you if you'd like to sit on the selection committee in a couple of weeks' time. We all have to do a turn, you know, and he thought it might be interesting for you. I can't do it because I've proposed one of the prospective members.'

Jayne smiled when she remembered how nervous she'd been, and how she'd gradually got off on the idea of performing before the formal-looking bunch. She now knew they'd seen it all before, of course. It would be fun to watch some other poor innocent going through the same initiation process. 'Sure, I'll do it.'

'Fine. It'll be in the evening, so we'll have to put your intro on video. Tony won't like it, but sod him! For once he'll just have to lump it. Now we'd better get cracking or he'll be having fits and we don't want to get into his bad books, now do we?'

Jayne had been looking forward to her trip to Frankfurt but when she had to get up at six in the morning after only getting to bed at two the night before it seemed rather less attractive. After a shower and some black coffee, however, she felt half human. The taxi arrived and whisked her off to London City airport, where Stella and Harry Lucas were awaiting her.

'Good gel!' Harry said in his usual bluff manner, giving her a wet kiss on the cheek.

The tiny six-seater plane was equipped with a bar and restroom. Harry had brought his 'secretary' along with him, a chubby blonde called Sandra with little to say for herself, and a beefy chap in a chauffeur's uniform called Spike, who looked as if he doubled as a bodyguard. It was soon evident that he doubled as a pilot, too.

'Champagne, everyone?' Harry beamed as they left the runway and took a running jump at the dawn sky.

'Ugh, not before breakfst!' Sandra shuddered.

'Where's your spirit of adventure, gel?' Harry grinned, popping open the cork.

Jayne had hers with orange juice and croissants hot from an insulated bag. En route Harry outlined the programme. They were to arrive around nine thirty but their first engagement wasn't until noon: an interview with a local radio station. Once they'd got into the costumes that would be provided for them they were free to wander around the stalls or peep in at the various video showings that would be taking place through the day.

'Ours is being shown at four thirty in the afternoon,' Harry explained. 'So you ladies must be on hand then for photos, signing autographs and so on.'

'Sure, Harry,' Stella said, knocking back her third glass of champagne. 'We'll do anything you say, won't we, Jaynie?'

'Within reason,' she smiled back.

Their arrival at Frankfurt was followed by a speedy drive in a luxurious Mercedes until they came to the hotel where the 'Four F's', as it was affectionately known in the trade, was taking place. A banner with four F's in a swastika pattern was flying at the entrance – rather a tasteless touch, Jayne thought. But once they went through into the lobby she was dazzled by the brilliance of the décor. A notice declared that everyone had to pass a strict dress code before they were allowed into the conference hall, but Harry said they'd been booked a suite so that they could change in comfort.

'You're VIPs today, girls!' he told them proudly, as their bags were taken into the lift ahead of them.

Upstairs, in the Kissinger Suite, the three women were left alone to get ready while the two men waited downstairs in the bar. There was an array of exotic clothes in the wardrobe for them to pick and choose. Sandra squealed in delight as she took first grab at a silver lurex dress that appeared to be just an arrangement of straps and triangles.

'Here, let me help you on with that,' Stella volunteered, throwing Jayne a wink.

The pudgy blonde was soon in the altogether, squeezing into the outfit with difficulty. When all the triangles were strategically placed Jayne had to admit that she looked rather sensational. Her small, fat breasts were poking through the tight straps with just the nipples covered, and her belly undulated between the straps around her hips like corrugated cardboard. From the rear, her flabby buttocks bulged through in jelly rolls that no doubt some men would find very attractive.

'I think I'll wear these over the top,' she smiled, drawing out a black suspender belt and matching stockings.

'How about you, Jayne – seen anything you like?' Stella asked at last.

'Well, I was wondering about this,' she replied, doubtfully holding up a white satin corset generously trimmed with maribou.

'Oh yes, that would look fantastic!' Stella enthused. 'But you'll need help getting into it. And what about your lower half?' She began to rummage in the wardrobe. 'This might do.' She drew out a transparent plastic skirt with hoops of gold around it, like a crinoline.

'Yes, that's fun!' Sandra declared, still admiring herself in the three full-length mirrors. 'Wear this gold tanga with it. Ooh, I do *love* dressing up, don't you?'

While Jayne stripped, Stella found herself a black leather catsuit that covered her from top to toe except for two heart-shaped cut-outs: one for each cleavage, front and back. She helped Jayne into the corset and began to lace her up tightly at the back, pulling so tightly on the strings that she found it difficult to breathe. When the figure-hugging corset was finally secured it formed a kind of armour-plating over her chest so that she could only breathe shallowly or her ribs were squashed.

'How does anyone put up with this?' she gasped. But the maribou down was deliciously soft against her cleavage, and she felt ultra feminine.

'You'll get used to it,' Stella replied, fastening the hooped skirt around her waist. 'Now step into these.'

The silky pale stockings were fastened to the suspenders that dangled from the corset, then Jayne found a pair of high-heeled shoes with cut-outs at the toe. They fitted her perfectly. She pirouetted in front of a mirror and realised that she looked amazing. With her waist cinched in her breasts jutted out more than usual and her nipples played peekaboo with the white feathers around the neckline.

'So sexy!' Stella murmured, as she clambered into her leather suit and asked Jayne to zip her up at the back. She gave a gasp and closed her eyes in bliss as the leather moulded itself to her intimate contours.

There came a discreet tap on the door, followed by Harry's voice. 'Gels, are you ready yet? Don't want to rush you ladies, but we're expected downstairs.'

Sandra opened the door a crack and blew him a kiss. 'Just coming, Daddy-o!'

After much last minute retouching to make-up and hairdos the trio emerged in their finery. Harry's eyes nearly popped out of his head when he saw them. 'Wow, you've really done me proud, ladies!'

They went through into the conference room and at once entered another world. The blinds were down and the lighting was subdued, which was a bit of a shock in itself at that time of the morning. Although the hall was nowhere near filled to capacity, there were about a hundred people milling round the twenty or so stalls that lined the walls. They were all dressed in fantastic creations of leather, plastic, vinyl – even in one instance, chainmail – with the sexes evenly represented. Jayne was interested to find that the weird soon became the commonplace and in a few minutes, her eyes became so accustomed to seeing naked nipples, bulging bottoms and pierced pricks that she no longer registered any surprise.

At the far end was a screen, currently showing a video that appeared to be set in a girls' boarding school, and there were half a dozen small, dark rooms leading off the main one for the showing of more films. Jayne was irresistibly reminded of a cathedral with side chapels as she walked down the centre aisle on Harry's left arm, with Sandra on his right and Stella bringing up the rear. She noticed that their progress was causing quite a stir. People were staring and whispering, throwing them admiring or envious glances, and one man was standing at the far end with an expectant smile. With his immaculate suit of black PVC, and well groomed silver hair streaked with pink, he had the air of being the head honcho.

'Ah, Harry! How good of you to come and provide us with such a feast for the eye!' The man smiled as they approached.

'Nils, let me present to you my constant companion, the lovely Sandra.'

Nils bowed low, took her hand and kissed it with relish. 'Sandra. Short for "Cassandra", I believe. Do you have the gift of prophecy, my dear? If so, I shall not believe a word you say!'

His erudition was lost on Sandra, who merely simpered and preened. Harry then introduced Stella and Jayne together, as 'The Stars of the Eye Spy video'.

'Really? Then I look forward to seeing you both perform.'

His curiously yellow-tinged eyes lighted on the deep cleft between Jayne's breasts and she felt a light shiver, as tangible as if he had touched her there with his lips or fingertips. Was he some kind of magician, she wondered. Or hypnotist? He offered her his arm, saying, 'Let me take you on a guided tour of our humble Temple to Venus, my dear.'

Jayne couldn't help feeling rather honoured that he had singled her out. Everyone's eyes were on her as they began to inspect the stalls and she knew that the other women were envying her her handsome escort. The wares on display ranged from fetish fashion and sex toys to 'herbal elixirs guaranteed to stimulate the libido' and erotic prints from India, China and Japan all 'guaranteed authentic'.

'In England I believe you have festivals of the Mind, Body and Spirit,' Nils told her, adding with a smile, 'Well, this is a festival of the Dirty Mind, the Sexy Body and the Adventurous Spirit. We celebrate sex in all its forms, without shame and without censorship. May I suggest that we two get together later on in one of the private rooms for a more personal celebration of the procreative urge?'

Jayne was taken aback. Such was the aura of the man that she felt she could hardly refuse, yet there was something peculiarly decadent about him and she didn't know whether she wanted to be drawn into his sphere.

While she hesitated Stella came up, letting her off the hook. 'There's a man over there who wants to photograph you,' she said. 'Excuse me, Nils, but he's from *Lech* magazine and I think Jayne might end up on the front cover.'

'Lucky Jayne,' Nils murmured dryly, releasing her arm. But as she turned to go he whispered, 'Room seventeen, eleven a.m.'

Stella led the way across the hall to where an eager young man in lurex tights and a straitjacket was flaunting a head of bright ginger hair and a Leica camera with equal pride. He also had a stonker of an erection, which he was wearing with studied nonchalance. He was grinning from ear to ear as she approached. 'Take your photo darlin'?' he said.

'All right. How do you want me?'

'Holding a copy of *Lech* please. We need some promo material. If we use you there's some dosh in it. Not a lot, but every little helps, eh? As the bishop said to the actress.'

Jayne stood in front of the stall holding the magazine up with a smile. The photographer took four shots, then asked her to take off her skirt, bend over and balance the mag on her behind. She did her best but it kept slipping off. Then Stella had the bright idea of sellotaping it to her buttocks.

'Great! Sign here and we'll be in touch if we use any of 'em,' he told her.

While Jayne was getting back into her transparent skirt Nils came up, and she realised that he'd been watching from a distance. 'You look infinitely more desirable without the skirt, you know,' he said. 'Leave it off, do.'

She threw Stella an enquiring look, but she just shrugged. Jayne wondered what to do. She felt undressed in just her underwear. Not that the skirt made her much more decent, it was simply the feel of it. Although she was no more indecent than if she were in a bikini, the sexy provocativeness of the corset made her feel more open, more vulnerable.

'Please?' Nils said, seeing her hesitation. 'Just for me?'

She smiled back at him. 'Okay. I'll just take it back upstairs.'

'No need.' Nils snapped his fingers and three of the girls who were patrolling the hall with trays of drinks rushed to his side. 'Take this garment back to wardrobe please, Elsa,' he said to a blonde beauty in a topless waitress outfit.

Then Nils looked pointedly at his watch. 'Ten forty-five,' he said with a smile before drifting off.

Jayne decided to take advice from Stella about whether to keep her appointment with Nils. When she told her, the other woman laughed. 'You'd be a fool not to go, Jayne. That man is one of the most powerful guys in the porn world. If he likes you, you're in.'

'But what will I have to do?'

'I've never had the privilege of finding out. But since we have that radio interview at twelve the longest he can keep you is fifty-five minutes, and I reckon that would be time well spent.'

Jayne was still cogitating when she noticed it was five to eleven and Nils was nowhere to be seen. She went up to Harry and told him that he'd asked to see her privately.

Harry clapped her on the shoulder. 'Lucky gel! Don't worry, he won't ask very much of you. But it's good news for our video. If he likes you . . . what time did you say, eleven? Hurry along, then. He's not known for his patience.'

Jayne's stomach felt as if it were revolving slowly while she walked out of the hall, through the lobby and into the lift. She was aware of the curious eyes that followed her progress and wondered if any of them knew that she was about to keep her appointment with Nils. Although no one raised a brow at her she felt selfconscious in her semi-nakedness and longed to be away from public view. But what would happen once she was closeted with Nils in his room? Her stomach seemed to be performing rapid gymnastics at the thought.

She tapped at the door of room seventeen and it was immediately opened. Nils was wearing a black quilted robe. He smiled broadly at her. 'Ah, good! I was hoping you'd keep our little appointment.'

The room was luxuriously furnished with a huge bed and a fluffy white fur rug in the centre of the floor. There was a huge bouquet of flowers on a table in the window and a television was on in the corner but with the sound turned off. Jayne was startled to see herself on screen, in her tennis dress.

'Oh! You're playing our video!'

'Yes, and quite delightful it is too. You especially, my dear. Will you take a glass of champagne?'

She thought it might steady her nerves. Although Nils was being the perfect gentleman she knew he had some kind of agenda. When would he get around to the business in hand?'

They sat together on the sofa and Nils toasted the success of the video. 'I'm sure it will sell like hot cakes!' he murmured, his pale eyes surveying her thoughtfully. He glanced at the screen where her bare behind was visible beneath the short skirt as she made a shot. 'Or perhaps "hot buns" might be more appropriate!'

She laughed at his little joke and he put his arm around her shoulder, his fingers resting lightly on her bare skin. His right hand was on her knee. Why did she think there was something creepy about him? He was good-looking, around forty-five she guessed, and he certainly had a powerful aura of masculinity about him. Yet he also had the air of one who led a clandestine sex life. As she now did herself, Jayne realised with a faint shock.

'You look so gorgeous in that costume,' he murmured, his fingers trailing down her arm and across the plump top of her breast. His other hand crept up her thigh, softly teasing her. Despite herself Jayne was becoming aroused, half attracted and half repelled by his insinuating smile and manner.

'Thank you,' she said primly, finishing her champagne. It was her fourth glass that morning and the room was blurring before her eyes.

'Of course it's your legs that turn me on the most.'

'They do?' Jayne turned in surprise to see him smiling suavely at her.

'Or should I say your feet? In those exquisite shoes.' Before she realised what was happening he was kneeling before her, his hands caressing the black leather, an expression of rapt attention on his face. 'There's something I want you to do for me,' he rasped, his self-control clearly wavering. 'It may strike you as strange, but it would give me a great deal of pleasure.' He sighed, his fingers reaching her bare ankles and stroking them softly. 'Oh yes, a great deal!'

Nils seemed to suddenly come to his senses. He got up and walked to the centre of the room where the luxurious white fur rug was spread, then slipped out of the black robe. Underneath he was wearing only a pair of black underpants, and his erection was very obvious. 'I want to lie down on this while you stand over me,' he told her, his voice low and throaty with emotion. 'Will you do that for me, please?'

Jayne put down her glass. 'Of course,' she smiled. She began to walk over to him, but he held up his hand. 'No, wait! Let me get comfortable first.'

She watched him lie down on the rug, wriggling into the warm nest of fur. He looked faintly ridiculous, but she didn't dare laugh. Instead she glanced towards the TV where her own image was smiling out at her, bare-breasted, while she licked Ralph's cock.

'Now you can walk towards me, slowly, looking as snooty as you like,' he told her.

His attitude struck her as grovelling. Was he the kind of man who got off on being abused by women? She stuck her chest out and approached him with haughty disdain, seeing the pale eyes darken and turn inward as some long cherished fantasy kicked into play. At last she was standing between his outstretched thighs, looking down at his twitching prick. He looked absurdly like a parody of a naked baby photographed on a bearskin rug.

'Let your nipples peep out, just a little,' he instructed her, dreamily.

Jayne delved into the cups of her tight-laced corset and managed to extract both her nipples. They protruded over the white feather trim, red and swollen. Nils gave a long sigh of pleasure then murmured, with greater urgency, 'Now I want you to put your right heel into my belly button.'

She smothered a grin, raising her leg slowly and bringing the heel of her shoe down into the shallow depression of his navel. He gasped as she pressed it home. 'Yes, grind it a little!'

Jayne rested her toe on his stomach and waggled her heel around. His hands travelled up her calves in a kind of supplication, and his pale blue eyes were tracking back and forth between the exposed nipples and the silky triangle between her thighs.

'Now play with your nipples!' he gasped.

Obediently Jayne took each nipple between her thumb and forefinger and began to twiddle. Nils groaned, hardly able to keep his eyes open as the sharp ascent towards orgasm was evidently in progress. He evidently found it uncomfortable to have his organ trapped within the constricting pants and impatiently pulled it free. The purple-skinned glans reared forcefully out of the undergarment, like a creature coming up for air.

Suddenly Nils' hands seized her shoe and removed it gently, bringing the heel up to be kissed with as much reverence as if it were a holy relic. Jayne was at a loss to know what to do next, but his instruction was hissed under his breath, 'Stroke my penis with your sole!'

Carefully she placed the arch of her foot over the thick, short shaft and began to roll it beneath her. Nils started one long, continuous moan that grew in volume as his frenzied licking and kissing of her shoe accelerated. Jayne had heard about foot and shoe fetishists before but the reality was even more bizarre than she had imagined. Yet it was titillating to see the man so worked up over her own footwear. Her nipples were extremely hard and sensitive, sending erotic messages down to her crotch which was responding by becoming puffy and moist.

Nils was sniffing her shoe now, and his glans was becoming sticky with the impending release of his seed. When he finally spurted, with an agonised groan, Jayne let her foot drop out of the way. She moved to his balls which she gently massaged with her toes, evidently prolonging his ecstasy. He had the whole of her shoe heel in his mouth now, and was gagging as the paroxysms shook through him in a wave of convulsions.

'Oh God, you don't know what that did for me!' he exclaimed, when he'd pulled the shoe out of his mouth and the last, shuddering throes had died away.

'I think I have some idea!' she giggled, removing her stockinged foot and pulling up her bra cups again.

He sat up, staring at her with his faraway eyes. 'No, you have *no* idea!' he said, sternly. 'Only another who shares my fetish knows the peculiar delight it brings. You like to think that you were humouring me, playing a silly game. But you have no idea. No idea at all.'

She turned away from that intense, slightly demonic gaze, feeling uncomfortable. He got up from the rug and picked up the discarded shoe. Taking a tissue from the embroidered box near the bed he dipped it in the champagne that remained in his glass and carefully wiped all over the heel. Then he handed it back to her with a smile.

'There you are, madame. Your champagne slipper.'

Jayne put it on, glad to be on an even keel again. The heels were just too high for her to feel comfortable balanced on one. He offered her another drink, but she smilingly declined.

'I have a radio interview at twelve, so I think I'd better keep a clear head. Not that it's all that clear, even now.'

'Would you like to lie down and rest for half an hour?' he suggested, resuming his earlier rôle of gracious gentleman. 'I know you had to get up very early this morning.'

Jayne hesitated, wondering if he expected more sexual services from her. He seemed to guess what was in her mind. 'I have to return to the hall but I'll make sure you're called at eleven forty-five. Feel free to use my shower if you wish.'

Jayne glanced at the clock by the bed. Had they really only been at it for fifteen minutes? She muttered her thanks and took off her shoes, lying down on the large, luxurious bed. She watched him stop and remove the video, replace it in its cover and carry it under his arm to the door. 'People are going to love this!' he said, emphatically, as he reached for the handle.

With a sigh Jayne closed her eyes and let a drowsy languor take hold. She knew she wouldn't sleep, she was far too nervous and excited, but it was good to have a rest. Her body was full of pent-up excitement but she was too tired to do much about it. This was a state she found herself in a lot these days. What a shame she couldn't vent her sexy feelings on Mick. The thought of him threatened to depress her, so she shut him at the back of her mind and thought about the impending interview.

Stella had promised to do most of the talking. But when, an hour later, the pair of them were face to face with outrageous Polly Darton from YBA Radio she pointedly addressed most of the questions to Jayne. It was hard to take the woman seriously, however, dressed as she was in a purple parody of Madonna's circle-stitched bra worn with baggy, see-through plastic pants and thigh high rubber waders. The rude tattoos on her behind were clearly visible through the pants when she turned around. Her hair was rainbow streaked and she had diamond glitter attached to the ends of her long, black fake lashes which she insisted on batting seductively at Jayne throughout the interview.

'I think she fancies you!' whispered Stella at one point, before collapsing into giggles.

Polly wound up a series of rather pointless questions with, 'So, Jayne the Vain – and with looks like yours vanity must be your besetting sin! – what are your plans for the future? Apart from planning to have as much sex in as many ways as possible, of course.'

'I . . . I don't know,' Jayne faltered, suddenly unable to envisage any 'future' for herself. Not of a kind that this weird woman and her audience might understand, anyway.

'We hope she'll go on working for us, presenting our special films in her inimitable fashion,' Stella jumped in. Jayne threw her a grateful look.

'But what about making them – films, I mean? Are you going to give us any more glimpses of that gorgeous body of yours, Jayne? I had a sneak preview of *Love All* earlier today, and I have to say that your boobs were sensational. They could act the ass off Kim Basinger's any day. I mean, your nipples are so . . . eloquent!'

'Well I might make another film . . .' Jayne glanced enquiringly at Stella again, who gave her a nod. Encouraged, she continued with more enthusiasm. 'I enjoyed making *Love All* so much that I think I probably will.'

Once the interview was over Jayne breathed an audible sigh of relief. To her surprise, Polly gave her a hug and a gentle bite on her earlobe. 'You were marvellous, darling. All that wonderful English reserve. My fans are going to love you to bits, just like me!'

Jayne shrank from her predatory gaze, realising that the

woman must be a rampant lesbian. She'd hoped to make a swift exit with Stella, but then she heard her accept Polly's invitation to go to her room and 'play'. Realising that she was included in the invitation, she wondered if she were ready for such an experience.

Yet if not now, when? She told herself that this was the perfect opportunity to try out something, to decide whether she liked making love with other women or not. She was away from home and unlikely to meet up with Polly again. And Stella was no real problem. She felt comfortable with her now they had romped together for the video, but equally she felt able to tell her if she didn't want to continue with a certain activity. Besides, she was still hot from her encounter with Nils earlier on, and didn't much mind where her satisfaction came from.

The three of them went up to Polly's room while Harry and Nils were deep in conversation at the buffet table. There was plenty of time before their last engagement, being introduced to the audience at the showing of their video. Maybe there would even be time for a sleep, Jayne thought hopefully, though by the look of her Polly was perfectly capable of enduring a marathon sex session.

More champagne was on offer once the door was shut behind them and this time Jayne accepted willingly. She couldn't imagine going to bed with someone as bizarre as Polly when she was cold sober. The radio presenter tuned in to her own station, which played raucous music almost non-stop, and began to dance while she drank from her glass, beckoning the other two to join her. Soon they were all three prancing in a kind of parody of the Three Graces until they collapsed in a giggling heap on the bed.

'Help me get out of this medieval bra, someone!' Polly demanded, rolling over onto her stomach. 'It's nipping my nips something cruel!'

Stella duly obeyed, struggling with the four heavy-duty hooks and finally freeing the huge breasts which flopped almost to her waist when she sat up. They were covered in freckles and had enormous flat brown nipples too. When she saw Jayne looking at them she grinned, wryly.

'Not as beautiful as yours dear, are they? I'd die for a feel of your tits, Jayne. They look so fabulous in that corset, don't they, Stella?'

'Mm.'

Stella was kneeling behind Polly now, her hands lifting up the weighty mammaries while she nuzzled her neck and hairline. Jayne felt a bit out of things until Polly reached out and began to unlace her corset. She gave a relieved sigh as her chest became less constricted and she could take proper breaths again.

Soon the cups were hanging loosely over her bosom, making it easy for Polly to reach in and touch her breasts. An expression of utter bliss passed over her face as her fingers found the rigid nipples and proceeded to fondle them. Jayne groaned, wanting to lie down.

'Why don't I take this thing off?' she suggested, her words coming out in a nervous croak.

'I'll tell you why,' Polly answered with a smile. 'Because it's more fun with it on, that's why! Makes it seem naughtier, don't you think? More predatory. You can put your hands inside my pants if you like, and I'll pretend not to notice.'

Jayne was uncertain whether this was an invitation or a request, so she did nothing. But Stella put one hand down inside the plastic pants from behind and started caressing the woman's generous arse, which seemed to satisfy her. For the time being, anyway.

As their activities proceeded Jayne felt there was a strange, dreamlike quality about the experience. She was unsure what this was due to: her early rising and champagne on an empty stomach, making her feel faint and disoriented? The weirdness of being at the Fuck-Film Fest surrounded by strange people in strange garb? The fact that she was unused to being made love to by a woman, let alone by two? She wondered what she should do and, being unable to decide, did nothing.

But her passivity seemed quite acceptable to the others. After a while she lay there letting them do what they liked to her, and it was certainly very pleasant. While Stella found her way into the nooks and crannies of her pussy, just as she had for the video, Polly seemed perfectly content to wallow around her breasts, kissing and licking her nipples to perfect peaks while her hands delved beneath the corset to squeeze handfuls of flesh. By the time she felt Stella's finger move under her panties and, with relentless determination, into her vagina, Jayne found herself on the verge of orgasm.

A few thrusts of Stella's fingers while her other hand massaged her clitoris was enough to propel her into a shattering climax that throbbed its way around her body from head to toe. She could hear Polly cooing and gurgling at her breast throughout, gaining some kind of vicarious satisfaction from seeing her come, and then the three of them lay back exhausted in a triple embrace. It wasn't long before Jayne actually fell asleep, thankful for the dual release from sexual tension and fatigue.

When she came to she was alone. Seeing she had barely half an hour before the video showing, she began to get up but her head was reeling so she lay down again. What would Mick think of her, she wondered, if he could see her now? In some ways she longed to tell him about her new, secret life. Invite him to share it, even. Yet she was unsure how he'd react.

So much seemed to have happened since Stella first told her about the Eye Spy Club. Jayne felt far removed from the woman she had once been, and from her partner, too. Their past lovemaking, satisfying though it had usually seemed at the time, now seemed naive and uncomplicated. Not that there was anything wrong with that, but would it be possible for her to go back to straight sex after trying all these

weird and wonderful variations? Somehow she didn't think
so.

It would all be up to Mick, she decided with a sigh. If he
were willing to develop his sexuality and explore wilder
shores of eroticism with her, there might be hope for them
as a couple. If not, they would certainly have to part.
Pushing such dismal thoughts aside, Jayne rose from the
bed with a determined effort and set about making herself
look presentable again.

Chapter Ten

Jayne dozed most of the way back to London in the little plane. It had been a tiring day, and she still had a job to do that night. But both Harry and Stella were pleased with the way things had gone. The video had been rapturously received and they'd been treated like minor celebrities, with people asking for their autographs or wanting photos. Jayne had enjoyed it all immensely, and the sex had just been the icing on the cake.

They said goodbye to Harry at the airport and took a taxi to the ETV building. Before they got there, Stella suddenly said, 'I wonder if you'd do me a favour, Jayne. A friend of mine wanted me to interview someone for her magazine, but I'm up to my eyes in working on the new *Hot Club* series. Do you think you could possibly do the interview for me?'

Jayne was wide awake at once, eager to know about anything that might further her career. But she'd never interviewed anyone before. Stella was reassuring. 'All you have to do is take along the list of questions I've typed out and record her answers on a tape.'

'And who is she, this woman I have to interview?'

'You probably know her by sight. She's a club member, but it's her professional life that you'll be asking her about. She works as a dominatrix.'

'A what?'

'You're not familiar with the term?' Stella's eyes glittered with a mixture of amusement and disbelief. 'She likes to dominate and punish men. That's what her clients pay her for, or rather her girls. She doesn't take many on herself these days.'

'Will you let me see the questions beforehand?'

'Sure. Soon as I've typed them up.'

'Okay. What do you want me to do?'

Stella opened her bag and produced a card with *Lady Odile* and a telephone number. Nothing else. 'Do you want me to ring her?'

'Please. She already knows about the interview. Just say you'll be doing it instead of me. She won't mind.'

Although Jayne was nervous at the prospect she knew it was going to be a good opportunity. She'd always fancied going into journalism. With her experience before the camera and a bit of interviewing under her belt she might make it into some other branch of the media. For the rest of the journey she sleepily daydreamed about having her own chat show. Maybe she'd suggest it to Stella if her interview with this Lady Odile went well.

The mysterious dominatrix answered the phone herself. She had a cultured accent, rather distant, but when Jayne introduced herself her tone became warmer.

'Of course I don't mind you standing in for Stella. I'm sure you'll do the job just as well.'

'To tell you the truth, it will be my very first interview,' Jayne admitted. Somehow she felt that honesty was the best policy. She would rather be treated as a struggling novice than despised as an incompetent professional.

Lady Odile gave a dry laugh. 'In that case, you'll probably be even more nervous than me, dear! I rarely give interviews. My work is, by its very nature, confidential. But I agreed to do this one as a personal favour to Stella, seeing as we are fellow club members.'

'Er . . . I'm a member of the same club, actually.'

'Are you now?' Odile sounded richly amused. 'In that case, I'm sure we shall get along very well. What day and time would suit you? I'm only available in the early evenings, between six thirty and nine thirty.'

They agreed on seven, the following night. Stella had said she was under some pressure to deliver the article and would be glad to have the raw material as soon as possible.

Jayne set off soon after six with the list of questions in her bag, along with a discreet cassette recorder. Mick had wanted to know why she was leaving so early, and she told him she was going to interview someone. 'It could mean a change of direction for my career, if I handle it well,' she told him, with a smile.

He had given her a brief hug and muttered his congratulations, but it seemed a mechanical gesture and momentary sadness had seized her. Once he would have been overjoyed, plied her with questions about her interviewee, wished her luck. But the days when they took such a keen interest in each others' careers were over.

Jayne realised she had no idea what was going on in Mick's working life either. If he got promoted, would he bother to tell her? The chill despair that surfaced whenever she contrasted their present coldness towards each other with their past passion threatened to overwhelm her, and she hurried from the flat and into her waiting car.

It was years since she'd driven down the King's Road and now it had an air of sober respectability about it that was foreign to its once swinging image. She missed the turning for Lady Odile's mews abode and had to backtrack, but she was standing outside the smartly painted and brass-furnished door just as a nearby clock struck seven. A pretty girl in a maid's uniform answered the doorbell.

'Lady Odile will receive you in her private apartment,' Jayne was told with a smile. 'Follow me, please.'

The mews 'cottage' was a great deal bigger than it appeared from the outside and Jayne suspected it consisted of at least two buildings knocked into one. Lady Odile's apartment was over the garage, and turned out to be a very pleasant sitting room with a couple of doors leading off into other rooms. The Lady herself was seated on a floral settee with a fabulous smoky grey cat on her lap. The animal's jewel-green eyes glowered at Jayne when she entered, reminding her of Dean's. Its enormous whiskers quivered and its tail gave a couple of warning twitches.

Jayne instantly recognised the elegant woman before her and fancied she saw an answering gleam of recognition in her large, blue-grey eyes. She had been at the last club meeting, wearing some kind of black leather outfit, and was memorable not only on account of her beauty and the air of authority that surrounded her, but also because she was over six feet tall. Now the long, shapely legs were slanted to one side and crossed at the ankles, in a model girl pose. She wore a fluffy pink jumper and black, close-fitting ski pants with gold sandals, and her platinum-blonde hair was done up in a French plait.

She smiled, her naturally severe expression melting into sweetness. 'Ah, you must be Jayne. Forgive me if I don't get up, only Toyboy here is such a cantankerous creature when disturbed. Do pour yourself a drink if you need one, dear. There's a selection in that cabinet, with some glasses. I wouldn't mind a sherry myself.'

Glad of the sympathetic gesture, Jayne went over and poured them both a sherry while the cat growled its token protest at her presence and was soothed by his mistress's fond reprimands. Odile took the sherry and set it down on the small table beside her, then said, 'Take your time dear, I'm in no hurry. The girls are under strict orders not to disturb us except in an emergency and the answerphone is on. So . . . you work with Stella then, do you? Haven't I seen your face on TV?'

'Possibly. I present the late night film shows.'

Odile's laugh was surprisingly, dirtily raucous, more like a man's. 'Oh, that tripe! Pardon me, but you have to admit their offerings are pretty tame compared with our homegrown club variety. I thought your performance was excellent, by the way. You've become quite a star in the members' eyes already, did you know that?'

Jayne blushed at the frank way the other woman was looking her up and down, knowing that she'd seen her in the nude being pleasured by three other people. Noticing her embarrassment, Odile smiled. 'Don't ever be ashamed of your body, Jayne. Keep it in trim, then you won't ever need to worry. I work out every day, and I don't mind telling you that my figure is trimmer today, now I'm in my forties, than when I was your age.'

'Really?'

'But maybe I'm pre-empting your questions?'

Jayne glanced down the list. 'Well there is one about whether you're enjoying life more now than when you were a famous model.'

She snorted. 'I knew Stella would put that one in. She won't let me live my past down, the minx! But look, why don't we make a start? Get that machine of yours running – here, you can put it on this table if you move my glass – and fire away.'

Jayne was relieved that they were getting down to business at last. She took a sip of her drink, set the recorder working and asked, 'Lady Odile, is that your real name?'

'Odile is one of my names, yes. And the title is not assumed, as most people presume. I am distantly related to a certain Duchess, who shall be nameless to spare her blushes. When I modelled, however, I used my mother's maiden name: Fortunata, meaning "lucky". It seemed too good an opportunity to miss.'

'So your mother was Italian? Oh, sorry, that's not in the script.'

Odile laughed. 'Don't worry, I'm sure Stella won't mind if you improvise! Yes, she was Italian and a fiery redhead. I get my domineering ways from her, so my brother tells me. I don't mind, it's made my fortune!'

Jayne glanced down at the list of neatly typed questions. 'About your modelling days, did you make contacts then that were useful to you in your present career?'

She laughed. 'Oh my word, yes! Models get invited to all sorts of parties, you know, by all sorts of people. And I accepted every invitation that came my way. I even attended a function on the Royal Yacht *Britannia* once, but I won't go into that now.'

'Um . . . how did you move from modelling into . . . what you do now?'

'It was a gradual process really. But the time I was in my mid-twenties I realised that my photographic and fashion modelling days were almost over. That wouldn't be so true today, but things were different then. I had a particular friend, a member of the aristocracy who shall be nameless, and he liked me to be very strict with him in private although he preffered me to act sweet and biddable in public. He got off on the contrast between the way I was in company and the way I behaved when we were alone. We didn't have sex or anything, but he did like me to make him clean out the toilet and things like that.'

'Really?' Jayne's brows shot up.

Odile laughed. 'Yes, I was like you – ignorant of such things. But I very soon learnt when I confided in a friend. She told me men would give good money to be treated that way. I didn't know it at the time but she was working in a Mayfair salon. A kind of upmarket massage parlour. And some of her clients were that way inclined.'

Jayne realised that it would be more interesting to pursue this line than to ask the next question. She would have to make it up. There was more to this interviewing business than she'd at first thought. 'Er . . . can you tell me a bit more about that?' she asked, lamely.

'What do you want to know?'

'How did you find out what she did, this girl?'

'Ah! Well, we had an affair, you see.'

Jayne knew she was blushing again, she couldn't help it. 'I see,' she said, her voice faltering.

'I've always been bisexual,' Odile continued, matter-of-factly. Seeing the look on Jayne's face she added, 'Oh sorry, is that on your list too?'

'No, it's okay.'

'But I expect you'd like me to expand.' Jayne nodded, taking another nervous sip of her sherry. 'I was exclusively lesbian at boarding school. Had to be, it was a girls only convent and very strict. But during the long summer holidays I was passed from relative to relative with my brother and no one much wanted us. So we had a pact. I'd make friends with girls and introduce him, and he'd return the favour with boys. I think I had the better bargain. There weren't many fancy-free girls around in the countryside but lots of randy boys. I had them all, farm hands, public schoolboys home for the hols, sons of vicars and doctors, even a couple of married men.'

'So you were lesbian in term time and hetero in the holidays,' Jayne grinned. 'But what about when you left school?'

Odile's seductive teal blue eyes turned dreamy. 'Oh, it was wonderful! When I was just turned seventeen I was spotted by Georgie Bates who ran one of the top model schools in London. She stopped me in the street, for heaven's sake! It was every girl's dream.'

'That must have been wonderful!'

Jayne recalled how she'd felt when Stella and Steve picked her out from twenty-seven interviewees to work for them. How excited she'd been, but how nervous too! She watched Odile stroke the now-purring cat. The woman was obviously enjoying the chance to reminisce.

'I had to go to bed with Georgie, of course. All the girls did, but it was no big deal to me. That woman was rampant, with an insatiable appetite, and I knew that she'd soon tire of me and want someone new. I only slept with her three times in all, but it was worth it. She launched my career and I've never looked back.'

Jayne felt slightly shocked by the way Odile was talking, as if such behaviour were commonplace. Perhaps it was, in the exotic world of modelling. She went on to the next question. 'Have you any comment to make on your notorious "three in a bed" romp with a certain cabinet minister and his mistress?'

That dirty laugh came again, making Toyboy growl menacingly and jump off her lap.

'I thought people were sick of hearing about that! I suppose you want juicy details. Okay. It was all set up by Lavinia, as I expect you know. She contacted me because poor old Charles was having trouble getting it up. And Lavinia – we were in school together, by the way – was no slouch between the sheets, let me tell you. She'd tried everything: aphrodisiacs, porn films, costumes, devices, toys. Even tried peeing on the old fart, all to no avail. His tadger seemed to be permanently disabled.'

Jayne found it peculiarly exciting to hear such frank talk expressed in such upper class tones. It sounded both worldly-wise and slightly sarcastic. She was also fascinated, since although she knew the bare facts of the story she'd been too young at the time to take any notice of the published details in the Sunday rags.

'Anyway, she thought if we both had a try he might get more excited. She knew I'd had a lot of experience by then. Mostly with that aristo I told you about. So I went along with my little bag of tricks to his *pied-à-terre* in Chelsea where Lavinia was waiting for me and we gave him the full works. He had strawberries and champagne laid on and soon the three of us were covered in the stuff, licking it off each other. Then I realised he was getting off on seeing Lavinia and I together. She hadn't thought of that, of course, seeing as their affair was top secret. So we tied him up and made him watch while we went through a great show of making love.'

'Only a show?' Jayne asked with mock innocence.

Odile smiled. 'I told you, we were at school together. We'd done it before, but we had to keep the old boy interested so it was all multiple orgasms and moaning in stereo. He ended up with a stonker of an erection, but before he could do anything with it the door burst open and there was a cameraman flashing away.'

'He must have felt dreadful!'

'It was a bit of a shock at first, naturally. But when the photos were splashed all over the *Nudes of the World* it did his reputation no end of good. He lost his cabinet post, of course, but apparently he was due for the chop in the next reshuffle and he wanted to retire anyway. But there he was, romping with two nubile women all over the tabloids, with a hard-on you could hammer nails with. After being impotent for a couple of years he was pleased as Punch. He was quite a celebrity in the night-spots after that, of course.'

Jayne knew Stella would be pleased with that little story, but she had to move on. 'Tell me how you set up in your present business.'

'Funnily enough, it was old Charlie who lent me the money for the deposit on my first flat. Nothing like this of course. Poky place, not much of an address, but it was a start. I was skint, and the modelling jobs just weren't coming. Been a silly girl, really, didn't salt any away for a rainy day. I did all the work myself to start with, advertised in girlie mags, even stuck cards in phone booths. Definitely the sleaze end of the market in those days. But word went around and I started getting a better class of client.'

'You mean . . . upper class?'

'Some. Some foreigners, Arabs and such. I'd go to their hotel rooms, or to country house parties. With clients like that I could afford to raise my fees. Within a year I'd moved into this place. Or the place next door, I should say. When this one came on the market I snapped it up. I've got my eye on the one the other side, too!'

She gave a wicked grin, and Jayne couldn't help admiring

her guts. She'd obviously worked hard to get where she was. Glancing down at the paper on her lap she was relieved to see she was almost through the questions. 'How many girls do you have working for you at present?'

'Just six now. Two got married, so I'm looking for replacements. Interested?'

Jayne had been caught completely unawares. She felt the heat rise in her cheeks again. 'Are you serious? I mean, I don't know anything about what you do, really.'

'The best way to find out is to take part. You could do that, you know. Or you could just watch, it's up to you. But if you wrote it up afterwards Stella wouldn't half have a hell of an article, wouldn't she?' She gave her raucous laugh. 'Always a good idea to get in the boss's good books, don't you think?'

'Well, I don't know, I . . .'

'Think about it. You don't have to decide right now. Back to the question . . . I like to have different types of girl working for me, different figure types, ethnic types. Right now I have one black, one Asian, one redhead, one brunette and two blondes. They can wear wigs, of course, but they can't change their bra size overnight! Most of them are well stacked but some men prefer their girls a bit slimmer. That's why I thought you might fit in.'

'I'll think about it,' Jayne promised, but she was already intrigued. 'And – this is the next question on the list, by the way – what kind of man likes to be dominated?'

Odile frowned and, for a moment, Jayne thought the question had offended her. But then she said, 'All sorts. You'd be surprised. Not only do they come from all walks of life but they're all personality types too. There's this cliché that it's mainly powerful men who order other people around all day, and want the responsibility taken from them sometimes. We get quite a few of those. But we also have clients who don't fit that image at all. Artistic types, musicians, macho sportsmen, farmers. We even have a landscape gardener, for heaven's sake.'

'How much an hour do you charge?'

'Sorry, that's confidential.'

'Okay. What do they get for their money, then?'

'Whatever they want, within reason. When a client comes to me for the first time he generally has only a vague idea of what he wants and it's up to me to make suggestions. But after they've been coming for some time – pardon the pun! – and get to know the ropes . . .' Jayne giggled. 'Oh, there I go again! There's no stopping me, is there? As I was saying, when they get a bit more familiar with the set-up they often suggest things themselves. Coming to us seems to free up their imaginations, gives them the confidence to act out their fantasies. We very rarely fail them, I can tell you that.'

Jayne began to realise that if she wanted really detailed information about what went on behind the scenes she would have to take up Lady Odile's offer and become more involved herself. Whenever she tried to pin her down she was fobbed off with generalities, so that the last three questions on Stella's list were not answered very satisfactorily at all.

Then she had a brainwave. 'I wonder if I might meet some of your girls, Lady Odile?'

'I'm not sure who would be free right now. Excuse me.'

She went over to a leather-bound book on a gilt table and opened it, running her finger down the appointments marked there. 'You could see Cherry and Layla for five minutes. But don't expect them to break any confidences, and I shall have to be present throughout.'

'That's fine.'

A tinkling bell summoned the maid who had answered the door to Jayne. The girl was very demure, bowing her head before her mistress and curtseying when she entered and left. She returned very soon with two other girls, each wearing a silk robe loosely tied at the waist.

'This is Cherry,' Odile smiled, bringing forward the girl with short blonde hair, blue eyes and tanned skin. She was quite tall, with long slim legs, and beneath the robe her breasts jutted solidly, nipples pressing against the navy blue silk. 'Hullo,' she smiled.

'And this is Layla.'

The Asian girl was a beauty, with lustrous brown eyes and black hair. She was shorter than Cherry and much smaller in proportion, but she also had a large bust which was accentuated by her incredibly slim waist. 'Hullo,' she smiled, rather shyly.

Jayne had the distinct impression that both girls thought she was a new recruit. It gave her a secret thrill. What if she were to throw in her job at ETV and join them here, working under Lady Odile? Maybe she should take up her invitation and give it a try, after all. The prospect excited her, she had to admit.

She asked how long they'd been working for Lady Odile. Cherry said around two years, and Layla a year. Then she asked if they enjoyed their work. 'Oh yes!' they both replied, with enthusiasm. Jayne figured they would have to say that, with their mistress sitting there. So then she asked, 'Why? What is it you enjoy about the job?'

The two girls looked at each other and giggled, like conspiring schoolgirls. Then Cherry said, 'Well it gives me a chance to dress up and try different rôles, for one thing. Maybe I'm just a frustrated actress.'

'Not too frustrated, I hope?' Odile broke in, with a smooth smile. The girls giggled again, and Layla said, 'It's nice being able to order the men about. I spent my whole childhood being abused by my male relatives. Now I can get my revenge. Not on them in particular, of course, but on men in general.'

'There is a bit of that in it,' Cherry agreed. 'And of course it's nice to make lots of money.'

'Do you have your favourite clients?' Jayne asked.

'All the girls do, they can't help it,' Odile broke in. Jayne began to wish she would let her girls speak for themselves. Was she afraid of what they might say?

'One of my clients worships the ground I walk on,' Layla said, with shy pride. 'He calls me Kali – that's an Indian goddess, you know. She's very powerful, and very fierce. I liked being associated with her.'

'My favourite client calls me Kipling!' Cherry grinned. 'You'll never guess why!'

'Do tell us,' Odile said.

'It's after Mr Kipling, you know, those cakes? They do some called Cherry Bakewells that have white icing with a cherry in the middle. He says they remind him of my tits. Not so much now, of course, since I've been using the sunbed.'

Layla picked up Toyboy, who was insinuating himself around her legs, and began to stroke him in her arms. 'Another thing I like is the way you see grown men turn into little boys again,' she said, thoughtfully. 'Sometimes I feel I'm being the strict mother they would have liked but never had.'

'I know what you mean,' Cherry said. 'But I don't waste time on psychoanalysing them. You'd end up going daft yourself. All you need to know is that they get off on it.'

'They certainly do!' Odile smiled. 'Do you have any more questions, Jayne? Only both my girls have clients soon and they need time to get ready.'

'Just one.' Jayne looked from Cherry's blue eyes to Layla's dark ones. 'Do you get any sexual satisfaction yourselves from your work?'

Cherry didn't hesitate. 'Only when I work with other women. Otherwise, it's just a power trip. I don't have real orgasms when I'm with a man, only fake ones.'

'Sometimes I like to bring myself off,' Layla said. 'Most men get off on that. But I've never let a man make me come. Never!' she ended, emphatically.

'Thank you,' Jayne smiled. 'You've both been very helpful.'

'Off you go now, girls. Mustn't keep your clients waiting,'

Odile said briskly, taking the cat from Layla's arms. 'And I'm afraid I must ask you to leave as well, Jayne. I have some business of my own to deal with. But don't forget my offer to let you see what we do at first hand, will you? Just give me a ring if you decide you want to take this further.'

Jayne left feeling oddly elated, and drove slowly back towards the television station with her mind full of what she'd heard. She played back the interview as she went, concluding that Stella ought to be very pleased with what she'd managed to glean in the way of information. It certainly gave a tantalising glimpse into another world.

Yet when she saw Stella the following evening she seemed less than satisfied with the tape. 'I'd hoped you would get more concrete detail,' she frowned, when they met in the cloakroom. 'I wanted to end the article with a dramatised account of what goes on. I could base it on videos I'd seen at the club, but it wouldn't be quite authentic. I want to know what a real client would experience at the hands of real girls to whom he pays real money.'

Jayne pursed her lips, trying to suppress her indignation. 'I tried my best.'

'Yes, I'm sure you did. I'm not blaming you. But now I'm wondering whether it would be possible to go undercover in some way, to find out what really goes on.'

Jayne hadn't intened to take Lady Odile up on her offer of participation in a session, but now it seemed that was exactly what Stella would want her to do. She felt uneasy about it, scared of entering deep waters. On the other hand, she'd joined the club to gain more sexual experience, so what was the difference?

At the club it seemed lighthearted, just for fun, but when people were paying for the privilege it was a different matter. She imagined that the men involved would take it all very seriously indeed, and she was wary of betraying their trust in the girls they paid such high sums to.

Stella sensed her hesitation. 'Is there something you're not telling me, Jayne?' she asked.

Jayne nodded. 'Actually, Odile did offer me the chance to take part if I wanted to. I didn't mention it because . . . well, I'm not sure I want to.'

Stella gave her a piercing look. 'Why not? It's the sort of thing we get up to at the club sometimes. What's the difference?'

'I don't know. I just felt uneasy. But if you really want me to . . .'

'It would be extremely useful. I don't see how else I'm going to get the kind of detail I need for my article. I don't have the time to do it myself, and my deadline is the end of next week. I'd be awfully grateful if you could bring yourself to have a go for me.'

There was a subtle edge to her voice that made Jayne aware she was being offered a chance to place Stella in her debt. And who knew how that debt might be repaid? Suddenly she felt like a naive beginner in a game that both Stella and Odile had mastered to perfection. Were they using her like a pawn in some obscure game of sexual politics?

For a few seconds, fear and caution battled with curiosity and excitement for possession of her soul. At last she said, 'All right, then. I'll do it.'

Stella hugged her warmly, bestowing a kiss on her cheek. 'Thanks, Jayne. You're a real pal! You won't regret this, I can promise you.'

'I hope not,' Jayne muttered, under her breath.

She phoned Lady Odile early the next evening. The dominatrix sounded delighted that she'd decided to join in their frolics rather than just observe from the sidelines. 'It will be with Cherry and Layla, since you know them already. And the client is a relatively new one. He's opted for the Deluxe Mystery option, and I think you'll be quite surprised when you see exactly what that entails!'

Jayne felt a thrill of danger ripple down her spine. She was playing with fire, not knowing what effect the experience of playing the whore would have upon her. Suppose she liked it and wanted to continue? Suppose she became another Odile, earning good money by dominating men, working her way up to the point where she was entertaining rich and powerful clients?

But then the whole idea struck her as ridiculous. Who did she think she was, silly little Jayne Sanders, to have such wild and wicked dreams?

Chapter Eleven

Mick felt frustrated waiting for Stella to get back in touch with him. Since Jayne had made that trip to Frankfurt she seemed more distant towards him than ever, but he still had sexual needs to satisfy and he was tired of doing it himself. In the end he decided to ring Lady Odile's number again. He realised now that he stood no chance of getting the lady herself, but his experience with Cherry had been more than just pleasant. It had opened up new possibilities to him, drawn his attention to hidden desires within him that had never been given free rein before. He'd discovered that he rather liked to be dominated by women.

The same cool voice answered when Mick phoned in the late afternoon. When she asked him what services he required, however, his mind went blank. She asked him if he'd been before and when he told her about Cherry she said, 'Maybe you'd like to try our Deluxe Mystery option?'

'What's that?'

She gave a low chuckle. 'I'm afraid I can't tell you, or it wouldn't be a mystery any more, would it? But it's a hot favourite amongst our clients. It will cost you a little more, of course.'

The figure she quoted was almost twice what Mick had paid last time but he thought, 'What the hell?' He wasn't spending much on his social life. 'What social life?' a voice in his head enquired, bitterly.

He agreed to the Deluxe Mystery and made an appointment for the following Friday evening. Lady Odile wouldn't even give him a girl's name, so he had no idea what he was in for. That made it all the more exciting, of course. But as he drove down the King's Road he was a bit apprehensive too. Much as he'd enjoyed the mild beating and trussing that Cherry had given him, he hoped they wouldn't think he was into serious bondage or S&M.

There were collywobbles in the pit of his stomach, reminiscent of his first date. It had been with an older, more sexually experienced girl, who had masturbated him to orgasm and then expected him to do the same for her. He hadn't had a clue, of course, so she'd tried to show him. But he had been hopelessly clumsy and in the end she'd had to finish herself off. Not very good for his self-confidence, he thought wryly.

Although he had several girlfriends in quick succession after that, losing his virginity to a married woman in one brief, heady fling, it was only with Jayne that his sexuality had really begun to flower, his overwhelming feelings for her making up for his lack of expertise. He'd quickly learnt what she liked best: the spot behind her ear where his kissing drove her wild; the way she liked him to stroke her inner thighs, wending his way very slowly up to the secret folds between them; the combination of slow and vigorous thrusting she preferred when she was on the way to a climax.

But in all the time he'd been with her Mick hadn't given much thought to what *he* liked, what *he* wanted. Jayne had given him plenty of blow jobs, and very nice they had been too, but her imagination didn't seem to stretch very far beyond that. Sometimes he'd had vague urges that he would have liked her to satisfy. He preferred it when she was on top, and he particularly liked to be stretched right out, with his arms above his head. Sometimes he imagined what it would be like if his wrists were tied, and the thought filled him with a warm, wicked glow.

But she liked it better with him on top, and only did it the other way when he complained of being tired. Mick hadn't wanted to mention his strange predilection for fear that she would think him unmanly, and a bit weird. He had been so afraid of losing her, he now realised, that he'd always gone along with what she wanted in bed rather than suggest things himself. It was ironic really, since it looked as if they were drifting apart anyway.

Now the thought that he might be about to explore the darker reaches of his sexuality was a real turn-on, and as he drove into the cobbled yard in front of Lady Odile's mews cottage his heart was beating rapidly in his chest. He was a little early, but this time he didn't want to go to the pub. Somehow the idea of imbibing alcohol did not appeal. He wanted to be fully alert to the experience that he was about to undergo, whatever it entailed.

The same perky maid opened the door to him and this time he felt confident enough to return her cheeky grin. 'Lady Odile is expecting you, sir. Would you like to wait in the drawing room? Someone will come to prepare you soon.'

Prepare him? For some reason those words evoked a peculiarly keen anticipation in him. While he sat leafing through some girlie mags in the plush and gilt room Mick felt a fluttering within. It was a bit like waiting for the dentist, but also how he'd felt getting ready for his first proper date with Jayne. Somehow he'd known, even then, that she was going to be very important to him. His mind insisted on wandering back to their first full sexual encounter. Evidently he was in a nostalgic mood that evening. Replacing the magazine on the small table beside him, he thought about how it had been for them both.

Because he'd still been seeing another girl, Kath, he and Jayne had made secret rendezvous for a couple of months after that first meeting at a party. Looking back, Mick was ashamed of the way he'd strung both girls along like that, but he hadn't wanted to upset Kath. Correction: he had been *scared* to upset Kath. She'd had him just where she wanted him for months, and it was only his love for Jayne that finally gave him the courage to break off the affair. Kath had behaved hysterically, as he knew she would, but in the end he knew he'd done the right thing.

For a while he and Jayne had to make do with furtive fumblings in the back of his car, but then a friend had offered them the use of her flat while she was away for the weekend. Mick would never forget the blissful freedom they'd enjoyed for the first time. He remembered diving deep into her warm, wet cunt as if into a tropical lagoon and wallowing there for ages before he came. Sex had never seemed quite as good after that, he recalled wistfully. Perhaps it had been due to the combination of long expectation and intense frustration, his desire heightened to fever pitch and then satisfied abundantly, completely, in one ecstatic afternoon.

'We are ready for you now, if you'd like to come this way.'

The maid had entered silently, her words shattering his thoughts. Mick rose stiffly and followed her out into the hall then into another small room, where the girl showed him the strange suit that was laid out on the bed. It was a black rubber wet suit, but with holes cut out back and front in the lower half of the torso. There was a mask that fitted over it with straps and buckles, incorporating a breathing tube but enclosing the head completely.

'Lady Odile requires you to wear this,' she said, non-committally. 'I'll help you get into it.'

Mick stared at the alien costume with a mixture of terror and fascination. Inside that get-up he'd look like some monster out of *Dr Who*, and wouldn't be able to see or hear a thing. Although he'd never felt more than mildly claustrophobic the idea of being so completely enclosed was nerve-wracking. Was this to be some kind of 'back to the womb' experience?

'It's all right, you know. Our clients always enjoy this.'

The maid was smiling at him reassuringly. She stepped forward and put her hand on his arm. 'Shall I help you off with your clothes now?'

Dumbly he nodded, sitting on the bed to let her unlace and remove his shoes, then his socks. She worked with silent efficiency, like a nurse, and soon he was stripped completely nude. What would that tightfitting rubber feel like, he wondered. A second skin?

It didn't take him long to find out. The sensation was very strange at first, reminding him of when his cousin had made him an apple-pie bed as a child. In the dark he had found himself caught up in the bedclothes with no way of escape, and his cousin had crept in to hold the sheet down over his head. He had almost suffocated.

Now Mick stood there with the latex clinging to his flesh with clammy pressure, except for the holes where his genitals and buttocks protruded. The soft material moulded itself to every curve and hollow, excluding the air. He'd used Jayne's washing up gloves, but this was nothing like that. The tight embrace was total, the surface of his skin completely enclosed so that if someone touched him he felt the sensation through a double layer. Was this something akin to what animals felt like, having a thick coating of hair or fur over their skin?

He was still relishing the new sensations when the hood was placed over his head and tightly buckled, blocking out all sight and most sound. The maid's voice came, muffled and faraway although he sensed she was talking quite loudly, shouting even. 'You're ready now. We're going into another room.'

Mick felt her clasp his hand through the rubber and guide him towards the door. Slowly, warily he put one foot before the other, like a child learning to walk. He wanted to put his arms out in front of him, like a somnambulist, but she held his left hand tightly. He had a mental picture of the doorway as they went through it, but he soon lost his sense of direction completely as she led him on.

Insulated from the world, he sensed that he had entered another room but he had no idea what was going on. Something was fastened around his chest – ropes? A harness? There were two pairs of hands deftly working on him, pulling the thing tight, then looping what felt like ropes or chains around his elbows and wrists. He let them handle him according to their agenda, lost in a mysterious world of dark passivity.

Oddly, Mick felt quite devoid of desire. It was they – his anonymous companions – who were being driven by some unknown urge to toy with him, their blind, deaf and dumb creature. Did they want him to play a flesh-and-blood Ken in their Barbie games? Suddenly he felt completely disorientated as his whole body swung upwards. There was no way of knowing how high, or in which direction he was facing. He might as well have been floating in space. Now he was literally in suspense, his moorings tight around his wrists and ankles, constricting his ribcage. Did they intend to swing him around, drop him from a great height? At the thought a fairground giddiness assailed him, despite the fact that he could see and hear nothing.

Then came the faint sound of music, tinkling bells and softly vibrating strings that teased his enclosed ears with their half music: not quite melody, not quite harmony, but with a gentle throbbing rhythm that synchronised with his pulse. Might even have been his own heartbeat, the sound of blood rushing through his inner ear, a kind of tantalising tinnitus.

With the music came the scent, something oriental that must have wafted through his breathing tube, but again very faint and teasing to his olfactory nerves. Mick felt all his senses straining through the tight suit, endeavouring to pick up clues about his environment. His muscles ached already, strained by the punishing position he was in, and he began to long to know what his unknown tormentors had in store for him.

Mick didn't even know how many women were in the room with him. Although his ears strained to catch the sound of voices, nothing filtered through his bizarre costume. Perhaps the maid had left, to go about her other duties, and he was all alone. Or was he merely being watched by someone, in person or on camera, like some laboratory specimen in a cage? Who had devised this special torment for him, he wondered; could it be the mysterious Lady Odile herself?

It was amazing how active one's mind became once the senses were more or less disabled. Of all his deprivations he missed touch the most. Not being able to feel his own body, to let his hands brush against his sides or to scratch an itch . . . Oh no, dear God! Don't even think about itches! Within his rubber armour he could feel his hair squashed to his head but that was about all. It had a strange effect on him, forcing all his attention inward, making him question his identity. The image of a human being as a soul locked within a dark fortress of flesh seemed compellingly real now.

Then he felt, or thought he felt, the slight brush against his buttocks of something soft and delicate. There was a long pause. Had he imagined it? No, there it was again, the same tentative and brief contact between some external stimulus and his own hypersensitised skin. He moaned softly within his prison and the vibrations bounced back at him. Enjoying the effect he did it again, and this time something brushed against his balls that were hanging loose from the rubber suit. Oh, exquisite! He desired it again with all his might. But next time the brief caress was delivered to his penis, a featherlight brushing up his shaft and a momentary sweep across his glans which made him shudder deliciously.

There was a different scent wafting down his tube now, and he sniffed deeply to identify it. Something floral – jasmine or rose – but mingled with the unmistakable odour of female flesh on heat. Mick would never have believed it was possible to play the detective to that extent, but he was convinced that some woman was getting off on what she was doing, on playing with her live doll. 'Inaction Man,' he thought with grim delight.

The knowledge that he was in one way communication with that unknown woman and through that most basic of senses, touch alone, thrilled him. He had to trust that she, or they, would not seriously harm him and yet he had no idea how far this little game might go. There was a rush of blood to his cock as it dangled outside his artificial second skin and he felt the beginnings of an erection, proudly defiant in the circumstances. Was she pleased to see what effect her tentative approaches were having on him?

Something else touched his behind, something icy cold and wet that made him shrink back within his rubber coating and utter a silent scream of shock. Ice cubes! After she had slid them around the taut globes of his flesh they left a wet trail that seeped into the crack of his arse. Inside the suffocating helmet, Mick smiled. But then his mouth opened involuntarily in another stifled scream as those same ice cubes were applied to his balls.

Almost immediately he felt a strange hot wind blowing over his naked buttocks. A hairdryer? He fancied he could hear the rattling hum of a motor. After the cold it was blissful, and it dried him off too. She brought it round to his genitals and, feeling the hot air blow across his cock, he groaned with voluptuous delight. He had a decent hard-on now and, fanned by the warm breath of the dryer, it blossomed and grew until it stuck its head up with proud fearlessness, like a pallid sunseeker revelling in Mediterranean warmth.

Oh, rash and cocky phallus! The sudden return of the ice cubes threatened to shrink his dick back into insignificance again. But the sensation was momentary and quickly followed by something new. His prick was being squashed between something soft yet firm, warm and fleshy. No it was not one thing but two. They were massaging his shaft with blubbery . . . balloons? He heard giggling – surely he was not mistaken? – and had an intuition that she was using a part of her own body. It felt too much like flesh, the pneumatic flesh of a pair of breasts. Yes, that was it. It had to be!

Now he'd identified them as boobs he could feel the rubbery nipples – ha, rubbery! – as they travelled up and down his shaft. Then the friction stopped and he was left hanging there, not knowing whether to expect any more or not. For a full minute nothing happened. Was he alone? The word 'suspense' was taking on a new meaning for him, a subtle combination of the sweet taste of desire and the bitter taste of fear. To fill the hiatus Mick began to fantasise about what he'd *like* his unseen tormentress to do to him.

If only she would take his cock between her lips while she stroked his buttocks he would be in seventh heaven. It wasn't too much to ask, was it? He felt his erection jerk wildly in the air at the mere thought of it. To have all his attention focused on what she was doing to him, just like when she'd played that trick with the feather, the ice, the dryer, would be wonderful. He wouldn't have to worry about anything else, just enjoy it. Too often, while making love to Jayne, he'd been distracted by the fear that perhaps she wasn't enjoying it as much as he was, that perhaps he should kiss her here, stroke her there.

But the pleasure he'd already felt in this weird predicament was unique, and the ultimate pleasure of an orgasm would surely be incredibly intense. Mick sighed within his mask, wondering how much longer she would keep him waiting. He tried to relax into it, the waiting, but it was hard not to be impatient. His limbs felt heavy and yet weightless, his body hot inside the confining suit.

Then, when he was least expecting it, came the oily blob on his behind. He gasped and bucked as the cream – gel, gloop, whatever it was – seeped in between his buttocks and deft fingers massaged it in, opening him wider and sliding about in there. Another hand (same person?) slapped some more lubrication onto his frontal parts, smearing it all over. He was a quivering mass of jelly, front and back orifices smothered with the stuff, the two most vulnerable parts of his body feeling as if they were melting into slime.

Once the first shock was over, and Mick started to relax into it, he found new heights of sensual discovery opening up to him. The hand that was ministering to his rear settled into a gentle, rhythmic routine: into his anus, round his right buttock, round his left buttock, into his arse again. The hand that was attending to his front portions first squelched his balls in a gentle squeeze then slid up the greasy pole of his shaft to the glans, where delicate fingertips traced around the ridged perimeter and across the oozing slit until the hand moved down to his scrotum again. It was all extraordinarily pleasant, and when Mick gave up wondering which part of him to concentrate on he found that it no longer mattered. Raw, unadulterated pleasure diffused through him from front and back, meeting in the central pit of his stomach.

Mick knew it wouldn't be long before the gathering force in his balls gushed up the length of his penis and cascaded out into space. Already the sensual currents were swirling around in a maelstrom of dark excitement, the invading fingers in his arse making him feel dirty and super aroused. He could hear, even through the rubber, the faint sucking sounds that his flesh made as it was probed and massaged. But then, just as he was poised on the edge of the abyss and sure that the impending orgasm would be the most mind-fucking he'd ever had, the caressing hands withdrew completely, leaving him stunned and bereft. He gave a single sob within his tight mask, his heart thuddding painfully beneath the tightly encased ribs, and slumped forward, his capacity both for agony and for ecstasy utterly exhausted.

Mick had no idea how long he hung there, semi-conscious,

a broken puppet on a string. Suddenly a stinging blow on his naked buttocks brought him sharply back to self awareness and his head jerked back as if on invisible wires. 'God!' he moaned, the taste of rubber against his lips. 'Whatever next?'

But if she – they? – heard him they made no comment. The chastisement continued for a few seconds then ceased, to be followed by more oily massage. This time the hands pinched and scratched at his flesh and made jagged red lightning flashes of pain appear before his eyes. Optical illusion, he told himself, but it didn't stop the hurt. Other fingers began working his erection back again, slipping and sliding up and down until he was firm, then solid, then rock hard. Oh, please! Mick's prayer was silent, inarticulate. He knew what he meant. And, if there was a god of pain and pleasure he would know what Mick meant too.

And then, when 'she' had got him hoping and fearing in equal measure, had him on the brink of an abyss that might lead to heaven or hell, the sudden releae came. Mick's whole body strained against the rubber straitjacket as the first jet-propelled bursts came from his prick accompanied by a volley of farts from his rear. A double relief, a shameless celebration of his bodily functions, an orgy of wild, uninhibited triumph of the flesh! His whole being felt as if it were strung out amongst the stars like some titanic god, his nerve paths making brilliant constellations, his blood warmed with celestial fire.

The racking bliss slowed and faded, leaving Mick with a sense of profound loss. He wanted to curl up into a ball in some dark place but still he hung there, like a tattered banner after the show is over. His body was throbbing quietly, but now his head ached as well as his limbs and torso, and he felt like a burnt-out fuse. Careful hands applied hot wet flannels smelling of lavender to his private parts, then gently towelled them dry. He was glad to know that he was not alone, but when the breathing tube was removed he felt quite incapable of talking to anyone.

Once the helmet was pulled off, light struck Mick's blind eyes with terrible force and he held up his rubberised fingers to shield them. It was only a low-wattage lamp in one corner of the room, yet it was bright as the sun to his light-deprived vision. When he grew accustomed to it he saw that the maid was about to release him from his harness. He took deep breaths of the still scented air and looked down wonderingly to see that his feet were about six inches off the ground. His prick was flopping down between his thighs looking sad and spent.

'We'll soon have you down,' she said, soothingly. 'Then you can have a nice rest. Did you enjoy that?'

Mick stared at her uncomprehendingly. It was like asking if he'd 'enjoyed' riding on Nemesis. He nodded vaguely, and felt himself being lowered gently to the ground. It felt strange under his rubber feet. The suit was unzipped and peeled off him, letting him feel the air against his skin again, fresh and clean. It was like a rebirth.

'You can lie down on that bed,' the maid told him, pointing to the low couch that he'd only just noticed in the corner behind him. Now he could see the strong hooks in the wall and ceiling from which he had been suspended by a system of ropes and pulleys. No wonder he ached all over! She led him by the hand, supporting him around the waist because he was still weak kneed, and he sank thankfully into billowing silken luxury.

Sleep must have followed almost immediately because, a round twenty minutes later, he woke himself up with his snoring. The memory of what had happened rushed back into his mind like water through a sluice, and he gave a slow, self-satisfied grin. Something momentous had happened to him here tonight. He had pushed back the boundaries of his sexual experience to the limit and found he could take it. Why he should feel proud of himself he had no idea, but he did. Still grinning like an idiot he rose from the couch and put on the black silk robe that the maid had left for him, then he strolled out of the room feeling heroic for the first time in his life.

Jayne and Odile were sitting upstairs drinking tea and conducting a kind of debriefing of the Deluxe Mystery session with a detachment that Mick would have found astonishing.

'Delaying his climax was a very shrewd move,' Odile told her, approvingly. 'But it must be judged carefully and it can't be done too often. If laboratory rats are overstimulated they lose interest, you know.'

Jayne laughed. 'I always said men were rats!'

'Hm. I think the jury's still out on that one!' She gave a smile and her tone became more conversational. 'Stella tells me you're going to be on the membership committee next week.'

'Yes. I don't know why, since I've only just joined myself.'

'Quentin thinks a lot of you, dear. He believes you have a natural instinct for these matters. And I'm sure you won't prove him wrong.'

'I'm still very nervous. How many of us will there be? And how many applicants?'

'About six members sit on the selection committee as a rule, with equal numbers of men and women if it can be arranged. Usually novices are assessed one at a time.'

'Novices!' Jayne laughed. 'You make it sound like a convent!'

Lady Odile reflected on this as she uncrossed her long legs so that Toyboy would leap into her lap. She pinched the tuft of hair at the nape of his neck and he cringed, acknowledging her dominance. Then she let him settle and began stroking his long, smoky-grey back with a firm hand, making him purr contentedly.

'I suppose our club isn't all that different from a religious order,' she said. 'We have our rules and regulations. When we close our doors the outside world vanishes from our minds. We have our ceremonies, our temples of worship, our rewards and punishments. We celebrate that vital spirit that is within every man and woman on this earth in varying degrees, the eternal spirit of sexual love.'

Her blue-grey eyes, that had been staring into the middle distance, refocused on Jayne and she gave a self-deprecating laugh. 'My goodness, that was quite a speech!'

'I'd never thought of it like that, but I suppose you're right. We're all dedicated to exploring sexual experience to the limit. Do you think that man liked what we did to him tonight?'

'I certainly hope so, he paid enough for it! I suspect he is only just discovering the nature of his own preferences. When men come here for the first time they often aren't sure of what they want. It's up to my girls to give him what he wants, even though he can't put it into words. That's why they are amongst the highest-paid in their profession. They've learnt to size a man up, to reveal his secret desires to him. Any woman who can do that is worth a fortune to a man.'

Jayne couldn't help thinking about Mick. Had she tried to discover what he really wanted? She was ashamed to admit to herself that she hadn't. It was probably too late to do anything about it now, but she could bear it in mind if she got herself involved with another man.

Realising that she was taking up Odile's valuable time, Jayne rose to her feet.

'I'd better be going now. But I can't thank you enough for letting me take part like that. I enjoyed it enormously.'

Odile's shrewd eyes narrowed a little. 'You did? Then maybe you should think seriously about joining my little stable.' She laughed. 'How appropriate for a mews property! Maybe I should start training some pony girls.' Jayne looked blank. 'Never mind. It's been a pleasure meeting you, my dear, and I know our paths will cross again. Good luck with the interviewing next week.'

As Jayne stepped out into the cobbled yard she realised how deeply she had entered into the private world that Lady Odile had created for her clients. She felt disoriented. Not to the same extent as that anonymous client, of course. But her head swam when she thought of driving to work and performing for the camera as usual. Still, it had to be done. Walking towards her car she took some deep breaths and tried to focus her mind on where she might obtain some cheap petrol at this time of night.

Chapter Twelve

The phone call from Stella came not a moment too soon. Mick had been on the verge of contacting her, impatient to know when his interview with the club committee would take place. She rang during a meeting and left a discreet message on his answerphone, saying that his appointment had been arranged for eight o'clock on Friday.

He felt enormously relieved. After the dramatic session at Lady Odile's Mick had been filled with an overwhelming desire to explore the further reaches of his sexuality. He felt like an adolescent again, in the control of forces he scarcely understood but which totally obsessed him. Even a photo of a man surfing in a wet suit gave him an unexpected thrill when he came across it in a Sunday supplement.

Mick knew he wasn't just a rubber freak, though. There had been so many elements of pleasure in his Deluxe Mystery experience that it was difficult to separate them. Once he'd got used to it, he'd found the experience of being helplessly bound, and of being some woman's passive toy, very satisfying. Then there was the sensory deprivation, at first so frustrating but after a while strangely liberating. The jelly they'd applied to his tender parts had been a real turn-on, and he'd even enjoyed the mild beating. But one factor had prevailed throughout, and could be summed up in one word: suspense.

With Jayne everything had become so predictable, he now realised. He knew exactly how she would respond if he performed this action or that, knew when to increase the pace and when to slow down, when to move from erogenous zone A to zone B. What the Eye Spy Club offered him was an invitation to explore the unknown, to boldly go across the final frontier into the hidden depths of his own psyche, and it was an invitation he couldn't resist. All he hoped was that, after the interview on Friday, that invitation would not be withdrawn.

Jayne seemed in a strange mood when he came home from work on Friday. She was quite jumpy, snapping at him a couple of times, so he asked her if everything was okay at work.

'Yes, fine. I . . . er . . . don't have to be in so early tonight, though. Not sure what time I'll be back . . .'

Mick wondered why she looked so shifty, but thought no more of it. He showered and changed, telling her that he was going to meet a friend at a pub and that he too had no idea what time he'd be home. He wanted to keep his options open. Maybe he'd pop into Stella's afterwards to tell her how his interview had gone. Or maybe he'd try and pay another visit to Lady Odile, if she could fit him in at short notice. He had a feeling that he might be in need of some outlet for his feelings of frustrations after the ordeal by committee was over.

Jayne left by taxi only about ten minutes before he did, so he took the car and drove to the West End hotel that Stella had mentioned. When he mentioned his false name at the desk the receptionist smiled brightly. 'Ah yes, Mike Clark. Your meeting is in the Kensington Suite. Third floor, lift to your right. You can't miss it.'

Mick stepped out of the lift into a carpeted corridor. A free standing wooden sign pointed the way and he soon entered a room that appeared to be some kind of ante-room to the main suite. Another noticeboard, prominently placed, had a message on it: 'Prospective Club members are requested to wait until they are summoned for interview.' That was all. A row of chairs and a table bearing copies of

The Tatler, *Vogue* and *Sporting Life* were the only furniture, and the decor was neutral tones of beige and illuminated by concealed lighting. There was something faintly sinister about the atmosphere, as if it were a waiting room for some clandestine organisation. Which, Mick realised with a grin, was exactly what it was.

Leafing impatiently through a magazine Mick found the print blurring as his mind kept drifting to the ordeal ahead. He hadn't felt so nervous since he was interviewed for his present job. Well, maybe his last appointment at Lady Odile's qualified too, he thought wryly, although this time he didn't expect to gain the same kind of pleasure from it.

After what seemed an interminable wait, he heard a buzz of voices behind the double doors opposite and then footsteps approached. The door was opened by a suave-looking young man in a dress suit and Mick instantly worried about his appearance. Was he dressed too casually for the occasion? He'd put on a Kenzo jacket and some smart black trousers with a white shirt, remembering to add a tie, but now it was one more thing to be anxious about.

'Mr Clark, the committee is ready for you now,' the usher said, his tone quiet and respectful.

When Mick entered the room he was so nervous he hardly looked at the six faces lined up behind the long desk. The man in the middle stood and held out his hand and introduced himself as Quentin, but after the greeting Mick took his seat on the leather chair in front of them and stared fixedly at the middle ground between them, suddenly overcome by embarrassment.

Quentin began the proceedings in a calm, controlled voice. 'Well, Mike – we're all on first name only terms here, by the way – I presume you are aware of the general nature of our little society. What makes you think you would fit in as a member?'

The question threw him and, in his panic, Mick glanced from one end of the row of faces to the other. With a gasp of horror, that he rapidly turned into a cough, he recognised Jayne. Having had more time to absorb the shock of seeing him she was now staring at him with a fixed ironic smile, her eyes brimming with curiosity. One eyebrow was raised quizzically but as he opened his mouth to speak she slowly shook her head, cautioning him against revealing their relationship.

Flustered, and with a hundred questions humming in his brain, Mick did his best to address himself to the question in hand. 'I . . . er . . . don't know whether I would fit in or not until I know more about what you . . . er . . . do . . .' Still in shock, he glanced at Jayne but she gave him no help. Her eyes looked very green, enhanced by the emerald velour top she was wearing that emphasised the proud swell of her breasts. Quite irrationally, Mick found himself fancying her more than ever. His dick was starting to swell beneath the tight fitting trousers, making him shift his position on the chair.

Still, he knew he wasn't doing very well in the interview. Quentin said, smoothly, 'Of course we understand that, Mike. But perhaps you could tell us something about your sexual experience to date?'

Again his eyes flew helplessly to Jayne's, searching for clues but getting none. He guessed she must have been introduced to the club through Stella, but was it all a put up job? Were the two women conspiring to take him out of his sexual rut and into some swinging scene? Was this Jayne's way of getting him off her hands? It was all very confusing and he longed to talk to her about it, but first he had to keep up this absurd pretence of not knowing her.

'Well, nothing much to tell actually.' Jayne's grin widened perceptibly. 'I suppose my sex life has been pretty conventional up to now.'

'Until recently, you mean?'

Quentin's dark eyes were probing his with amusement and Mick suddenly remembered his experiences at Lady

Odile's. 'Ah, yes.' Determinedly not looking in Jayne's direction he continued, 'I did visit a . . . certain establishment where I discovered some new things about myself.'

It was Jayne's turn to look startled. She leaned forward attentively as Quentin said, 'About your sexuality, you mean?'

'Yes.'

'Can you describe what happened?'

Mick briefly scanned the line of waiting, expectant faces. They were all good-looking individuals, but even amongst the three attractive women Jayne stood out. He suddenly felt very proud of her and a burst of confidence followed.

'Yes. I made two visits. The first time a prostitute dressed as a cowgirl tied me up and whipped me, then made me suck her off.'

He glanced at Jayne to see how she was taking it. Her eyes glittered warmly at him, sharing a private joke. He felt his cock harden and longed to plunge it into her wet quim. His hopes were rising too. If she was already part of this set up she must be interested in sexual experimentation too. To think he'd read her wrong, all this time. But maybe it wasn't too late to make amends. Maybe after this was all over he could take her home and roger her senseless.

'And you liked it?' Quentin's suavely insistent tone brought him back into the interview.

'Yes, although it felt a bit weird at first. Like it was happening to someone else. But she began to rub her fanny all over my chest and that triggered me off.'

'You enjoyed the bondage element?'

'I suppose I did. Because when I went back the second time I ended up having the works and that felt fantastic!'

Quentin gave a dry smile. 'The works. Could you elaborate, please?'

'Okay. First they put me into this rubber wet suit affair. I was completely enclosed from head to toe, even had to use a breathing tube. It was a bit frightening at first, especially when they attached chains to my wrists and ankles and hoisted me off the ground.'

'So you were completely helpless, at the mercy of unknown hands. Was that it?'

Mick nodded. 'The strangest thing was not being able to see or hear anything much. Just a few faint sounds, like I was under water. And not having my skin exposed to the air. I got hot and clammy under all that rubber, but I got used to it. The suit seemed to embrace me, really tightly all over, and I grew to like that.'

Again Quentin gave his dry smile. 'It's been described as a primal experience. Womb-like.'

'I suppose so.' Mick glanced at Jayne. She'd stopped smiling now and was looking thoughtful, her green eyes glazed. Something was going on inside that pretty head of hers.

'And you enjoyed the feeling of helplessness once more, right?' Quentin said.

'Yes, but there was more. The suspense. And what I think is called "sensory deprivation".'

'Ah yes. We block off the interface with the real world to experience more fully the subjective hyperreality.' Mick looked at him blankly. He smiled. 'Forgive my jargon. Perceptual Science is a little hobby of mine. I trust that your satisfaction was enhanced by the experience?'

'I should say so.' Mick grinned, and couldn't resist looking at Jayne who smiled back. 'Not all of me was covered up, you see. The naughty bits were exposed.'

'And stimulated?'

'In various ways. But everything they did to me – slapping, tickling, massaging – seemed so much more . . . intense.'

'Quite. You have begun to discover your secret, sensual self, Mike. Consider yourself very fortunate. Most people go through their whole lives without realising their full potential for ecstasy. It is to the pursuit of that fulfilment that we, as club members, dedicate ourselves.'

'I still don't know what it is you do, exactly. I mean, how you run things.'

Quentin smiled, his waving hands indicating those on either side of him. 'We run things by committee, like all the best societies. Yet we like to think we are a democracy too. Naturally we practise safe sex. We are not a suicide club. So we have rules and regulations, like any other organisation, and we ask prospective members to sign an agreement to keep them.'

'It all sounds a bit . . . formal.'

The man laughed. 'Sometimes formalities can be titillating, don't you think? Take this interview, for example. Here we all are seeming very prim and proper, wearing nice clothes and seemingly on our best behaviour. Yet I know that you are secretly excited by your descriptions of past pleasures and your fantasies about future ones. I also know that every other person in this room, myself included, is enjoying the fact that we know exactly what the Eye Spy Club is all about, but you have only the vaguest idea.'

'When will I find out?' Mick asked, suddenly tired of all this fencing.

'Only if and when you are accepted as a member.'

'And what are your criteria for admitting people?'

Quentin placed his elbows on the desk and steepled his long fingers beneath his chin in contemplation. At last he looked up with a grin. 'Do you know, I believe we've never actually formulated it? We tend to go on consensus, you see, a kind of group intuition. Depending on how the candidate performs in the test we set him or her, of course.'

'Test?'

Mick felt the hairs prickle on the nape of his neck. Stella had said nothing about any test. Was there to be some kind of initiation, then? Jayne must know what he was in for. She must have been through it herself. He looked at her for some kind of sign, but she was just smiling enigmatically at him.

'We shall first blindfold you.' Quentin rose, taking the paisley scarf from his neck as he did so. 'I believe you would like to be at our collective mercy,' he smiled as he walked around the long table behind the others. 'Not knowing what will happen to you, nor who will be doing it to you. You will enjoy that, I think. The surrender to the sensual self.'

There was a mesmeric quality to his voice, his expression as he came up to Mick's chair and stood before him with the scarf pulled taut between his hands. For one terrible moment, Mick thought he was going to strangle him. He could feel the adrenaline rushing through his veins, his heartbeat thundering in his ears. Was this all an elaborate plot that Jayne had devised to have him done away with? The very absurdity of the idea seemed to give it credibility.

Quentin walked behind him slowly, savouring the moment. Mick's eyes flicked over to Jayne's. She was still smiling, sitting perfectly still with her eyes looking towards him, unfocused. He thought she looked like a statue of an ancient Egyptian queen. He scarcely noticed the two women flanking her, the buxom brunette or the bubble-haired blonde.

The scarf was laid over his eyes and pulled tight, knotted at the back of his head so that he could sense the light but see nothing. What were they doing now? He heard footsteps, whispers, chairs being pulled back. Already he was making up for the lack of visual information by keenly listening, feeding all the audio cues back into his overactive brain. His balls felt hot and heavy. It was desire, but not the kind that was familiar to him, the automatic response to stimulus. This was something deeper, more primitive. A hunger for something lost, something buried deep inside him in the place where memory and intuition were identical.

The voice of Quentin came again, soft, soothing, insinuating. 'We shall not tie your hands and feet since you are held here by your own desire, your desire to become one of us. But you must do exactly as you are told, do you understand?'

Mick nodded, terror and excitement curdling in his bowels. He tried to gain comfort from the fact that Jayne was amongst them, but the thought that she might wish to exact some kind of revenge continued to torment him. What if . . . what if? His imagination was working overtime as scenario after scenario unfolded before his blind eyes.

Then hands began to go to work on him, taking off his jacket, undoing his belt, loosening his tie, removing his socks. Mick felt like a small child again, being undressed by his mother, and buried emotions began to well up in him. He fought back the tears and let them strip him with professional ease, like nurses. There seemed to be several people at work but he couldn't calculate how many or whether they were male or female. Oddly it didn't seem to matter one bit. In the background faint music was playing and there was a nostalgic scent in the air which he couldn't quite identify.

Suddenly he felt himself being lifted bodily into the air by the arms and legs with someone also supporting his head. After they'd carried him a few paces he was laid down on some sort of bed, probably the couch he vaguely remembered seeing as he entered the room. There was a sheet under him and still that powerful, elusive smell. What was it?

'Baby . . .' a female voice whispered. And then it came to him. The unmistakable smell of the nursery. There was a rubber sheet beneath the cotton one on which he was lying, and its odour was mingling with the comforting scent of talc. They were treating him exactly like a baby, for heaven's sake!

Once Mick had got over the shock he realised that this was the ultimate in fantasies of helplessness, and he settled back with a kind of relief believing there could be no harm in it. Already gentle female hands were stroking his limbs, his forehead, making delicious soothing noises. There was the tinkly sound of a music box playing nursery rhyme tunes. Evidently this game had been well thought out and prepared. He was impressed. If these were the lengths they were prepared to go to in order to please their members then he very much wanted to join this club.

There was a clanking, slopping sound and Mick strained to try and make out, through sound alone, what might be going on. Jayne's voice said, in tones of quiet authority, 'I think his bath is ready now, mother. Test the temperature with your elbow, as you've been shown. Then make sure you have everything you need.'

It dawned on Mick that the women were playing out their own game of 'new mother'. One was pretending to be the mother while Jayne was acting out the nurse, advising her on how to care for her newborn infant. But this was not the Jayne he knew. There was something strangely exciting about the way she sounded, quite detached, as if she'd never met him before in her life. Evidently she didn't want anyone to suspect that they already knew each other.

Mick heard a splashing noise and then strong arms lifted him off his bed and lowered him into a small bath of warm water. He was too big to lie down in it, of course, but he could feel an arm around his shoulders supporting him as he squatted in the waist-high water.

'Good, now get the soap,' Jayne said in her nurse's voice. 'Make sure you get into all his little folds and crevices.'

Mick felt his penis swell at the thought, and soon he was being soaped all over. Careful fingers pulled back his foreskin and washed him thoroughly. His cock thrust impatiently againt the caressing fingers as they massaged silky foam into his glans. 'Oh, he is a well developed baby!' the nurse cooed as the mother cradled his balls in her slippery palm.

He could have lain there all night, wallowing in the attention his body was getting, but eventually they lifted him out again and onto a large bath towel. He lay there dripping wet while two pairs of hands rubbed him vigorously with another towel, a procedure which resulted in a tangible increase in his erection.

'Pop his nappy on first, mother, then you can feed him,' Jayne's efficient voice said. An erotic thrill rippled through his genitals when she said 'feed'.

Cool fingers began to smooth antiseptic-smelling cream into him, rubbing it a little way into his arse crack and then all around his bollocks. She didn't touch his cock though, much to his disappointment.

Jayne said, 'I much prefer the old fashioned terry type of nappy to the disposable ones. You can fasten them so snugly, and baby feels more secure. Now I'll lift up his little botty while you slip the nappy underneath.'

Mick felt strong arms pull up his legs until his behind was almost in the air. When he was let down again it was onto warm, fluffy terry towelling. A flap was pulled up between his legs and the corners folded in tightly before the second flap was pulled up, then he felt safety pins being secured. The nappy felt like a soft cocoon around his sexual parts but his erection had been maintained throughout and now he could feel his shaft thrusting urgently against the tightly constricting material.

'That's right, mother, now the plastic pants.'

There was a slight sting of elastic as his legs were put through and the pants pulled up over the nappy. Mick was slowly subsiding into a heavenly state of passivity. He even found himself unconsciously sucking on his thumb. When he first realised what he was doing he blushed and took it out, but then he heard Jayne say, 'Do you want any help with your nursing bra, mother, or can you manage yourself?'

Another woman's voice, sweet and low, said, 'No, I can manage thanks. I'll try him with my right nipple first.'

Mick felt a surge of excitement pass through him at those words and his mouth actually began to water, as if he were really hungry. His head was hoisted onto a female lap, then he felt something nudge against his lips: a nipple! He took it eagerly into his mouth and began to suckle. It was huge and rubbery. His hands seized the surrounding flesh and he realised what a large, firm breast it was. He reached out with the other hand and found its twin.

The anonymous woman playing the nursing mother had bared both her delightful breasts for him and let him handle them freely while he nuzzled and sucked at the long, juicy nipples. It wasn't long before everything had merged into a contented haze, even his cock lay quiescent in its novel underclothing.

'He's a good feeder,' Jayne said, admiringly. 'He loves the breast, that one.'

'Oh yes,' his 'mother' murmured. 'And I love the way he suckles and caresses me. It's quite a turn-on.'

Up to now Mick had been so immersed in his infantile regression that he hadn't thought about giving the woman pleasure too. Realising that she was probably enjoying it as much as he was made his prick surge again, desperate for satisfaction. It was no longer enough to wallow in mindless bliss. He began to kick his legs and gurgle, baby fashion, as a signal that he was feeling frisky.

It worked. He heard Jayne say, 'Baby seems a bit restless, mother. I think we'll take a look in his nappy, shall we? I'll do it while you go on nursing, if you like.'

Mick gulped as careful hands unpinned his nappy and parted the folded layers to reveal his rampant organ. 'Oh dear!' Jayne said in mock dismay. 'Baby *has* been getting excited, hasn't he? Never mind, some soothing cream should do the trick.'

Rolling his tongue around the still tumid nipple, Mick gave a grateful sigh. It seemed he was about to be thoroughly sati ied after all. Soon Jayne's capable hands were rubbing cream into his cock, sending hot spirals of sensation up his body and making him suck even harder as his progress towards orgasm accelerated. The deft fingers dropped to his balls, delicately working the sticky cream into his taut skin. He clutched at the great round globe of the breast with both hands, feeling it become his whole world as the mind-blowing stimulation of his erection took him to the outer limits of primordial bliss.

Locked into an automatic reflex, Mick continued squeezing and caressing the pneumatic flesh as the inexorable rise towards orgasm sped to its conclusion. By the time the crisis was reached he was almost unaware of where he was or what was being done to him, even the sense of his own identity was minimal as the buried child in him reared into active life along with his prick.

When the first spasms shook through him Mick bawled like an infant, half in relief and half in disappointment that the exquisite feelings were almost over. Cradling hands held his head as he moaned out his long protest, and when he began to return to normal he felt equally tender hands caressing his body, bringing him slowly back down. He felt totally spent, as if the climax had drained him of all his blood and energy as well as semen.

'There, there!' cooed a feminine voice. A blanket was thrown over him and he was left to recover, dozing quietly.

After a few minutes the full memory of his situation returned to him and he sat up in horror, ripping the blindfold off his eyes. He was completely alone. His clothes were neatly folded on a nearby chair but all the paraphernalia that the women had used – bath, toiletries, nappies, towels – had disappeared. So unreal did he feel that, for a moment, he wondered if he'd hallucinated the whole experience under the influence of some drug. But then he remembered Jayne.

Had she gone home already? A strange diffidence overtook him as he remembered how he'd been at her mercy. Yet his curiosity was unbounded. He wanted her to tell him everything: how long she had been a member of the Eye Spy Club, who had introduced her, what she had done at their meetings. He had so many pressing questions that demanded answers and he wouldn't rest until he knew the truth.

Yet as he got dressed Mick became more circumspect. He didn't want Jayne to know about his relationship with Stella, in case she thought they'd been having a clandestine affair. His experiences at Lady Odile's establishment she already knew about of course, but there was no need for her to know the name and address of the dominatrix. After making himself so open and vulnerable to her, Mick felt the need to keep some secrets to himself.

Since no one had appeared by the time he was dressed, Mick walked out of the door and through the waiting room to the corridor, where he made for the lift. He still felt strange, oddly disoriented. The only time he'd felt like this before was when he'd been in hospital for a spell and had to make his own way home by taxi. There was the same lightheadedness, the same feeling of insecurity and aloneness. It occurred to him that perhaps he was unfit to drive, and he thought about phoning for a taxi.

But as soon as he came out of the lift there was Jayne waiting for him in the hotel lobby, smiling with the same green light in her eye that had driven him wild earlier.

'There you are! I thought you'd never appear,' she said, putting her arm through his and walking him confidently towards the exit. 'Don't worry about getting home. I came by taxi so I can drive us home in your car. I assume you're in no fit state?'

Her glance was quizzical and she was clearly enjoying the joke, the shared secret. Mick found himself quite unable to speak. He let her lead him through the swing doors and out into the chill evening. The shock of the street, after the cosy sensuality of his experience in the hotel room, struck him like the trauma of birth. Jayne seemed to sense it and held him close with a firm pressure of her arm, walking steadily towards the hotel car park.

Even in the familiar surroundings of his car Mick couldn't bring himself to say much. He listened in silence as Jayne told him what had happened *in camera* after they'd left him sleeping. 'We took a secret ballot on whether you should be a member, but only Quentin knows the result. The discussion about you was very interesting, but I'm sworn to secrecy.'

'Of course.'

She gave him a sidelong smile. 'But between you and me, I reckon you're in!' When he said nothing she went on, 'How did you get to hear about our club, anyway?'

He'd been prepared for that question. 'I saw an ad in a magazine.'

'Really?' She was looking at him quizzically in the driving mirror. 'That's strange, because we never advertise. Word of mouth only, that's the rule. We're supposed to sniff out likely candidates then see if they're interested. I wonder who headhunted you, Mick. Was it the woman who introduced you to all those exotic delights?'

'Yes. I got her number through a mag. That's what I meant to say.'

Jayne shook her head, mockingly. 'I don't know, visiting houses of ill repute now, are we? Still, I can't blame you. You must have got fed up with me working night after night. I can see that now. But things are going to be different from now on, aren't they?' Her voice dropped, becoming low and sexy. 'Very different.'

Mick absorbed everything she said slowly, as if he were hearing it through cotton wool. He still didn't know quite where she was coming from, what was going on in her head. She had the upper hand, no doubt about that, but he still had his secrets. Stella, for instance.

'Why aren't you going to work tonight?' he asked.

'Stella let me have the night off.'

'What did you tell her?'

'Oh, just that I needed some time off.'

Evidently Jayne wasn't going to let on that Stella was also a member of the Eye Spy Club. But she must know that Mick would find out eventually. She didn't know he already knew, of course. This was a real game of cat and mouse they were playing and he was enjoying all the subterfuge. But how long before his cover was blown?

They arrived home around midnight and Mick followed her indoors, feeling more together now but also rather apprehensive. Was he in for another inquisition? It was too much to hope that he might be in for something more pleasant. Jayne's manner was ambivalent, impossible to decode, as she strode through the door into the flat and went straight to the drinks cupboard.

'Whisky?' she offered, taking the bottle out. 'I could do with one myself. The strain of trying to pretend I didn't know you has taken its toll.'

'Why did you pretend?'

She turned towards him with a reflective smile. 'I don't know really. Partly because I didn't want to spoil the fun, I suspect. And also because I was enjoying seeing you squirm. I'm sure no one else noticed a thing. But now we've started on this we'll have to see it through. They are a bit fussy about members not meeting out of club hours.'

Throwing off her jacket she came up to hand him his glass. Her emerald top showed off her rounded breasts to perfection and Mick felt renewed desire for her. But now he was so unsure of her. He had put himself in her hands completely, hers and that other anonymous woman's, made himself look a bloody fool and all because he'd followed his dick to Lady Odile's. If she wanted to, Jayne could exploit his vulnerability, expose him to ridicule.

She picked up the bag she'd carelessly tossed on the sofa and took out a video. She held it between her breasts, smiling. 'What's that?' he asked.

'The video of our performance tonight.'

His blood froze.

Chapter Thirteen

They watched the video together. Jayne knew she had been taking a risk in asking Quentin if she could borrow it, but she had convinced him that she needed to go through the experience again since it had made such a powerful impression on her. He'd made her sign a slip of paper saying she would not show it to non-club members or use it for commercial gain, and she'd had to promise faithfully that she would bring it to the next club session or have it sent back by special delivery.

'If we admit this young man we shall follow tradition and show it at the first meeting he attends,' Quentin had said. But from the way he said it Jayne knew that the vote had already gone in Mick's favour. The thought eased her qualms as she switched on the TV for them to view the video. She was as good as showing it to a fellow member already.

As the first shots of Mick sitting there in apprehension came on the screen Jayne understood the true nature of her urge to give him a sneak preview. She'd wanted to protect him from the shock and humiliation that she'd had to go through at her first club meeting, seeing herself masturbating while others looked on, both on screen and off. Now, seeing him being blindfolded and stripped, she wanted to hold him in her arms. Perhaps she did have latent maternal instincts after all.

She compromised by snuggling up to him on the sofa. The questions they needed to ask each other were held in abeyance as the compelling images unfolded. Jayne felt a further surge of compassion as she saw her lover stretched out, blind and naked, like a human sacrifice or a martyred saint. She had once, when things were going really badly between them, thought him wilful and obstreperous. Now she saw him as a needy child, and her heart went out to him. Was this what he had secretly needed all along, to be *more* dependent on her, not less?

Watching herself and Karen playing nurse and mother respectively, Jayne felt a warm glow spread through her loins and realised that she really liked the idea of being in total control. It was a bit of a shock, to say the least. Raised on the conventional stereotypes of masterful men she had never considered the possibility that she might be attracted to more passive types. Was that what had been lurking beneath the surface of her affair with Mick?

He certainly seemed to be enjoying himself. The images of him suckling at Karen's ample breast showed him totally absorbed, his sturdy erection testimony to the erotic power of the situation. Jayne saw herself stroking the slick shaft of his cock and remembered how she'd longed to be able to mount him and satisfy herself thoroughly, but it would have been inappropriate to the scenario they were enacting so she'd remained frustrated. Now, watching it all again, she felt the same wild urges.

'God, you were so turned on!' she exclaimed.

Mick turned to her with a grin. 'Yes I was, wasn't I? Strange, but true!'

'I wanted that prick of yours inside me.'

'You did?' His brown eyes widened. 'To be honest I wasn't thinking about the effect on you and the other woman at all. I was completely immersed in my own private world. I felt I was genuinely recapturing all those baby feelings. Do you think I was?'

She shrugged. 'Who knows? But does it matter? The fantasy worked for us both, that's what really counts.'

'Mm.'

Jayne heard the husky desire in his voice, knew that he was feeling the same way she was. She put her arms around him and drew his head down to her breast. He clung to her as she whispered in his ear, 'Now are you going to be a good boy and come upstairs? We'll skip the bath routine tonight, I think. It's way past your bedtime.'

She stopped the video at the point where Mick lay dozing after his orgasm and they went upstairs together, his hand in hers. Meekly he lay down on the bed for her to undress him. She'd done it before, mostly when he'd been too drunk to do it himself, but this time it felt very different. Jayne caressed his feet after she'd pulled off his socks and he gave a contented, sleepy sigh. She liked him in this state, not trying to impress her, not following any script, just going with the flow.

'Would you like me to massage you?' she asked. It was something she used to do when they first lived together, but she had let it lapse. 'I'd really like that.'

'Me too.'

When he was completely naked she poured some of the Body Shop oil she still had into her palm and began to work it into his face as it lay on her lap, cradled between her thighs, his head hair mingling with her pubic hair. Slowly she began the intimate rediscovery of his body. In some ways it was a painful experience, reminding her of what their relationship had lost. Somewhere along the line they'd stopped making time for each other, and it had taken a chance encounter at the Eye Spy Club to bring them back together like this.

Chance? She still wondered about that. Was Mick hiding something from her? Had someone masterminded their meeting? The only candidate she could think of was Stella, but as far as she knew her boss had never met her lover. But those awkward questions were threatening to spoil her mood so she thrust them to the back of her mind to be resurrected at a more convenient time. Right now all she wanted to do was wallow in the peace and contentment that was flowing through her. She could feel the good vibrations – for want of a better term – flowing through her fingertips into Mick's compliant flesh and feeding back in a kind of loop. Despite his passivity their enjoyment was mutual, deeply so, in a way she had forgotten was possible.

Jayne's hands glided down the long valley of his chest to his flat stomach, where she made circular motions for a while. His erection was still half there, and it wouldn't take much to get it solid again, but she was biding her time. As she circled his navel with rhythmical strokes she observed the thickness of his shaft and watched a bead of liquid seep from the slit in the bulbous head like resin from a tree trunk. To her surprise she felt her mouth watering.

Wanting to increase the suspense for them both Jayne moved down his thighs and shins to his feet. While she massaged them her eyes were on the heavy sac between his legs and the pale stalk above, surrounded by curly brown hair. The combination of his butch maleness and the softer, more female, side of him intrigued her. She had the feeling that he had cultivated the former because it was what society expected of him, but his most secret satisfactions were the province of his other self. Like a shy child that *alter ego* had lurked within his psyche until now, fearful of exposing itself. Well, she would nurture and encourage it, just to see what happened. The fact that it complemented her own newly emergent sexuality was a fortunate co-incidence.

Slowly she let her fingers drift upwards, over the hard bone of his shins and the knobbly plateau of his knees to the lean flesh of his thighs. Jayne let her knuckles brush against his balls and heard him sigh contentedly. She pushed into the little bag of skin, feeling it yield, and kneaded it a little. His cock twitched. Between her own thighs she could feel arousal taking place, her soft tissues swelling and moistening, the secret centre of her opening up and becoming receptive. Her womb swooped with longing, her cunt ached to be filled.

Jayne moved her knees further up the bed, straddling his legs, until her crotch was on a level with his. Her hands cradled his penis, feeling the long wand of turgid flesh grow hot and ready between her palms. She wanted to impale herself upon it, to use his member as the instrument of her fulfilment just as she would make use of any other tool. Once she would have thought it necessary to let Mick take the lead, to flatter his manhood. But now, tonight, she felt under no such obligation. She had seen him willing to be humiliated before strangers, to make himself look ridiculous in his quest for strange gratification. His grown up mask had slipped, and she had glimpsed the baby face beneath.

Feeling her own lust for fulfilment gathering force in her, Jayne let her thighs slide easily over his until their pubic hair mingled. She gathered his scrotum in her hand and began to rub her open vulva with it, gasping at the longed for contact of flesh on flesh, feeling her labia swell and spread in her eagerness for stimulation. Her fingers found the thrusting nub of her clitoris and she gave it a few teasing strokes before gliding on upward. At last the delicate, exposed folds of her sex were in contact with his rigid rod. She gave a long sigh of pleasure.

Mick still lay immobile, caught up in some private fantasy she guessed, letting her do with him whatever she wished. And now Jayne knew exactly what she wanted. Parting her love lips with her fingers she began to rub her clitoris against his cock, feeling the sharp sensations course through her, raising her erotic temperature by several degrees. A low moaning issued from her lips almost without her realising it, as sheer abandoned greed for satisfaction drove her nearer the summit of ecstasy.

When her clitoris was throbbing impatiently and the

hollow ache inside was clamouring to be filled, Jayne at last raised herself up onto her knees and positioned the shiny, taut glans at her entrance. She waggled it around between her labia, making glorious squelchy noises as her juices ran fresh and free, teasing herself by imagining how it was going to feel when she eventually took the plunge. Her breasts were tingling, her nipples hard as glacé cherries, and she took a few seconds out to tweak them between her fingers while her pelvic muscles played with his glans, squeezing it rapidly and bringing her desire to a head.

Unable to bear it any longer, Jayne seized his sturdy cock and thrust it inside herself with a loud groan, rising up onto her knees the better to force herself down onto it. At once she was filled up with its hot solidity, her inner walls rippling in sensual delight as she rode rapidly up and down. After the first eager movements, however, she decided to take her time. She withdrew until the tip of his cock was just engaged in her entrance then inched her way down, savouring the luscious feelings that were setting her soul on fire.

For a while she held him there inside her, relishing the tight embrace her cunt was giving to his erection, feeling the swollen clitoris move against the solid root of his cock as she wiggled and twitched her muscles. Her excitement was growing, all her senses heightened, and yet she revelled most in the feeling of being in command of her lover. Mick continued to lie there, eyes closed, quiescent, while she bent his rampant member to her will.

Slowly Jayne traversed the length of him once more, quivering on the very brink of orgasm but always stopping short of going too far. She wanted it to be special when it happened, and she knew that the greater her desire and titillation, the more cataclysmic the eventual explosion would be. Again she held him tightly, proud of the muscle tone that enabled her to clench and caress him internally, feeling how stimulating her actions were to the bud of pleasure that was throbbing with excitement at the top of her vulva.

Reaching down behind her spread buttocks, Jayne found his balls and began caressing them, which elicited a low moan from Mick. She rubbed the sac against her bottom, and squirmed around, feeling his coarse hairs brush against her wide-open lower lips. Her nipples were tingling again but this time she ignored them, knowing that the knife-edge of frustration they produced would only serve to heighten her eventual release. She was learning a lot about herself and her responses, she realised. Mainly because she wasn't concerned with Mick and his satisfaction. For once she was able to concentrate solely on her own. It was like masturbation only far, far better. Smiling, Jayne elevated herself for the final sprint home.

Now she wanted it good and hard, producing the rapid friction that would propel her into a climax. She was sweating and gasping by the time her efforts were rewarded. The erotic tingling in her clitoris and the molten voluptuousness in her quim merged into one tumultuous vortex of sensation. Her fingers flew to her breasts and she pinched her nipples tightly to both hasten and increase her gratification. Tipped over into a mind-shattering orgasm she heard herself making guttural noises as if from far off, and her world became one all-enveloping universe of sensual bliss.

The exquisite spasms seemed neverending but eventually they began to fade and left her both exhausted and yet longing for more. Still in a daze, Jayne tumbled onto the bed beside her lover's recumbent form and felt the strength ebb out of her as sleep rapidly followed.

As usual, there was little time to talk next day. Although it was Saturday Jayne had scheduled a mammoth shopping trip followed by tea with a friend in the afternoon, and Mick had already arranged to accompany a friend and his son to a football match. But over breakfast Jayne tentatively introduced the subject of the Eye Spy Club.

'If you do get to be a member, I was wondering how we'd both cope with being in the same club,' she began. 'I mean, jealousy could be a factor. I don't think they really like couples joining. I seem to remember . . .'

'I've thought about that,' Mick said. 'It's a risk I'm willing to take if you are. I feel we're entering a new phase, and things could go either way. Being in this club could make or break our relationship, I'm not sure which. But one thing I am sure of, we couldn't have gone on as we were.'

She reached out and put her hand over his on the kitchen table. 'I'm glad you said that, Mick. I've been feeling the same, only too scared to admit it. Last night was a big breakthrough for me.'

He grinned, his brown eyes gleaming fondly at her. 'Me too. It was wonderful, Jayne. Better even than the old days. But I feel there's more to explore in me, more to discover.'

'And you want to do it in the club, right?'

'I suppose we could try on our own . . .'

'We've been trying on our own for the past six months and it hasn't worked, has it? I think we both need some new input, new ideas, and the club will certainly do that for us. It's a safe environment for sexual experiments. But it could be a dangerous one for the emotions. Members are strictly warned not to get involved with each other outside club meetings. But what really bothers me is how you might react to seeing me making love with other men – and women.'

'And women – really?'

His grin spread wider. Jayne nodded. 'Sometimes. But if I thought you minded seeing me, either on film or for real, then I'd become self-conscious and it wouldn't work.'

'Maybe that's a risk we'll have to take. To be honest I can't see any alternative now. We both agree that our sex life has been in the doldrums, and we want what the club has to offer. Even if we both pull out and try to go it alone we'll be wondering what we're missing. And there's no guarantee that our sex life will get better. We'll probably just end up going our separate ways.'

'And then we wouldn't be able to rejoin the club. The rules state you only get one chance of membership. If you withdraw for any reason you can't reapply.'

'In that case we don't really have a choice, do we?' Mick took her hand up to his lips and tenderly kissed her fingertips. 'But I'd like to keep the fact that we know each other a secret.'

Jayne thought about Stella. She'd never met Mick, or Mike as he would be known in the club. There was something very exciting about the idea of pretending to be strangers. Okay, technically it was against the rules. But no one was asked for their home address, only a contact phone number. And if Mick gave his work number there was no problem.

'I suppose the chance to declare our relationship has already come and gone,' she said.

'Yes. I was taking my cue from you, you know. Why *did* you want to keep it a secret from the committee?'

'I suppose I was afraid I'd be asked to resign. And I'd already attended a couple of meetings. I'm finding it very . . . liberating.'

Mick grinned. 'I'm dying to find out what you do. Can't you give me a few clues?'

'You've already had one, that video. But I won't say more. That way I'm sticking to the spirit of the regulations, at least.'

'Okay.' Mick rose from the table, his familiar body now seeming strangely unfamiliar as Jayne viewed him with new eyes. He appeared more little-boyish, more sensual. The old Mick, who had sometimes alienated and frustrated her with his predictable ways and boring foibles, was being replaced by someone far more interesting.

That evening Jayne arrived early at ETV. She and Stella went for a drink at the studio bar which was almost empty at that time of night. They found a quiet corner and Stella asked the question she was obviously dying to pose, 'Well? How did you get on last night?'

'It was very interesting. I didn't just sit on the committee. I became involved.'

Stella's hazel-brown eyes sparkled, sensing Jayne's pent-up excitement. 'In what, exactly?'

'Well, Mick . . .' Jayne froze, afraid she'd given the game away. But then she continued smoothly, 'Or was his name Mike? I don't recall. Anyway, the candidate told us how he'd visited a dominatrix and enjoyed it. So Quentin gave Karen and me the nod to play the scene we'd arranged beforehand. It was one of the "adult baby" ones.'

'Ah, interesting! But did you enjoy it too?'

'Very much.' Jayne gave a well satisfied grin. 'I played the nurse and Karen was the mother.'

'In other words, she got his mouth round her nipple and you got his cock in your hand.'

'Oh! Do you know the game then?' Jayne giggled, surprised.

'Yes, it's one of the stock scenarios. Quentin only uses familiar ones at interviews, but he tries to tailor them to the individual needs of the candidates.'

'I wonder what "need" he detected in me then, making me masturbate in front of the committee!'

'He had you sussed as an exhibitionist, my dear. Of course we're all that to some extent. You have to be to belong to the club at all. Or maybe he just wanted to see you come. You never can tell with a man like Quentin. Anyway, do you reckon this guy, Mike, will be admitted as a member?'

'I think so. He played his part to perfection and really got into it.'

'Good.' Stella looked thoughtful, then said, 'Actually I

might see if I can use him in a little project I'm cooking up with a friend. We thought we'd do it as a live presentation at the next meeting.'

'Really? What's that?'

'It's a three-hander, two women and one man. I must have a word with Quentin. If he's agreeable Mike sounds just the man for the job.'

Jayne decided not to question Stella too closely, especially as she didn't seem inclined to go into detail. But inside she was eaten up with curiosity. The idea of seeing her lover perform with two other women was intriguing. More than that, she found the idea very arousing too. Would she be jealous? Somehow she doubted it. Knowing that he wouldn't be having a 'relationship' with them, merely allowing his body to be used for entertainment, put Jayne in the position of an actor's wife who had to get used to seeing her husband act romantic leads.

The next meeting of the Eye Spy Club was scheduled for the following Saturday and Jayne could hardly wait. Mick came home from work on Tuesday beaming from ear to ear.

'I got a call telling me I've been accepted as a member,' he announced.

'Mick, that's wonderful!' Jayne took him in her arms and they embraced warmly. 'Oh, one thing you should know. In the club I'm called "Miranda" so you must be careful not to call me by my real name. Just as I must remember to call you Mike, not Mick.'

'Miranda!' He grinned. 'Suits you!' He kissed her exuberantly, squeezing her tightly in his arms.

'I feel like cracking open a bottle of champagne. Maybe we'll get some when we're out.'

It felt absurdly as if he'd been given a promotion at work. Not that Jayne was in the least surprised. She had known that he was just the sort the club needed, sexually inexperienced (yes, she had to admit it, even though she was partly to blame) but also curious and adventurous. It sounded as if he was going to have a double adventure soon: first the live action on stage, then the shock of seeing himself on screen. She wanted to tell him that Stella had a treat in store for him, but didn't dare. Let him find out in his own good time that Jayne's boss was also a club member. It would only complicate things right now.

Saturday crawled by for both of them. Once Jayne and Mick had done the supermarket run they went their separate ways, Jayne in search of a new aphrodisiac perfume she'd heard about and Mick off to Silicon Mart to get an upgrade or two for his home computer. She returned first and ran herself a bath. After tracking down the sensual perfume she'd been tempted by the range of toiletries that went with it and had purchased some bath oil and body cream which she was dying to wallow in.

There was plenty of time for wallowing, too. Both Jayne and Stella had the evening off because Tony was having a special Gay Filmfest Weekend and had called in a couple of presenters from *Queer Films Inc* to host it. As she lay swathed in gorgeous, aromatic foam Jayne felt she hadn't a care in the world. Being able to talk to Mick openly about the club, to have him share in the fun, was an enormous relief. It was only now, when it was over, that she realised what a strain keeping it secret from him had been.

Of course they must continue to be circumspect so that no one else suspected. That meant travelling separately to and from the venue. They were meeting at the elegant Hampstead house where she had been interviewed, and which she had since discovered was Quentin's own residence. Mick had also been given the address, presumably when they told him he'd been accepted into the club. He would get his membership card when he arrived. Jayne smiled to herself, sinking below the foamy bubble once again. He was in for a few surprises tonight!

They ate a light supper together when Mick returned, then she suggested he should leave before her. It was strange seeing him set out alone, even though they would be ending up at the same place. But she knew that he had business to see to before the meeting, and more of it than he imagined. Stella would no doubt pounce on him when he arrived and invite him to take part in her little charade . . .

When Jayne decided it was time to go herself she felt a feverish glow of anticipation that lasted until she got out of the taxi at the walled mansion in Hampstead, when it was superseded by a nervous fluttering in her stomach. She felt calmer when she had entered the house, however, and delivered the video to Quentin. She saw a few familiar faces around the hall and stairs. Mick's was nowhere in sight, but she had expected that. As a new member he would be much in demand, one way or another.

The ladies' changing room was upstairs. Jayne found several women milling around in there, trying on the fantastic costumes that hung on portable rails at the sides of the room. Then a familiar face smiled at her from the crowd and came up to greet her. It was Karen.

'Miranda! Good to see you again, darling.' She gave her a sensual, lingering kiss on the cheek that sent prickles down her spine. Then Karen stepped back, displaying herself. 'What do you think of my outfit?'

It was certainly spectacular. The woman's impressive breasts were displayed in a red vinyl corset that emphasised the depth of her cleavage and tapered to a tiny waistline. When she twirled round, her pert buttocks peeped out from beneath the black lace trim at the bottom of the undergarment, almost completely exposed. In the front, a tiny black lace rosette was suspended over her obviously shaven pussy. Jayne found the effect very erotic, and said so.

'Perhaps you'd help me find some suitable size five footwear then,' Karen pleaded, taking her hand and pulling her over to where all the styles of boots and shoes were ranged on racks and graded according to size.

'These look good,' Jayne suggested, pulling out a pair of

black velvet laced boots with stiletto heels.

'Mm, I've had my eye on those myself.'

She sat down to try them on while Jayne browsed through the costumes for herself. At last she pulled out an alluring, skintight mini-dress in pink satin with transparent patches over the breasts and buttocks.

'That'll be good on you if you wear it without underwear,' Karen told her, authoritatively.

Quickly Jayne stripped, seeing her friend take in every detail of her figure with frank appraisal. She felt an odd shiver of pleasure at the thought that Karen desired her. Although they had met only briefly before they joined forces at Mick's interview, there was already quite a bond between them. Jayne sensed that the attraction was both erotic and friendly.

'I'm looking forward to tonight,' Karen announced as she stood up in her boots, teetering a little on the high heels. 'Any idea what's on the agenda?'

'Yes, our mutual friend!' Jayne grinned, as she pulled the dress over her head and smoothed it down until the 'windows' were in the right places. She looked down at her nipples peeking provocatively through the sheer material.

'Really? Are you quite sure?'

'Pretty sure. And since they'll be showing the video too he'll be starring in a double bill. Quite a début, don't you think?'

'Evidently Quentin thinks he'll go far.'

'Oh, I don't think it was down to Quen. Stella and a friend of hers have bagged him.'

'What are they going to do with him?' Karen's hazel eyes gleamed with anticipation.

Jayne shrugged. 'No idea. But I'm going to be on the edge of my seat watching it, that's for sure. I really got off on that scene we played out with him, you know.'

Karen moved close and whispered in her ear, 'So did I, darling. But it wasn't just Sonny Boy who turned me on.'

She emphasised her words by lightly running her tongue around Jayne's ear making her squirm with a mixture of dislike and delight. 'And if you want some extra stimulation this evening, I can provide you with it. But you'll have to meet me in the loo in five minutes.'

Before Jayne could reply, Karen had moved off into the throng, apparently searching for some accessories. Jayne felt half intrigued by the invitation and half repelled. Would she dare to meet the other woman in the loo? It wasn't a particularly appetising prospect. If there was to be a seduction scene she might have chosen a more romantic venue!

A pair of strappy, high-heeled silver sandals went very well with the pink dress, and Jayne received several compliments from other women as she tidied her hair and make-up in the mirror. But when she looked around the room Karen was nowhere to be seen. She must have slipped out, presumably to the toilet next door. Was she awaiting her in one of the cubicles? The five minutes was almost up. Jayne knew she would have to keep her strange appointment, if only to satisfy her rabid curiosity.

Uneasily, Jayne sneaked out of the room and into the cloakroom next door, feeling absurdly like a naughty schoolgirl. There were no rules about not having unscheduled sexual encounters on the premises, but she had a feeling they were supposed to take place either in the bedrooms or in public. This little assignation didn't seem to qualify as either. Tentatively Jayne opened the door and found Karen waiting for her, leaning against the window sill with an enigmatic smile on her face.

'I knew you'd come,' she said. 'And, if you accept what I have to offer you, you're going to come over and over again!'

'Really?' Jayne tried to act cool but she was buzzing like a wasp on heat inside.

Karen tipped her head towards one of the cubicles with a wink. Jayne followed her inside. She watched incredulously as Karen reached inside the right-hand cup of her corset and produced a pair of smooth ivory-coloured balls, linked by a short chain. 'What are they?'

'Chinese love eggs. I use them all the time.'

'How?'

'You put them in your pussy and squeeze them like a prick. When you've been doing it for a while you can climax at will. I came a dozen or so times during our little Nursing Mother game.'

'You did?' Jayne stared at her. 'I never realised!'

Karen gave a smug grin. 'That's because I've trained myself to come quietly!'

'And you've got those things inside you *all* the time?'

'Not quite all. Sometimes I have a cock in there, just for a change!'

Jayne laughed. 'Honestly, this is incredible! I can just picture you sitting in a tube train or queuing at a supermarket checkout and squeezing away like there's no tomorrow!'

'You got the idea. I don't know the meaning of "bored", I can tell you! Want to try it?'

'Okay.' Jayne took the smooth plastic balls into her palm and squeezed them. She lifted up the hem of her skirt and exposed her naked mons.

'Shall I put them in for you?' Karen offered.

Jayne nodded, her heart beating rapidly. Careful fingers began to probe between her already swollen labia and in through her already wet opening. Karen looked up with a grin. 'Nice and wet! I can see the very idea of it turns you on.'

'You'd be great as a sex-aids saleswoman!' Jayne said, trying to distract herself from the fact that a woman she was finding increasingly attractive was fingering her pussy.

'Funny you should say that, I used to be one!'

She pushed her fingers in and out a few times until Jayne was completely opened up, then inserted the pair of balls, one after the other. They felt satisfyingly hard and mobile.

Jayne clenched her internal muscles experimentally and her throbbing arousal increased considerably.

Then came the sound of a tinkling bell, a signal that the evening's entertainment was about to begin. Karen rose from the toilet seat taking Jayne by the hand. 'Come on, time to go. You've got the whole evening to work out how to climax with those things. See if you can beat my record of thirty-eight times in one hour!'

Chapter Fourteen

The atmosphere in the large, elegant room was electric. Jayne sat at one of the round tables next to Karen, and both women were wearing very smug smiles. On the raised platform at one end of the room Quentin was making his usual suave, witty speech before the first act began but Jayne hardly heard a word he said. She was far too busy attending to the wild sensations that were coursing through her body as a result of her internal gymnastics.

When she saw Mick appear on stage, however, accompanied by Stella and another woman, Jayne relaxed momentarily in order to take in the extraordinary sight. Her lover was stark naked except for a kind of black leather harness that was fastened around the base of his impressive erection. His hands were tied behind his back and he was blindfolded. The women led him to the centre of the stage and stood on either side, like attendants at a side-show. Jayne surveyed them curiously.

Stella was kitted out in full dominatrix gear, with her breasts exaggeratedly uplifted in a red rubber corset and her pussy encased in what looked like an elaborate leather chastity belt, complete with straps, chains and padlocks. Her friend looked equally magnificent. Jayne recognised her from a previous club meeting and struggled to recall her name, something beginning with O. Olive, was it? Or Odette? The woman was a statuesque blonde with large breasts that jutted firmly from her chest, and her locks flowed free over her bare shoulders. She wore a bikini of fake leopardskin together with some primitive tools in a leather belt around her waist: a crude dagger, a coiled whip and a club. The effect reminded Jayne of some primeval tough girl, Brigitte Nielsen as *Red Sonja* perhaps, or Raquel Welch in *A Million Years BC*.

Music began, raw and arousing, and the two women began circling Mick like wild beasts homing in on their prey. Stella pushed him down and he sank to his knees, then her friend suddenly pushed him forward and sat on his back with her long legs dangling over his shoulders. A wave of laughter, tinged with wicked delight, went round the room. The blonde beauty began to swivel her hips and thrust with her pelvis, rubbing her pussy against his bowed head and deriving obvious pleasure from the friction.

'Isn't Odile magnificent!' Karen whispered, leaning close to Jayne. 'How are your balls doing, darling?'

'Fine,' Jayne replied, but speech was difficult right then. The sight of Mick being subjugated by that gorgeous amazon was turning her on a treat.

On stage, Stella was showing signs of arousal too. She produced a key from her cleavage and made Mick take it between his lips. Then she knelt in front of him and managed to manoeuvre herself so that the key fitted into the lock of her chastity belt. She gave a brisk jerk of her hips and the lock opened, to enthusiastic applause. She proudly displayed her neatly trimmed bush of dark hair, held the now useless belt up in the air then tossed it into the audience. It was caught by a portly man with a moustache, who claimed it proudly as a trophy.

With her private parts exposed, Stella took a shiny black condom out of her cleavage and smoothed it down over Mick's still-solid erection. He made a blind grab for her breasts, but she turned away and got down on all fours, backed up until his cock could enter her from behind, then guided him in. The audience cheered and clapped as she slowly wiggled her behind with voluptuous enjoyment, and

Jayne couldn't help wondering why she didn't feel the least twinge of jealousy. Was it because of her own naughty little secret?

The sneaky love balls were moving around to devastating effect as she squeezed and released them with rhythmic contractions of her vaginal walls. Jayne crossed her legs tightly to enhance the stimulation, and gasped as the final dizzying rush towards a climax began. She glimpsed Karen's knowing smile then closed her eyes as the full onslaught of her orgasm hit home. Shivers of delight travelled up and down her spine, her thighs trembled and her lips uttered low moans as the thrilling spasms ran their course.

When she opened her eyes again, Jayne saw that Stella had reached a similar state and was bucking and gasping her way through a climax that looked very convincing. Mick looked pretty far gone as well. His mouth was hanging open – a detail she recalled from their own lovemaking– and even at a distance she could see the beads of sweat trickling down beneath the dark hairs of his chest. Odile was still sitting astride his shoulders, wriggling her furry pants so furiously that she might have had ants in them, her magnificent cleavage streaked with perspiration too.

Suddenly a crashing chord rang through the room and Odile leapt off his back and pulled out her whip, which uncoiled itself into a long leather thong. She cracked it a couple of times, letting it snake across the floor, and then flicked the tip of it across Mick's naked shoulders. Jayne winced, but the look on her lover's face was not one of unmitigated pain. He'd been shocked, that was obvious, but once the first stinging impact began to wane it was replaced by a faint, but undisguised, smile of gratification.

Jayne couldn't see his eyes of course, no one could, but the way he resumed his thrusting into Stella's willing pussy with new enthusiasm suggested that he was responding well to a taste of the whip. She was amazed. Although she had by now got used to the idea that Mick enjoyed being dominated, it hadn't occurred to her that he might revel in pain. Was he some kind of masochist? She felt both close to him and distanced from him as she contemplated this possibility.

Now Stella was obviously close to her second coming. Her eyes were half closed in bliss and her body was on autodrive, buttocks clenching and hips thrusting as she worked herself up into a sensual frenzy. Suddenly the whip cracked again, this time over Mick's bare buttocks, and he gave a loud cry as this second lashing pushed him finally over the brink, triggering his climax. Odile rapidly returned to her former position and began grinding her mons hard against the back of his head. The audience applauded loudly as Stella and Odile reached orgasm at the same time, turning the threesome into an erotic spectacle of sweaty, pulsating gratification.

Karen seized Jayne's hand and held it tightly, signalling that she was also in the throes of supreme delight. The thought of so much synchronised ecstatsy was too much for Jayne, who clenched her balls tightly once again, feeling another wave of unfettered bliss fill her veins and turn her into a mass of sensually vibrating flesh. 'Oh God!' she breathed softly, as her body was once again suffused with erotic heat.

The continuing loud applause of the audience allowed her gasps and shudders to go unnoticed – except by Karen. Even as the woman was reaching her own climax she was gazing at Jayne with a peculiar look on her face, part envy and part admiration, apparently longing to share in her orgasmic experience. Jayne was watching her through half closed lids, fascinated by the ambiguity of her expression.

When she next glanced at the stage, the trio were taking their bow and then Mick was gone. Quentin returned, his smile showing how pleased he was that yet another of the 'little entertainments' had been so well received.

'I'm sure you were already familiar with the talents of those gorgeous ladies, but the newcomer was Mike, our special novice of the evening. You will now have a chance to appreciate once again his particular penchant for placing himself unreservedly in the hands of beautiful, domineering women. Bring down the screen please, Justin.'

He strolled off and the room darkened so that everyone could see the large video screen that was unfurling. Jayne settled back in her chair contentedly. Although she'd both taken part in the scene and viewed the video, she was looking forward to seeing how it was received by the others. Slowly she clenched her pussy over the quiescent balls, feeling like a child with a gobstopper in its mouth that got sucked from time to time. The erotic feelings resumed, making her sigh with pleasure.

A shadowy figure crossed the room and came to sit on one of the empty chairs beside her. It was Stella. 'What did you think of our little playlet?'

Jayne leaned towards her ear and whispered, 'Great! You were both magnificent.'

'What about Mike, isn't he the perfect submissive? I hope you noticed that he kept it up throughout. He's going to be a very useful chap. Can't wait to see the video.'

Jayne smiled to herself. She would have to get used to talking about him as if he were just another club member, but right now it struck her as very amusing. She'd never had quite so much fun keeping a secret before.

The familiar image of Mike sitting in the middle of the hotel room and looking embarrassed filled the screen. Jayne squeezed hard on her love balls and felt her arousal take a quantum leap. She hoped Stella and Karen would just keep quiet from now on and not distract her. With luck she could manage two or three orgasms before the video had ended.

Someone else was coming over to their table and soon Jayne realised it was Mick. He pulled up a chair on the other side of Stella and threw her a wink. Then he leaned across and said, in a stage whisper, 'See which of my performances you prefer, Jayne – the live one or this one.'

It took Jayne a few seconds to register his gaffe. Then she began praying hard that no one, least of all Stella, had noticed. Her cunt clutched frantically at the pair of balls for comfort, sending shivers of heightened sensation throughout her lower regions, but the experience was more frantic than erotic. She kept on squeezing and squeezing, her muscles locked in nervous spasms. Those love balls were fast taking on the rôle of worry beads.

Even in the semi-darkness Jayne could see Stella's eyes widen in recognition. 'Yes, *Miranda*,' she said with pointed emphasis, 'let's see which of Mike's performances turns you on the most.'

She was looking from one to the other of them in a very hostile way that made Jayne's blood run cold, but Mick didn't seem to notice. His eyes were riveted to the screen, revelling in his own image. Stupid, stupid man, Jayne thought irritatedly. She blamed herself for not impressing on him enough the importance of using her pseudonym. But how much did his faux pas really matter? Stella was now aware that he knew her outside the club, but so what? She didn't know they lived together.

But it irked Jayne that she felt unable to mention it. She would just have to wait and see if Stella said anything. Her anxiety would not go away, however. Although she sat with her eyes on the screen they were unfocused, her mind far away. What was her best course of action: to sit tight and hope it would blow over, or to come clean and throw herself on her boss's mercy? She'd never felt she knew Stella all that well, despite having worked with her for so long. What if the woman had some grudge against her, and this was just the chance she needed to take her revenge?

'Stop being so paranoid!' Jayne told herself, as the scene on the screen swung into sexy action. Everyone else was clearly enjoying it, smiling and applauding sporadically

She couldn't help noticing that some of the women were fingering their nipples or had their hands buried between their thighs, while several of the men seemed to be doing surreptitious deeds beneath the tables. But it was impossible for her to become as involved herself. She sat on tenterhooks, scared to death that Mick would call her 'Jayne' again, since it evidently hadn't occurred to him that she was supposed to be 'Miranda' now.

The film ended to enthusiastic applause, then Quentin appeared on stage again. He said a few words, asked Mick to get up and take a bow, then announced that the 'live action' video for the evening would be a lesbian romp featuring 'three of our most attractive and adventurous young ladies'. Jayne, looking steadfastly away from Mick and Stella in case she caught their eye, caught Karen's instead.

The other woman leaned over to her and whispered, 'Personally, when it comes to lesbian frolics I'd rather perform them than watch them. How about it?'

For a moment Jayne had no idea what she meant and gazed at her blankly. Karen said pointedly, 'I mean, how about coming upstairs?'

'What, right now?'

She nodded, smiling. 'Why not? There will be plenty of rooms free.'

At once Jayne realised this would give her the exit visa she needed. If she left the room with Karen she could stop worrying about whether Mick would address her by her real name again. Then maybe she would go home alone, just to be on the safe side. But she was going to give Mick a rocketing when *he* got home!

They slipped from the room while everyone else was staring at the screen and Jayne followed Karen up the wide staircase to the landing above, where there were six doors. Evidently familiar with the layout, Karen headed straight for one of the doors and opened it to reveal a small bedroom, tastefully furnished and with erotic prints on the walls.

'This is my favourite,' she smiled, sitting on the bed and kicking off her heels with a 'pouf!' of relief . . . 'So intimate, don't you think?'

Her large hazel eyes, fringed by gorgeous dark-brown lashes, stared provocatively at her as she tossed back her shoulder-length mane of auburn hair. Jayne felt herself coming out in goosebumps. With her lesbian experience limited to a few adolescent skirmishes and her brief encounter with Stella and the remarkable Polly, she had no idea what she had let herself in for.

'I've been enjoying the effect of those love balls,' she said, rather shyly, uncertain what else to say.

Karen laughed. 'I should hope so! They're great for going solo, but even better when . . . come here! I'd rather demonstrate than talk about it!'

She pulled Jayne close, her hands around her waist, until they were both sitting on the bed. 'I've been wanting to get you alone ever since I saw your video,' she murmured, throatily.

Jayne squeezed hard on her balls, relishing the feelings that careered up her spine. At the same time Karen's lips moved to hers, enclosing her mouth with soft, moist flesh. She opened her lips slightly and a thick wet tongue slipped inside, making her shudder with delight. As their kiss deepened she felt a nipple being flicked through the see-through hole in her dress while another hand stroked her thigh. Lost in a sensual haze, she lay back to allow her female lover freer access to her body.

There was a musky, sweet smell emanating from Karen's cleavage that Jayne found incredibly arousing. She breathed in the faint perfume with a sigh and felt the lips move from hers while dextrous fingers went behind to find the zipper then pulled it down her back, allowing the dress to be peeled away from her breasts.

'Beautiful!' Karen murmured, taking each exposed nipple between her lips in turn while she caressed both straining globes of flesh.

The sudden stimulation of her breasts heightened Jayne's arousal to fever pitch and she moaned aloud, rapidly working her muscles against the teasing balls. Wasting no time, Karen's right hand found her naked vulva and began expertly to work her clitoris. It took only a few seconds for the combined external and internal contact to bring her to a mind-shattering climax. No sooner had it begun, however, than Karen moved rapidly down between her thighs to lick and suck at her overflowing pussy.

At first the rapture was wonderful, exquisite. But then it began to seem as if the spasmodic waves would, quite literally, never end. Jayne was overheating, the sweat running off her in trickling, tickling rivulets, her thighs trembling with the repeated paroxysms. And through it all Karen's eager lips and tongue continued working, keeping the orgasmic fire alive. Yet as her muscles clenched the balls over and over, with increasing force, the pleasure verged on pain and Jayne felt her tolerance level was being severely tested. Just how much continuous rapture could one woman take?

When the climax finally started to fade Jayne sighed with relief and fell back slackly onto the bank of pillows. Her breathing was ragged and her pulse raced alarmingly. For one terrible moment she thought she was having a heart attack. The strength of her response had amazed her. She never would have believed she was capable of enduring such a prolonged and violent assault upon her senses.

'Are you okay, kiddo?' she heard Karen enquire from her side. A gentle hand smoothed a strand of hair from her sweaty brow.

She opened her eyes and grinned weakly. 'I think so. That rather took me by surprise.'

'Yes. I call them "ball-crushers"! I did warn you that with those things inside you would come more intensely.'

Jayne leant back and closed her eyes again. The memory of her prolonged climax was waning but her muscles still ached from her waist down. She needed to rest.

'Look, I hope you don't mind if I go downstairs,' Karen said. 'Only there's some people I want to see.'

'Fine. Go ahead,' Jayne said, sleepily.

Once the other woman had left, however, Jayne rose from the bed and splashed her face with water from the vanity basin in the corner. She found a hairbrush on a table and ran it through her tousled locks until she looked almost respectable, then she left the room. Instead of returning to join the others she went into the ladies' changing room and found her clothes. Quicky she changed back into them, then slipped out through the front door without anyone noticing she had left.

The night air felt fresh and clean on her cheeks, soothing her still-fevered brow. She walked out of the gate and found herself in a quiet street, but there was a taxi rank just round the corner so she headed straight there. Fortunately a cab was waiting. Feeling rather like a fugitive she directed the driver to South Quays. Somewhere along the line the evening had gone sour, and now she couldn't wait to get home.

Mick was so absorbed in the spectacle of three nubile young women giving each other a good seeing to that it took him a while to realise that Jayne had left the room. At first he thought she must have gone to the loo, but then he noticed that the other woman had gone too, the one who had played the nursing mother. He hoped she'd be back. He rather fancied her.

But by the time the video was over and the lights went up Jayne had still not returned. He began to feel anxious. Soon after he'd arrived she began to act strangely, almost turning her back on him, which worried him. Stella was acting stiff and cold towards him too. His enjoyment of seeing the buxom blonde perform cunnilingus on the raven-haired girl while she fondled the small breasts of the Chinese girl was somewhat marred by his unease.

Then he saw that the other girl had returned alone and was chatting to some people near the door. He excused himself to Stella and walked casually in her direction. When he got there she gave him a half-smile. Encouraged, he approached her.

'Do you know where Jayne is?'

'Jayne?'

The girl seemed genuinely puzzled. Mick said, 'Yes. You were sitting next to her and I saw you leave the room with her, about twenty minutes ago.'

'Oh, you mean Miranda!'

He stared at her blankly, then it dawned on him. Of course! Jayne had said that was her pseudonym. How stupid of him! He'd been confused because Stella used her own name, but he should have realised. After all, everyone was calling him Mike instead of Mick.

'Yes, Miranda.'

'I left her in one of the rooms upstairs, lying down.'

Her hazel eyes danced mischievously at him and Mick's imagination began to work overtime. Had Jayne and her friend been indulging in similar activity to what he'd just seen on the screen? It hardly seemed likely. But then this club was supposed to offer a sexual free-for-all. Surely not all the action could take place on video!

He found out which room Jayne was supposed to be in and went to ascend the stairs. The room in question had obviously been recently occupied. The bedcover was rumpled, there were drops of water round the basin and the hand towel was wet. He even saw some fair hairs in a brush that looked suspiciously like Jayne's. But if she had been in there, she no longer was. Where the hell had she got to?

Mick spent the next half hour drifting around the room downstairs, being congratulated on his performances and made to feel welcome by all – all except Stella, that was. Every time he looked in her direction she seemed to frown or look daggers at him. At last he went over and took her to one side.

'Excuse me, Stella, but I need to know why you're angry with me.'

'Angry?'

'Yes. Ever since I came to sit beside you. Was it because I called Jayne by her real name?'

Stella's brown eyes turned almost black as she frowned again. 'You should have told me you were acquainted outside the club. I thought I was the only member you knew. You could get me into trouble with the committee for proposing you.'

'Why?'

'The rules state that members aren't supposed to have intimate relations outside the club. Now I don't know what your relationship with Jayne is, but . . .'

Mick decided it was time to deflect her attention away from himself. 'Okay, so what's yours?'

'We work together, actually. But Quentin has known that from the start.'

Mick hated her supercilious tone. Although he knew he would regret it, he delivered his icy riposte. 'Well we *live* together, *act*ually!'

'What? Jeez, you're joking – I hope!'

Mick shook his head, tight-lipped. Stella stared at him for a few seconds, her eyes like molten fury, every blink indicating another unwelcome thought. 'So the pair of you thought you could deceive me, did you?' she said at last, her voice breaking like splinters of frosted glass. 'You'll regret this,' she ended, turning on her spiked heel and walking away from him.

Mick had that awful sense of having done something irrevocable. He hadn't had that particular sinking feeling for years, not since he'd told Kath that he was in love with

Jayne and had decided to move in with her. And now the sense of impending doom was even stronger than on that occasion.

There didn't seem to be any point in staying around after that. Mick went to the changing room and found his clothes neatly hanging or folded as he'd left them. He supposed he would have to tell Jayne the bad news, and as soon as possible. Much as he disliked the prospect, he wanted to get it over with. When he was dressed he made for the door and, without knowing it, ended up at the same taxi rank Jayne had used just half an hour before.

The taxi crawled through the labyrinthine streets on its way to South Quays, compounding Mick's agony. All the way he was thinking about how to tell Jayne about his blunder, and hoping that she wouldn't be too angry with him. In the past Jayne's anger had been little more than a transient mood, but just lately everything seemed to have changed between them and now he had no idea what to expect from her.

There was a light burning in the front window of their flat as he got out of the taxi. She was there, waiting up for him. A bad omen. He paid the driver and went on in, his heart starting to pitty-pat in his chest. As soon as he went through the door he could feel her waiting for him. There was something tangible in the air, an atmosphere of controlled anger and dark suspense that he found extraordinarily exciting.

In the front room Jayne was standing with her back to the window, legs astride, hands behind her back. She was wearing a black push-up bra and matching panties, suspender belt and dark sheer stockings, with shiny black high-heeled shoes. Her face was made up more than usual, with dark-shadowed eyes, lustrous black lashes and very red, shiny lips. She looked extraordinary. The minute Mick appeared she gave him a withering glance.

'You have been an extremely naughty boy!' she said in a

low voice that thrilled him to the core. 'And you must be punished.'

'Yes, I know. I'm sorry, Jayne . . .'

'*Mistress!*' she barked.

'I'm sorry . . . Mistress.'

'That's better. But saying sorry isn't enough to make up for what you did tonight, wretched creature. You betrayed my trust, revealed our secret. Now take off your clothes.'

Obediently, Mick stripped until he was facing her stark naked. Fortunately she had put the central heating on but he shivered nevertheless, more from excitement than cold. He knew she had some plan, some punishment lined up for him, but he didn't know what and that was the source of all his perverse delight. She walked towards him very slowly, and he saw her flesh gleam peachily in the glow from the lamp in the corner. His cock lifted its head.

'You used my real name,' she said in that same low, menacing tone. 'Even though you knew it was taboo, you called me by my real name. That is a serious offence, a flagrant breach of the rules, and I intend to punish you severely. Now, kneel!'

He did as he was told. Jayne stared down at him with frozen eyes, increasing the voluptuous terror that was giving him an adrenaline high. His head was on a level with the mound of her pussy, sitting pretty within the black panties. She put her arms around the back of her waist to release the catch of her suspender belt and then she unhitched the stockings which fell in silky folds around her knees. She pulled the belt taut between her two hands, the plastic suspenders clinking slightly. Then she walked slowly round until she was standing behind him, invisible. He dared not look round.

'Bend over and kiss the ground!' she snapped.

He obeyed, feeling the carpet's rough caress on his tongue. She kept him there for what felt like ages, his bottom stuck ridiculously into the air, his face buried in the pile of the carpet with its comforting woolly smell, like an old jumper. Then he heard a faint clattering whoosh and something stung him sharply across both buttocks. He gasped in pain, but it was bearable.

'I'll teach you to break the rules!' she snarled, lashing him again with her suspender belt. It hurt more this time, the knobbly suspenders quite effective against his tense flesh.

Jayne delivered six blows in all, and then another one 'for luck' as she grimly put it. Mick's bum tingled and burned, his eyes were watering, but the effect on his prick was far from deflating. He still had his erection, pointing proudly forwards as he knelt on all fours now. He watched Jayne's shapely legs return to stand before him. Slowly his eyes lifted until he could see the black pouch concealing her mons. He fancied that there was a damp patch in the fabric.

'All right, now you must show that you know how to please me.'

Mick looked up at her face. She was giving him a twisted smile as she put her hands down the front of her panties and levered them down. She bent forward until her cleavage was at his eye level, then stepped out of her underwear and pulled off the stockings, which were now pooled around her ankles. His eyes flew back to the magnet of her sex and he noticed that she'd trimmed her hair to the bare minimum so that her plump rosy love lips were clearly delineated beneath the sparse fur.

'Lick me now!' she commanded. 'Make me come!'

He moved his mouth up to the musk-laden heart of her, his tongue parted the tumid labia and found honey within. In profound gratitude he performed the way she liked it, with plenty of rapid tongue-tickling of her clitoris. She swayed on her feet as her climax approached, and he put his arms around her hips to steady her then found himself stroking the warm cushions of her buttocks. His mind was filled with visions of her all-powerful beauty, his body throbbed achingly, but so sweetly, with the increased sensitivity that her chastisement had evoked. His body spat fire in one brief, but thoroughly satisfying, climax. And his soul was profoundly contented.

The rapturous spiralling of her orgasm soared to ever increasing heights, making her moan and thrust against his mouth again and again, before she sank to the ground in trembling exhaustion. When he tried to take her in his arms, however, she snapped at him. 'No! Leave me alone now. Go to bed.'

Reluctantly Mick left the room, taking a quick pee then falling straight into the comfort of his bed without even bothering to brush his teeth. All his previous tensions spent, he soon fell into a deep sleep which lasted through until late morning.

When he awoke Jayne had gone out, leaving a note to say she was visiting a friend for the day and would go straight on to work in the evening. Mick was disappointed. He'd hoped that last night had started a new phase of their relationship, put it on a new footing. But perhaps it had. Jayne might be acting wisely in refusing to confront him or discuss it this morning. Although he was new to it all, Mick's instinct told him that perhaps they needed to distance themselves from each other at an everyday level in order to relate at a deeper one.

He couldn't stop thinking about it on his own, though. All day long he indulged himself by going over the events of the previous night, recalling how he'd felt on stage at the hands of those two gorgeous women and then the supreme satisfaction of being dominated and chastised by Jayne. His love for her had revived and was now stronger than ever, but he was fearful of what might happen at the club now that Stella knew about them. His copy of the club rules had clearly stated that such relationships must be declared at the time of joining. It all depended on whether Stella was prepared to keep their secret too.

Anxiety kept him awake that night, listening for Jayne's

key in the door. He dozed finally, awoke a dozen times imagining he could hear her, and finally he really did. She closed the front door and came striding straight down the hall to the bedroom. She flung open the door and flicked on the light, making him sit up and blink. Then, when his sleepy eyes began to focus, he saw how furious she was.

But this was no game. Her wrath was real. He cringed from her, afraid she would strike his face. Her eyes were a leaden, threatening grey and her lips were compressed into a hard line. Instinctively he backed away from her clutching the duvet. 'What's the matter?' he whispered, his heart sinking with the certainty that everything had gone horribly wrong.

'Your stupid mistake has got us thrown out of the club and me sacked!'

'What? But she can't . . .'

'Oh yes, she can. And she has.'

'Okay, so we broke club rules. But Stella has no right to *sack* you. You could take her to an industrial tribunal for unfair dismissal.'

Jayne's face was a mask of contempt for his naivety. 'No chance. You know I'm on a short term contract with only two months to run.' She towered over him, no longer the amazon beauty, more the harridan shrew. 'Get out of bed!'

He scrambled out, reaching for his dressing gown. She snatched it from him. 'No! Get dressed. You've ruined everything and I want you out of here. Out of this flat and out of my life. For good!'

Chapter Fifteen

Mick hadn't believed she really meant it, but here he was in the middle of the night with only the clothes he stood up in and nowhere to go. He felt like going straight round to Stella's and giving her a piece of his mind, but he doubted she would let him in. And he felt so damn weary. He got into his car and curled up on the back seat with the travelling rug over him, hoping to snatch some sleep.

After several false starts he managed to drop off around dawn. When he awoke it was bright day and he felt sore all over. Terrified that Jayne would suddenly appear and do something drastic, like puncturing his tyres, he got his engine into gear and drove off. It was like having the clock turned back to when Kath had pursued him vengefully. Her style had been to spray 'wanker' on his windscreen, make vituperative phone calls in the early hours and put his name on a whole series of mailing lists so that he ended up swamped with junk mail. He didn't think Jayne would react like that, but you never knew.

For an hour or so he wandered about aimlessly, his mind confused and his soul in turmoil. Then he rang his friend Jim and asked if he could stay with him for a few days, just until he 'got himself sorted out'. His mate didn't sound too pleased but at least he didn't refuse.

Mick drove back to the flat determined to get some clothes, at least, and if possible to have it out with Jayne. But the place was empty. He resisted the urge to take childish revenge – cutting her underwear into ribbons went through his mind, or putting superglue in her shoes – and merely concentrated on removing those things of his that he didn't want her to spoil. Then he drove to Jim's and went off to the pub with him to drown his sorrows. But it was frustrating not to be able to tell his friend any more than that he and Jayne had had 'a bit of a row' and by the end of the evening he was thoroughly fed up.

For several days he was in limbo, going to work during the day and then spending most of the evening at the pub so he wouldn't impose on Jim. When his sexual frustration reached a peak he was tempted to ring Lady Odile's number again and, on Friday night, he finally did so. She asked what service he required but he broke in saying, 'I'm Mike. Remember me from the Eye Spy Club?'

There was a short pause. Then her tone changed completely, becoming almost conspiratorial. 'What do you want, Mike? I heard about what happened to you and Miranda, and I'm not sure I should be talking to you at all.'

'I don't know who else I can turn to,' he admitted. 'Stella's given my girlfriend' – he shrank from calling her either Jayne or Miranda – 'the sack and she's thrown me out.'

'I don't want to get involved in your domestic troubles . . .'

'I'm not asking you to. I just wondered if I could see you.'

'My time comes expensive, Mike.'

'I'll pay,' he said, desperately. 'Just an hour of your time would do. I just need to talk to someone who knows about . . . what I need to talk about.'

'All right. Can you come along tonight at ten? I'm free then.'

'Oh yes, thank you!'

Mick felt pleased as he put down the phone. The prospect of being able to unburden himself even a little was a great relief. He sat in the pub for another couple of hours, being careful not to drink too much, then drove to the King's Road.

The maid opened the door as usual, then he was led upstairs to Odile's private quarters. She received him in a full-length rose-pink gown trimmed with lace and looking quite different from the amazonian creature who had used his head as a dildo at the Eye Spy Club. With a wry smile she gestured to a nearby armchair and poured him a very good single malt.

'I thought you sounded as if you needed this.'

Mick raised the glass gratefully. 'I do. Cheers!'

'So, let's not beat about the bush. What is it you want from me?'

'I don't know. I only know that you're the only person I can talk to right now.'

She held up a glittering, ringed hand saying sternly, 'Don't you give me that "you're the only one who understands me" shit, whatever you do.' Then her face softened into a smile. 'You're pissed off because just as you discover your true sexual nature you lose the means of expressing it. Am I right?'

He grinned back. 'Spot on. Only trouble is, the night before Stella sacked Jayne – I'm calling her by her real name because it doesn't matter any more – we had the most wonderful time. She punished me for using her real name in the club. It was almost as good as when I was here and . . .'

'That was Jayne too.'

'*What*?'

'She came to me on the pretext of wanting an interview. At least, I assumed it was a pretext. I said the best way to find out what we did here was to join in. Stella sent you to me, said she thought you were an excellent subject, and I invited Jayne to join in the fun. At the time I had no idea you knew each other, of course.' She shook her head and the blonde locks swished like a heavy curtain. 'Naughty woman. She's in my bad books too, you know.'

'Oh? Why is that?'

'Never mind. More whisky?'

'Better not. I'm driving.' A sense of urgency seized him. 'What am I to do, Odile? I want Jayne back, more than anything. But she blames me for spoiling her career and her sex life.'

Odile gave him a circumspect look. 'I *may* be able to help on both fronts.'

'Really?'

'No promises, and Jayne would have to agree of course. But I've been very impressed by what I've seen of the pair of you. Not just here, but in your club performances. I'm sure you both have great potential, and I need talented newcomers right now.'

'Need? For what?'

'I'm opening a second establishment.'

She paused, to let her words sink in. Mick stared at her incredulously. 'Are you offering us a chance to *work* for you?'

She nodded. 'It's work that some people might regard as play, but I take it very seriously. My clients pay top dollar for the services I offer and I have to offer them the very best. I think I could train you and Jayne to come up to my high standards.'

'Both of us? I don't understand.'

'I haven't explained fully. Here we offer the opportunity for submissive males to be dominated by gorgeous, skilled women who know exactly how to tease and torment a man to the height of ecstasy.'

Mick murmured his endorsement of her claim. But he was still mystified. 'I can see how you would want Jayne. She would make a magnificent dominatrix, I know that now. But what part could I possibly play?'

Odile smiled, coquettishly drawing her small feet in their rose velvet slippers up onto the couch beside her. 'The most important part, I assure you. What I have in mind is intended to satisfy women's needs, not men's.' She paused to let the information sink in. 'In my new place I shall provide male submissives, such as yourself, for my female clients to dominate.'

Mick felt a rush of anticipation ripple through his body, so exquisitely sensual it was almost an orgasm. 'You mean . . . they'll pay for *my* services?'

Odile gave a wry smile. Her tone veered sharply into business mode as she explained, 'Why not? Many women who are pushed around at work, or at home, would love to be able to take it out on some male victim without feeling guilty about it. I know quite a few lesbians who would jump at the chance too.' She leaned forward, showing several inches of cleavage, and picked up the glass of champagne from the table in front of her. 'I've done my market research, I've got my business plan approved by the bank, I've found my premises. Now I just need to find my personnel. Cheers!'

Mick knew this was a job made in heaven, perfect for him, but he still couldn't quite believe he would be getting paid for what he enjoyed most in the world. There must be a catch. And something else was worrying him. 'But what about Jayne? I can't see how she would fit into the picture.'

'I need girls I can train as supervisors. Both to train the men, and to help female clients who are new to the game and want some hints and tips. She would have to spend some time here, learning the trade, before I let her go on to the new place. Both of you would. I need men for my novices to practise on.'

'So, let me get this straight. Jayne and I would both be working here at first, then we'd go on to the new place?'

Odile nodded, taking a sip of champagne. 'I believe you know Karen – your 'nurse'? She's already in line for the new establishment. She shows great promise, but she still needs further training. I think she and Jayne would work together very well, don't you?'

Mick's head was spinning. So many possibilities, and yet he wasn't sure if Jayne would see it the same way. How could he convince her, when he was already shit in her eyes?

Odile seemed to guess what he was thinking. 'I know you want the job, but what about Jayne? Maybe Karen is the one who should approach her, not you. Leave it to me, Mick. I'll do what I can.'

As he got up, she added, 'There will be some lucrative spin-offs too, you know. Videos, for a start. There's a huge untapped market out there for classy Sub-Dom videos and we can supply the best because we won't be using third-rate porn actors. All my people will love their work, you see, and it will show. Job satisfaction, that'll be the key to our success.'

He left soon afterwards, realising that Odile had gone farther than he could have hoped in offering to solve his problems. Yet he still felt restless, longing to talk to Jayne but knowing that he was likely to get short shrift if he contacted her too soon. Needing to ease his frustration he cruised an area where he knew he could pick up a prostitute, hoping for a blow job, but when he saw the girls on offer he didn't fancy any of them and went back to Jim's feeling wretchedly unsatisfied.

Odile had his work number and had promised to ring as soon as she'd set up the meeting between Karen and Jayne. For the next few days he was on tenterhooks, unsure how his future was going to shape up. Should he look for a flat by himself? Jim was showing signs of wanting to be rid of him and he had nowhere else to go. But there had been no word from Odile, either.

Then, surprisingly, he had a call from Karen. She apologised for ringing him at work but said, cryptically, that she was 'under orders to convey some important information'. Mick found the situation amusing. If anyone had bugged his phone in the cause of industrial espionage they would have him down for a spy by now!

'I suggest you go home on Saturday night,' she said.

'Home? Are you sure?'

'Quite sure. Don't worry, it will be quite safe, I'm sure.

Just make sure you don't arrive till after midnight. Around twelve fifteen should be about right.'

'Can't you tell me what's going on?'

'No, that would spoil it. Look, I have to go. See you Saturday.'

'You're going to be there too?'

But he found himself talking to an empty line.

Karen's message had seemed to offer some hope, but still Mick felt restless and unsure. He went over and over Odile's offer in his mind. She obviously wanted both of them, but if Jayne refused to work as a dominatrix, would Odile take him on without her? Would he have to give up his day job? The thought was daunting since he'd been with the firm three years and had a career path mapped out with them. And how did Karen fit into all this? The idea that he was at the mercy of a bunch of machinating women was gathering strength. It was one thing to be dominated, but quite another to be hen-pecked, and Mick was afraid that what had started as the former was turning into the latter.

Nevertheless, Saturday night found him driving towards South Quays filled with an unstable mixture of optimism and trepidation. He drew up outside their apartment block and looked up at the window, surprised to see low flickering lights within. He looked at his watch: twelve fifteen exactly. Leaving the car a few yards away he hurried towards the porch and keyed in his number, praying that Jayne hadn't got around to giving him the electronic heave-ho just yet. The door swung open as it always had and, sighing with relief, Mick entered the familiar portal. He went up in the lift and as he approached his old front door was startled to hear noises like music and laughter and the buzz of conversation coming from inside.

'A party?' he asked himself. 'Surely not!'

It certainly sounded like one. He put his keys in the lock but before he could turn it the door opened of its own accord and Karen was there, looking dramatic in a black velvet cloak and, it seemed, very little else.

'Mick! I'm glad you made it. Quick, in you come.'

She led him into the bedroom – *his* bedroom, although it no longer felt like that. He just had time to notice that all evidence of him had been swept away before she told him to take his clothes off. 'Why should I?' he asked belligerently.

'Because you need to be like everyone else. We're playing a game of Blind Man's Buff.'

'I didn't come here to play party games . . .'

'Maybe not, but you're going to all the same. If you want to get Jayne back, that is.'

'Hey, what are you . . .'

'Shut up!' she snapped, rapidly undoing the buttons of his shirt. 'You'll find out later what this is all about. Just do as you're told for now.' She gave him a wicked grin. 'You're rather good at that, I seem to recall.'

When he was starkers Karen opened a drawer and took out a skin-coloured net. She held it up and he saw that it was some kind of body suit. It seemed a strange shape, though. Karen found her bearings and rolled it up until there was an elasticated hole at the end.

'In you get,' she smiled. 'You're going to love this!'

Obediently Mick dived into the tunnel of elasticated gauze, feeling as he imagined a lobster might feel as it entered a pot. Feeling his way with his hands he pulled the stretchy material around him, helped by Karen on the outside, and then realised that the stuff was going to cover his head and face completely. He also realised that there were no arm or leg holes. The weird garment was, quite literally, nothing more than a shaped sack.

Karen pulled and twisted the stuff around until only his feet were sticking out in the air and she judged it to be a snug fit. Mick found he could breathe through the micropores in the material but the netting was so tight that he was forced to keep his eyes closed, his hands at his sides and his legs tight together. He tried to move forward and had to make small, shuffling steps. Karen led him to the bed and told him to sit down. She knelt at his feet and pulled the sheath down until even they were covered, then she laced them up tightly with a drawstring.

'There, that's you sorted!' he heard her say. Her voice sounded faint, but quite distinct.

She allowed him a few minutes to become acclimatised to his strange new environment. Bound like a parcel he felt pleasantly secure, but he could only take shallow breaths and his balls were squashed uncomfortably. The rest of his body felt alien, immobile. His arms felt glued to his sides and since he could hardly separate one leg from another it was more like having a single stem to support him. He'd been suddenly transformed into a merman.

When he tried to 'walk', however, he felt more like a human pogo stick. Karen did her best to help him, putting an arm around his waist (the contact produced a line of sweat around his midriff) and encouraging him to progress in a combination of shuffles and hops. This must be a bit like learning to walk again after an accident, Mick thought grimly.

His slow progress was taking him into the sitting room. Despite the fact that he could see nothing, and was therefore relying on Karen to guide him, Mick was still capable of forming a mental map of the flat that was so familiar to him. He was guided by his ears, too. Although muffled by the clinging stuff, he was getting used to decoding the sounds of female voices and he knew that he was approaching the place where several women were gathered.

The door had opened to reveal him to the occupants of the room. He knew this even before he heard their gasps of surprise, because beneath his stockinged feet he could feel the metal bar that gripped the carpet either side of the threshold and t ere was a slight increase in temperature as he entered. He could also hear something he couldn't identify, a faint whirring sound. Was someone using a battery-powered dildo? The thought that he'd interrupted some lesbian fun and games was very titillating.

'It's Condom Man!' he heard a woman giggle, and the others responded with more laughter. Yes, he supposed he would look a bit like a giant johnnie. How many women were there in the room? He tried in vain to differentiate the voices as his feet shuffled through the thick pile. At least four, that was for sure. His skin, so thoroughly sealed, nevertheless was capable of feeling a kind of prickly heat triggered by the thought of being at their mercy. Even his cock was hardening, although the tight binding was making it difficult for him to attain a full-blown erection.

'What are we going to do with him?'

That was Jayne's voice, he would know it anywhere. He was standing in the middle of the room now, being inspected by the women. Would she recognise him?

'He's like a giant sausage in a skin,' someone else said. More giggles.

'What does he feel like?'

Their hands moved on him experimentally, sliding over the taut, smooth micro-netting, feeling the intimate curves and planes of his body that was almost naked, almost accessible, but not quite. They made little appreciative noises at first, mms and ahs that soothed him as much as their caresses, made him feel safe in their hands. The delicate female palms were running over his buttocks, his thighs, his calves, and then someone found his soft parts and gave a low squeal of delight.

'Feel his packet, everyone! It's kind of squidgy – ooh!'

One after one they squeezed his cock and balls, making him squirm inside his firm casing. The feeling wasn't exactly unpleasant, just peculiar. Until his erection began to grow, that was. Then it felt as if he were trying to lift a ton weight with his dick, or push through half set concrete. He imagined he was wearing underpants several sizes too small, the ones he'd had when he was seven perhaps. And his balls were hardening too, hot and heavy in their double layer of real and artificial skin.

'It's wonderful stuff,' someone said. 'So tight and elastic.'

'Yes, it's a kind of lycra with pores,' Karen explained. 'Almost literally a second skin. They developed it for use in surgical cases but now it has other uses.'

'Like turning men into mummies.'

The wave of laughter hit him like a blast of hot air. The longer he was in the suit the more sensitised to his environment he seemed to be growing. His nose made a small tent of the material in the centre of his face and through it he could smell the women on heat, their various perfumes failing to disguise the heady aroma of musky, seeping love juice. His erection gained another centimetre or so, but at terrible cost. Mick groaned aloud as the constricting web around his genitals refused to give.

'What are we going to do with our giant condom?' he heard Jayne ask.

'What do you usually do with a prick in a rubber suit?'

The laughter came again, this time inducing the first real tremors of fear in him. Inside this get-up he felt so impersonal, dehumanised. And from the way they were talking the women were viewing him as more of an object too. A sex object. Would they wreak some dark feminist revenge on him for the abuse that men in general had visited upon their sisters, from the beginning of time? He could well imagine Jayne thinking that way, now.

'Why don't we make him lie down?'

Several pairs of hands grasped him by the feet, hands head and waist, lowering him none too gently onto the carpet. He lay like a fallen idol while the women started to play with his body. Someone lay on top of him and began to roll around, the changing pressure on his flesh almost unbearable at times, the air rushing from his lungs as if they were burst balloons, her weight crushing his cock and balls, stifling his face with what he thought were her big breasts.

Suddenly he heard Jayne say, 'Sod this for a game of soldiers! He's not much use to us with his prick enclosed, is he? Now, where did I put those scissors.'

Mick froze in fear, his helplessness no longer a source of comfort but of terror. He lay there rigid, his breathing slowed, his eyelashes fluttering wildly on the trapped lids. Jayne returned and he felt her kneel at his side. At the touch of cold steel he gasped and shuddered, but there was no stopping her. She gouged her way through the cloth with the point of the scissors, inevitably nicking his flesh, and then he felt the first slight relief of tension as she hacked her way in a great arc around his stomach. The sense of release was incredible.

'I'm not sure you should have done that,' he heard Karen say.

'Sod it! We weren't going to get our jollies with him all gift-wrapped like that, were we? Nor was he, I imagine. Oh that's better! That's much better!'

He knew she was exclaiming at the sudden expansion of his erection. His penis was swelling to full size, free as a bird, and to have that part of him exposed while the rest of his body was still under tight control was an amazing experience. The women were fussing and giggling around him, but they might as well have been a million miles away for all he cared. While Mick was in a floaty state of bliss he knew they were wrangling over him in some way, and soon he was being roughly handled. His cock was pumped with eager hands and then lips took over, thick luscious ones that slid wetly up and down his shaft with the teeth behind grating lightly, evoking the most exquisite sensations.

But all the time he felt as if his organ were detached from the rest of him, like a pool of light in an otherwise pitch black room. The feelings were real enough, but something was blocking them off from that part of him that really mattered, that fully experienced things. Mick felt split into two parts: the larger part was in a state of blind torpor, and the smaller part was awake and dancing with life, but the two sections didn't seem properly connected.

Then, quite suddenly, he felt something take the place of the lips and teeth, something hotter and wetter and infinitely more voluptuous that slid with aching slowness down his cock until it had enveloped it completely like a glove of quilted velvet. He knew it was a pussy. Better still, he knew exactly whose pussy it was. In fact, there was no cunt in the world he knew better than that tender, caressing envelope of silken flesh.

Moaning softly he let Jayne ride him to please herself, not that he could do otherwise. She was obviously enjoying varying the pace, now thrusting vigorously, now gliding languidly, and as he relaxed out of the weird state he'd been in, Mick felt every bone in his body turn to mush and every muscle to jelly. Had she recognised him? Did he care? He was yielding utterly to her, his caged body along with his liberated penis, symbol of his spirit, and she was fingering his nipples through the cloth the way he liked her to do. She knew it was him, he was sure of it now. And was this her manner of forgiveness?

If so, it was the perfect reconciliation. Mick was in the paradoxical state of being held tightly compressed while his cock was running on overdrive, and it was incredibly arousing. His blood, after being constricted elsewhere, had rushed eagerly to the one place where it could flow freely, giving him the most substantial hard-on he'd ever had. Jayne seemed to be appreciating it too. She was rocking back and forth on his bound thighs with increasing abandon, her breath coming in the frenzied gasps that he knew signalled her impending climax.

The rest of the room was quiet, as if the other women had just melted away. Perhaps they had. Although the floor was hard against his back, Mick scarcely noticed any discomfort as the orgasmic tension grew in him, all the more powerful for being constrained within his rigid body. The stress on his immobilised muscles was enormous; he felt as if he were pumping iron.

Heat suffused through his body and the sweat formed a layer between his skin and the mesh that enveloped his head and torso. Breathing became difficult and he gasped aloud, feeling the threat of asphyxiation keenly for the first time. Since his hands and legs were immobilised, he began to clench his buttocks and raise his pelvis in rhythmical accord with Jayne's movements, actions which she seemed to appreciate. She pinched hard on his nipples and then he felt her start to come, the walls of her cunt rippling up and down his shaft and her cervix sucking against his glans, a phenomenon which invariably triggered him off too.

Mick had forgotten what a complete sexual union he and Jayne were capable of, so when all the old, familiar signals returned and he let himself slide into the perfect beauty that was his woman, he felt tears well up beneath his glued lids. And then his cock was weeping in sympathy, in floods and fountains, while every nerve in his body vibrated with ecstasy.

Then, just as he thought it was all over, Mick was amazed to find himself suddenly rocketing out of his body and into a bright space from where he could look down and see Jayne riding on him, her lovely face and breasts filled with radiance. His consciousness seemed to drift in ecstasy for a timeless period, then dissolved and reformed inside his inert body again. All, apparently, in the space of a few seconds.

Tender hands were unlacing the cords that bound his feet, rolling up the caul that he was caught in and freeing his body the way his spirit had been freed, just before. When the cloth was wound back from his face he took a great gulping mouthful of air and it tasted sweet as wine. He stretched his crushed, aching limbs and felt the blood course freely through them again. Finally he opened his eyes to see Jayne still astride him, looking down on him with a loving smile.

Mick was dimly aware of someone else in the room, hovering in a corner with a camcorder, but his focus of attention was on the woman he had lost and found again, his Jayne. Then he studied his beloved's face as if he were seeing it for the first time. Saw the almond-shaped eyes that hovered, like shot silk, between blue, green and grey. Saw the full moist lips, now flushed a deep pink, with which she expressed herself so well in word and deed. Saw the heaving swell of her breasts, crested with nipples, beneath which her heart beat steadily with love for him. At once Mick knew for sure that he was forgiven for what had been, after all, just a peccadillo. And he knew, with equal certainty, that they had a long and loving future ahead of them.

Jayne leaned forward until he could feel her warm breath on his face, and her nipples brushing against the flattened hairs on his chest. She said softly, 'Welcome home.'

Epilogue

'Thank you for calling Odile Partners. This is Lady Odile speaking. I would like to describe for you some of the services we have on offer for discerning clients such as yourself. My highly trained and experienced men and women pride themselves on being able to satisfy your every need and fulfil your wildest fantasy.

If you are a man, perhaps you would like to place yourself in the hands of gorgeous, blonde Miranda. She loves men who are obedient to her every whim. If you wish she will make sure you are fully restrained, and chastised when you fall short of her high standards. If you prefer to serve two lovely ladies, Miranda would be happy to join forces with the delectable Karina, who is also adept at putting a man in his place.

Both women are very versatile and can, if you prefer, offer you the opportunity to free yourself from adult responsibilities and regress to your childhood. They will take complete charge of you, and treat you with tender loving care. They will dress up for you, in any of a variety of authentic costumes, and if you have any special requests they will do their best to meet your requirements.

If you are a woman, Odile Partners can also cater for your very specialised tastes. Maybe you would like a chance to get your own back on the men who frustrate and torment you in your daily life? In that case, Mike is your perfect partner. He will do anything for you, and remain devoted no matter how harshly you treat him. You can indulge yourself with some power dressing from our fabulous wardrobe, and if you need any assistance we *have ladies on hand to guide and advise you in the subtle art of domination. Work with a partner, if you prefer, who will place her expertise at your disposal. Discuss your fantasies and deepest desires with her, then plan how they may be accomplished. We are sure that you will find the experience extremely liberating.*

Perhaps your preference is to have a submissive woman under your control, one who will adore you and indulge your every whim. Whatever your desire, male or female, Odile Partners can find a way to satisfy you. Call between the hours of eight and ten a.m. or four and six p.m. to discuss your options and make an appointment.

One last word. You may rest assured that everyone at Odile Partners performs for the sheer pleasure of it, and thoroughly enjoys their work. We do not believe in sexual exploitation, but in mutual satisfaction. Feel confident in coming to us that you will be getting not just a professional service but a very personal one.

— Thank you for calling Odile Partners. I look forward to making your appointment in the knowledge that I will be helping to fulfil your most precious dreams.'

More Erotic Fiction from Headline Liaison

VOLUPTUOUS VOYAGE

Lacey Carlyle

The stranger came up behind her and slid a hand round her waist while the other glided over her breasts. Lucy stared out into the darkness as he fondled her. She knew she should be outraged but somehow she wasn't . . .

Fleeing from her American fiancé, the bloodless Boyd, after discovering he's more interested in her bank account than her body, Lucy meets an enigmatic stranger on the train to New York. Their brief sensual encounter leaves her wanting more, so with her passions on fire Lucy embarks for England accompanied by her schoolfriend, Faye.

They sail on a luxurious ocean liner, the *SS Aphrodite*, whose passenger list includes some of the most glamorous socialites of the 1930s. Among them are the exiled White Russians, Count Andrei and Princess Sonya, and the two friends are soon drawn into a dark and decadent world of bizarre eroticism . . .

0 7472 5145 2

More Erotic Fiction from Headline Liaison

Vermilion Gates

Lucinda Chester

Rob trailed a finger over Rowena's knee, letting it drift upwards. She slapped his hand. 'Get off me,' she hissed, 'or I'll have you for sexual harassment.' Nevertheless, part of her wanted him to carry on and stroke the soft white skin above her lacy stocking-tops . . .

Rowena Fletcher's not having much fun these days. She's a stressed-out female executive with a workload more jealous than any lover and no time, in any case, to track one down.

Then she is referred to Vermilion Gates, a discreet clinic in the Sussex countryside which specialises in relaxation therapy. There, in the expert hands of trained professionals, Rowena discovers there's more than one way to relieve her personal stress . . .

0 7472 5210 6

Adult Fiction for Lovers from Headline LIAISON